THIS IS WHAT HAPPENED

Books by Mick Herron

The Oxford Series

Down Cemetery Road

The Last Voice You Hear

Why We Die

Smoke & Whispers

The Slough House Series

Slow Horses

Dead Lions

Real Tigers

Spook Street

London Rules

Other Novels

Reconstruction

Nobody Walks

This Is What Happened

Novellas

The List

The Marylebone Drop

THIS IS WHAT HAPPENED

MICK HERRON

Published by Soho Press, Inc.
853 Broadway
New York, NY 10003

Library of Congress Cataloging-in-Publication Data

Herron, Mick, author.
This is what happened / Mick Herron.

ISBN 978-1-61695-977-7
eISBN 978-1-61695-862-6

1. Psychological fiction. 2. Suspense fiction.
PR6108.E77 T48 2018 823'.92—dc23 2017015230

Interior design by Janine Agro, Soho Press, Inc.

Printed in the United States of America

10 9 8 7 6 5 4 3 2 1

To my sister, Anne

I wander thro' each charter'd street
Near where the charter'd Thames does flow
And mark in every face I meet
Marks of weakness, marks of woe.

London
William Blake

Part one.

1

The longer she sat there, the colder she became. With her back to the cistern, and her feet drawn up beneath her, Maggie perched on the closed lid of the toilet, and concentrated on being as still as possible. An hour earlier, a spasm in her leg had caused the overhead lights to switch on. Their electric hum had startled her more than the glare. Someone would hear it, she thought, and come investigate. But nobody arrived, and the spasm subsided, and a few minutes later the lights turned themselves off again.

"How long do I have to hide in the toilets?" she had asked Harvey.

"Until twelve. At least."

"The guard patrols all night long."

"But there's only one of him. And he can't be on every floor at once."

She had an urge to confirm that the flash drive was still in her pocket, but any movement would bring the lights to life, and besides, she had checked three times already.

Alone in the dark Maggie squeezed her eyes shut, tried not to shiver, and made herself invisible.

Quilp House was twenty-seven storeys high, each spreading out from a central lobby area where the lifts were, and around which the stairwells ran. In the lower half of the building the floors were open-plan, with rows of desks divided into three or four work-stations apiece. During the day a kind of electricity filled the air, which was not so much the ambient excitement caused by communion with the world's markets as much as it was the repressed emotions of people forced to work in close proximity, and thus hold in their baser reactions, their bodily rumblings.

From the twentieth level, the building changed character. Here, people worked behind closed doors, in progressively larger offices. Views became spectacular. The higher up you were, the further off you could see the weather.

On these floors cameras blinked at corridors' ends, little red lights above their lenses signalling vigilance. Occasionally they swivelled, redirecting their meerkat gaze.

"What about the CCTV?"

"There are two guards on the night shift," Harvey had explained. He was patient with her. Without having to be told, she knew he understood what it was to step across the lines that bordered daily behaviour. "One to patrol, and the other to watch the screens. The TV monitors. Do you know how many of these there are?"

She had a vision of a wall built of pixels, boasting as many views of corridors as there were satellite channels screening sport.

"There are six," he said. "And they alternate from camera to camera. Which means the odds are against your showing up on screen at any given time."

"So they don't automatically detect motion?"

"Maggie." He had reached across the table and put his hand on hers. Around them had been the usual clatter of young mums and earnest hipsters: like most of their conversations, this had taken place in the café where they first met. Where he had first approached her. "It's fine to be scared. It's fine not to want to do this."

"I do want to do it."

"And I wouldn't ask if I could see any other way of getting the job done. If you knew—"

He broke off while a young woman squeezed past with a tray piled high with dirty mugs, their rims laced with froth.

"I know you wouldn't," she told him.

Because she was his only hope.

Her wristwatch pinged when midnight struck.

For a moment, the sound confused her—she had not been asleep, precisely, but had entered a fugue state in which memories and plans collided, throwing sparks off each other—and she jerked upright, banging her head against the cistern. An image of her sister popped and vanished as the cubicle light flickered on, followed by the other bulbs in the lavatory. Her heart pounded. Someone would come. But nobody did, and after a moment Maggie unfolded her limbs, which were creaky with cold, and tried to rub life into them.

Pins and needles assaulted her fingers. She did not feel like an agent on a mission. She felt like a young woman up past bedtime, who wanted only to crawl beneath some covers and find warmth.

"What do I do now, Harvey?" she whispered.

It would have been nice if he'd been there, offering an answer. But it was up to her now. She was on her own.

Because it didn't matter—because the lights had blinked on anyway—before making her way out of the cubicle, she raised the toilet lid, pulled down her jeans and pants, and used it for the purpose for which it was intended. Then she rearranged her clothing, closed the lid, and had her hand on the handle before she caught herself—that would be all she needed, to send a watery alarm cascading through the building. She imagined security guards stomping up and down the stairwells, crashing into the lavatories on each floor, throwing open doors, looking for the culprit.

"Maggie, Maggie," she murmured to herself.

When her heart rate was normal she unlocked her cubicle and tiptoed to the door and opened it and peered out.

The corridor was in darkness. The motion sensors were sleepy, and wouldn't kick in until she stepped outside. Even then they allowed a second or two's grace, as if they needed convincing that they weren't rousing themselves for someone of no consequence. For a mouse, creeping its night-time way along an empty hall.

Rather than a spy. An agent on a mission.

"Trying not to make the lights come on will only stress you out," Harvey had said. "It can't be done. You have to move to get where you need to be, and the sensors will do the rest. So don't worry about them. You can't control the things you can't control."

It was nice that he was confident she could control the other things.

"Maggie, Maggie," she chided herself again. Here was the equation: if the lights were off, the guard wasn't on this floor. And if he wasn't on this floor, he wouldn't see the lights coming on.

Which meant it was safe to step out into the corridor.

But before she could do so the lights flickered and the door to the lobby clicked shut, and then—loud as a lion—she could hear the breathy whistling of the security guard as he rounded the corner, heading her way.

"I wish this were like the films," Harvey had said, "where you have an earpiece and a radio mic, and we're synchronised to the nanosecond. And I'd be hacked into the security system, so I could tell you when it's safe to walk down a corridor, and when to shelter under a desk. But life's not like that, Maggie.

This business isn't like that. We're a lot more . . . We're less James Bond and a lot more, I don't know, Mr. Bean or someone. We have to use what's at hand. And I wish I didn't have to ask you to do this. If I could do it myself, I would. If there were any other way . . ."

He had not finished his sentence. He hadn't needed to.

"And let me say this. You're a brave girl, a tremendous girl, and I couldn't be prouder of you. But if you want to back out, do it now. Because from here on, it'll be too late."

"I don't want to back out."

She did, though.

What he was asking was that she put her head in the dragon's mouth. It was so far removed from her daily life she might as well be watching it in one of those films it wasn't like, and even there at the table she could feel her innards contract, her thighs grow watery. She'd wobble when she stood, she knew she would. And she ought to tell him he'd picked the wrong girl, a nobody, who couldn't be relied on. She'd dissolve into panic at the worst moment. She wasn't icy cool and she wasn't super-hot. He'd plucked her from a crowd, and really, it would be sensible to let her subside back into it, and lose herself among the traffic.

But if she said that she'd see disappointment cross his features, that strange mix of the ugly and the sad on which she'd come to depend.

And besides . . . And besides, what he was asking of her was important. For Queen and country, he'd have said in the old days, though here in the modern world it was more tangible than that. What he was asking her to be was a cog in a larger wheel, on whose turning much depended. He was giving her the opportunity of helping ensure that something did not happen. That there was a fundamental anonymity to this—success measured as an absence of event—did not faze her. Anonymity was her natural setting, her personality's screensaver. Just ask Meredith.

"Good, then. Good." He fished about in his pocket.

For all he'd said about not being James Bond, Maggie had still expected something flashy, in a silver case perhaps, moulded to fit. But instead he'd handed her a very ordinary flash drive, the size of her thumb. It was black, with a white label so its contents could be indexed. This was blank, of course. When she reached to take it from him, he held it over her palm for a moment.

"But listen. Whatever happens, you mustn't let this fall into their hands. They mustn't know you've got it, mustn't know you've used it. Once it's done its job, you have to either get it out of the building, or hide it somewhere it won't be found. And they will be looking." His gaze was intense. She imagined this the look men used when sending other men to war. *You might not come back. But I will remember you.* "If they find you, if they know you've been there, they'll be looking for this. And they mustn't find it. I can't tell you how crucial that is."

"I understand."

"Do you?"

She could only nod.

He let go of the drive and there it was, on her palm.

Maggie made a fist round it, keeping it safe.

She melted back inside, letting the door close silently, and stood with her back to it, her heart's hammering the loudest sound in London. He would hear her through the wood, and see the light beneath the door. Or put a hand to it and push, the automatic gesture of the guard on patrol, and when he encountered the resistance of her weight, it would be over. Alarms would sound, or whistles blow. Those meerkat cameras would turn and point, and her image would plaster itself over the monitors downstairs—six of them? The other guard, the one whose job it was to lean back in his chair and eat doughnuts, would reach for the telephone. And it would not be the police he would call, Harvey had left her in no doubt about that. The people whose building this was, whose secrets it contained, they looked after their own. The last thing they'd do would be call the police.

But he won't see the light, she thought, because the lights are on in the corridor too. There'll be no telltale yellow strip painting the carpet. This was just another door, the ladies' loo, and why would he check that it opened? It always opened.

His whistling was familiar, a tune on the edge of her recall. It faded as he walked past, and the creaking of his tread on the carpet disappeared. The door he'd come through, from the lobby where the lifts and stairwells were, was off to her right, and if he completed a circuit of the floor he would not pass by again but enter the same lobby from the other side. But she didn't know his routines, whether he might halt halfway and retrace his steps, or whether he was heading for a particular desk, or for the vending machine in the kitchen area . . . She could slip out now, and run into him three seconds later. Or this might be as close as their paths would come, and the fact that she'd just evaded him—had all but felt his breath on her cheek—might itself be a token that her safety was now assured.

Maggie, Maggie . . .

There were no tokens, no guarantees. But what was certain was that the light was currently on. Slipping into the corridor would cause nothing to change. As soon as this thought took hold of her she acted on it, standing upright, opening the door, stepping outside. The corridor was empty. Choosing the direction the guard had come from, she hurried round the corner to the lobby door.

She had spent hours in the toilet on the eighteenth floor. This was seven flights below where she needed to be, but that had been planned for—had been her own idea.

"If they catch me—"

(An outcome that had to be acknowledged.)

"—if I'm caught, at least they won't know what I was really after."

"You're a natural." Harvey's ugly face broadened when he smiled, and the tips of his incisors showed. He had a high forehead, a receding hairline, and while his hair was clipped short, it had a noticeable curl, and left to itself would probably fall into ringlets. It was a light dirty brown in colour. He favoured open-necked shirts with a check pattern, and in cold weather wore a long black overcoat with a wide collar, of a kind she could imagine adorning gangsters. "You've done this before—admit it!"

He joked to put her at her ease, and it worked.

So now she was in the lobby of the eighteenth, and needed to climb seven storeys.

The doors required a security pass. She wore hers on a lanyard round her neck, and flashed it now across the face of the reader, which blinked red to green and allowed her through. The stairwell had no windows, and the lights were constantly on, a health and safety requirement. But the stairs were uncarpeted, and difficult to climb noiselessly. They made her trainers squeak. She tried to step only on the runners, two at a time, but still foot and stair conspired to produce this noise, like a cat's toy. If he reached the stairwell again—or so much as put his head round the door—he'd hear her. What good would speed do her then? Better to climb slowly, hugging the wall, out of the line of sight. She was just about to do this when a door, some flights below, opened.

"Remember, the building won't be empty."

"Even after midnight?"

Every so often a look would ripple across his face, like the shadow of a cloud, and in it she could see irritation, frustration—disappointment, mostly. She was adept at the art of reading disappointment. And when that happened it was as if a fish-hook tugged at her heart.

But Harvey had not let his feelings break surface.

"There'll always be someone. Not on the upper floors, but lower down, where the actual work gets done. You know, by ordinary people. Like you and me."

He was not ordinary. But she was, and this was the obstacle she had to overcome.

"The markets sleep for no man," he said. "But you should be okay. Overnighters are for junior staff. The top floors will be quiet. All the fat cats'll be home in their little palaces, or snuggling their mistresses in five-star hotels."

He'd actually said *snuggling*. The word distracted her from any number of questions, complaints really, worries—such as, What if I'm spotted? What do I say when I'm challenged? What if I'm caught in the stairwell, and someone shouts up at me:

"Hello?"

Tight against the wall, she tried to make herself smaller.

"Anyone there?"

She didn't move.

For what felt like a minute, nothing happened. Perhaps he had been convinced by her pretended absence. The only way of being sure was to lean forward and see him not seeing her, but to do so would break that spell. But if he came up the stairs to check, if he found her trying to hide—

Another door opened. The one Maggie had come through.

"Sir?"

A deep voice, a bass delight. The security guard.

"Oh, Joshua, hi—thought I heard someone."

"Just doing the rounds, sir."

"Yeah, you don't need to call me that—how you doing, anyway? All good?"

"All fine, sir."

Maggie recognised the rhythm of the exchange. A young man in a suit, and another in a uniform. White/black went without saying.

The younger man, the suit, came up a flight, so the two were only one level apart.

"You still turning out on a Saturday?"

Maggie heard a rustling kind of noise, as if he were miming something physical, the throwing of a ball, the wielding of a bat.

". . . Sir?"

"The old rugger?"

"I don't play rugby, sir."

"Oh, right, no, only I thought—"

"Don't go for sports at all, sir."

"Right. Must be thinking of someone else, yeah?"

"Sir."

"Well, I'd better be . . . Have a good night, Josh."

"You too, sir."

A door opened, closed.

Maggie's palms, flat against the wall, felt wet as well as cold.

"The old rugger," the security guard said.

After a moment, another door opened and closed, and she was alone in the stairwell once more.

When she was ready to move, Maggie crept up the remaining flights. She kept her back to the wall, and allowed time for her trainers' squeaks to subside between each step. It reminded her of being a teen again, slinking to her bedroom after a night spent with Jezza, desperate not to make a sound, knowing that the slightest creak would wake her parents' wrath.

At the twenty-fifth floor she let herself into the lobby.

Before the lights came on, there were men in each corner, four of them, waiting—a trap. But when the now-familiar flickering to life was done, the men turned into pot plants, their thick green leaves like rubbery imploring hands. Instead of earth, the pots were rim-full of smooth stones, between which, she imagined, each plant's roots twined and clutched. Low-maintenance vitality.

She took the right-hand door. There were offices here, but glass-walled, and she could see through them to the outside world—London after dark was a fairground whose wheels kept turning. Sleek buildings, already higher than they had a right to be, strained further skywards still, while in the spaces between them cranes clustered, resembling huge metal birds, building nests where the city allowed.

The streets were different at night too. Were colder, damper, and those who asked you for change did so in tones more aggressive than suppliant. The daylight hours taught them to know their place, and know it they did, and it was here, and now.

But she had a job to do. And once she was back on the street, Harvey would be waiting for her, bearing the thanks of a grateful Intelligence Service.

The office she was looking for was the largest on the floor, a corner suite. Ahead of her, the lights buzzed to life, and she knew that if she were observing this building from across the road, a story would be telling itself, one in which a lone woman—probably a cleaner—made her way through the night, scattering darkness as she went. But no one would guess her real mission. The door was not locked. She entered the room. *It will take two minutes, no more.* Harvey's promise. Before the lights had time to turn themselves off, she would be on her way back to the stairwell. She approached the desk, on which a laptop sat, locked to its docking device with a chain sleeved in plastic. *Two minutes.* She reached into her pocket for the flash drive.

It was gone.

Whatever happens, you mustn't let this fall into their hands.

She went through her pockets again—all of them. Even the ones the drive had never been in.

They mustn't find it. I can't tell you how crucial that is.

In her throat, a rising tide. It would all overcome her now, this mission she'd been chosen for, its importance, her own inconsequence. She could run away, hide under her bed, let the world go on without her. Except that that's precisely what it would do, wouldn't it? If she ran now, and failed in her mission, then the things Harvey had warned her about would happen, and the world would turn for the worse.

Once it's done its job, you have to either get it out of the building, or hide it somewhere it won't be found.

It hadn't done its job yet, and it was still in the building. It must have fallen from her pocket, would be on the stairwell, or somewhere between this office door and the lobby, or else—

The toilet.

There, where she'd crouched for hours, waiting for the office block to grow quiet and dim. She'd all but frozen in place, and even now her arms and legs felt heavy. But before leaving she'd had a pee, and that must have been when it happened, must have been when the flash drive wriggled free from her pocket. How could she not have heard it? But that was a useless thread to follow. For now, the choice was stark. She could return to the lavatory on the eighteenth floor, or . . .

Or the world would turn for the worse.

Maggie left the office. For no sensible reason she ran in a half-crouch along the corridor, as if that silent watcher in the neighbouring building weren't simply following her story but preparing to pick her off with a high-powered rifle. But the watcher didn't exist. She was alone, and hadn't been found yet, but she had no right to be here, and there was a guard on a floor below, and more people below that. All these nervy thoughts made her clumsy—at the door to the lobby her lanyard caught on a button, and in a brief slapstick routine she tugged its catch loose and her security pass fell to the floor. She bent to collect it and, as she straightened up, saw through the lobby door's porthole window the lift opening, and a man stepping out.

Once through the door, he stopped.

Was he sniffing the air, like a dog, for strangers?

Maggie had scrambled round the corner. She was now in a break-out area, so called, as if it were from here that workers might make their escape: an area three metres square, surrounded by high-backed sofas. She was lying on one in case he dropped to the floor and scanned for visible feet. Though it was more likely that he would simply walk past and see, not just her feet, but all of her, one whole young woman, twenty-six, very scared.

She closed her eyes, that ancient trick. *I can't see you, you can't see me.*

Harvey, what do I do now?

The man was talking. That same bass delight she'd heard in the stairwell. Joshua, the guard.

"Yo, yeah, I'm on twenny-five."

crackle

"No, it's juss, lights are on, man. Like something triggered them?"

crackle

"Pussy yourself, man. Doing a job here."

crackle

"Yeah, well, you get tired watching TV, we can always swap."

The crackling stopped.

Joshua paused.

He's by the pigeonholes, thought Maggie.

She knew those pigeonholes well.

And if he was by the pigeonholes, he was standing not far from where she lay. Might even be staring in her direction. If he had X-ray vision, she was caught already. And if she made a sound, a squeak, a rustle . . . She was trying not to breathe. To make herself smaller than small.

The floor creaked. He'd taken a step.

Towards her?

It was like a thought experiment. Any move she made to determine his whereabouts would give her own away.

Another creak.

Was that one closer?

The sofa was red, though this didn't matter. Of the other three, another was also red, and the remaining pair were blue. Big bright bold shades. There'd have been a meeting and someone would have passed round a catalogue and a vote would have been taken. Unless there was an underlying protocol which overrode democracy—a corporate livery, a company style. This didn't matter either. All that mattered was that she was curled up on the world's reddest sofa, whose tall back was the only thing shielding her from—

crackle

"Yo."

crackle

"Sweet, man, yeah, maybe a mouse. You know I put them traps down? The humane ones? Catch and release, right?"

The planet shifted, and if she hadn't already put a hand to her mouth, wasn't already biting down on her outstretched index finger, she'd have screamed.

He had turned and was leaning against her sofa. The back of his head had swum into her ken, a shaved and cratered moon.

"I'll release it I catch it all right. Release it from the window. Twenny-five floors, see if the little fucker lands on its feet."

crackle

"So yeah. Kettle on. See you in ten."

She could not breathe. She could not move. She could swear she could feel his heat.

Could smell the odour of smoked cigarettes.

The sofa moved again, crawled half an inch across the floor, and seemed to vibrate at the same time—what was he doing, was he toying with her?

Catch and release.

This was what cats did, they played with their food.

And then her heart flipped as he let out a huge sigh:

". . . Aaaaaaaaaaaaaaaahhhhhhhhhhhhhhhh . . ."

When Maggie realised what he was doing, that he was using the sofa's high back as a scratching post, she had to bite down on her finger again, this time to keep hysteria in. A big burly man, and he was giving it a real jiggle, reaching those places his own hands never could. It must feel so great, it must feel so grand, but oh God, what if he came round to push the sofa back into place when he was done? There she'd be, curled up like his special treat, and all he'd have to do was reach out and pluck her.

It didn't happen. The sofa stopped moving as he finished his scratch and then he was gone, back the way he'd come. She lay there while he, presumably, checked the nearest offices, their glass frontages making it unnecessary for him to step inside, and then she was hearing the lobby door open and close, after which there was only silence.

Five minutes later, maybe less, the lights went out.

Harvey, you should have been there.

She wanted to make herself happy, to turn this into an anecdote.

It was like being trapped up a tree, only the bear can't see you. And all it wants to do is rub its back against the bark.

But it wasn't working. Joshua was gone, yes, but she was still here, and the flash drive still seven floors below, in the ladies' loo—she hoped—and there was nothing funny about any of it. Maybe one day. Maybe when she was in a wine bar, and Harvey was pouring the last of the second bottle into her big glass. Then it would be funny. But not yet.

The seconds ticked by, followed slowly by the minutes. She wondered if it were true, if there were mice in the building, and with the thought came a phantom tickle up her thigh, and she yelped and slapped at her leg—couldn't help it—and the lights came on.

Which was, as it were, a wake-up call. Maggie stood and clenched her fists and hurried to the door. Let herself through to the lifts, whose numbers showed that three were at ground level, the other on the twelfth. This was as much a guarantee of safety she was going to get. Out on the stairwell the air felt colder, so much so her breath was visible. She counted the steps down: twelve per half-flight. One hundred and sixty eight in all.

On the eighteenth floor, all was quiet. There were no potted plants here, though, and it struck her she'd never noticed this before. At night, you have different eyes. Different details shuffle into view.

In the ladies', everything was as she'd left it. The door to the third cubicle hung open and the toilet lid was down. The automatic freshener had spritzed the air, and a tang of artificial pine prickled her senses, but on the floor there was nothing—no flash drive—and her heart slumped inside her.

Whatever happens . . .

Where was it?

. . . you mustn't let this fall into their hands.

If not here, where?

She'd have seen it on the stairs if that's where she'd dropped it. It would not have been possible to miss a thumb-sized wedge of plastic . . . This was the process her mind was going through, a logical one-step/two-step that, followed to its destination, would restore everything to how it ought to be, and leave her triumphant, the flash drive in her palm. But her body had ideas of its own, and even now was forcing her onwards, one extra step, beyond that final cubicle to the wash-space, where the basins lined the wall. And there, in the centre of the floor, having scuttled under the partition, lay the flash drive. It was with a peculiar sense of calm and rightness that she bent to retrieve it. All that panic, Maggie, and where did it get you? Just an unnecessary shock, when if you'd gone about things in a methodical way, you'd be out of the building by now.

It was time to take a grip. Drive firmly in hand, she left the toilets and headed up the stairs again. The lights on the twenty-fifth were still on, her recent presence still eddying the air. In the corner office she knelt by the desk, unfolded the flash drive so its male part was showing, and inserted it into its port. Then turned the computer on.

"What will it do?"

Harvey had looked at her thoughtfully, weighing up, she assumed, the exact degree of her right to know.

And if he had refused to say, would it have made a difference? She had come this far, after all—had allowed herself to be recruited. This might have made others bridle. Made them feel used. But being used was being shown that you were useful. And Maggie wanted to be useful.

Besides, he had already told her so much, so much.

"The company is not what it claims to be," for instance.

And: "If you could be part of something huge—something life-savingly important—what risk would you be willing to run?"

Nobody would know, of course. That had been clear from the start. The heroism he was offering was anonymous, deniable, and might even be deemed criminal if things went wrong.

Turning it over and over in his mind, the way she was turning the flash drive over in her hand.

"It will install a surveillance program into the company's network."

". . . That's all?"

"It's enough, believe me."

He had a halting way of speaking, a verbal dawdle that became more pronounced when he was at his most earnest.

"It will allow us to monitor all their internal communications."

"Can't you do that anyway?"

"Theoretically, yes. But not without using a much wider net. And that means bringing in GCHQ, and that means . . . I'm sorry, Maggie. We're outside your need to know here."

She said, "You're worried that the more people know, the more chance there is of someone leaking the operation."

"Maggie . . ."

"You're worried there's a traitor in your organisation."

He glanced around.

"Nobody's listening, Harvey."

She felt like they'd just swapped shoes—here she was, reassuring him. But they were talking quietly, and the café was its usual mid-morning mayhem. Infants in their carriages and mothers on their phones. They'd have more chance of being overheard if they'd been using semaphore.

Harvey said, "Certain operational . . . weaknesses have come to light. Which make this a particularly . . . sensitive matter."

"Which is why you need me."

He smiled that gently ugly smile of his. "Which is why I need you."

The drive weighed nothing. Weighed less than a snowflake.

"So I . . ."

"You plug it into the USB port, then turn the computer on."

"I'll need a password."

"Nope. You just wait until you're prompted for one. Then power down, and then remove the drive. Couldn't be simpler."

It was safe in her grip. Safe in her hand.

Couldn't be simpler.

The screen asked for a password, in that officious way screens had.

Maggie was tempted to key a retort, *Ha ha, screw you*, but had visions of a net dropping from the ceiling, of bells going off. To have come this far to get snatched now, well. That would be . . . disappointing.

She held the power button down until the machine emitted its yelp, then closed the lid, pulled the flash drive free, and put it in her pocket.

Job done.

All that remained to do was leave.

She took a glance round the office before doing so. The view through the windows aside, it looked ordinary, as if no grim business were conducted here. The desk, the furniture, the two armchairs posed around the glass-topped coffee table, were unassumingly anonymous. The art on the wall had been chosen not to draw the eye. She had a vision of whoever it was did business behind this desk, a blank-faced man, a featureless woman, with a circular face and an inked-in nose. And then she blinked it away, and headed for the lobby.

For a moment, she considered summoning the lift and dropping twenty-five floors in one fell swoop, marching past the front desk with a wave. Harvey was waiting for her down the road. He'd be standing on a corner, their appointed rendezvous, checking his watch. *My clever girl*, he'd call her, or something. Job done. Job done.

But the lift would be a mistake, a change of gear she had no business making. Careful steps had got her this far, and careful steps would see her home. She let herself back into the stairwell. Twenty-five flights, fifty sets of stairs. There was a rhythm waiting in them, and her feet found it soon enough, just at that tipping point between speed and safety. When Maggie looked down she couldn't see the ground floor, and when she looked up couldn't see the roof. Caught between two extremes, so much the opposite of her real life, she might as well have stepped, not into a stairwell, but through the back of a wardrobe.

There'd be time for thoughts like this later. For now what

mattered was these remaining flights, fifteen of them, fourteen and a half. Fourteen.

On the thirteenth floor, where else, the door opened, and she all but ran into his arms.

"Miss?" he said.

"Oh," she said. She came to a halt. Vocabulary failed her. "Oh."

"Can I ask what you're doing here, miss?"

"I was just . . . on my way home."

"But you shouldn't be up here, should you, miss?" Joshua tilted his big head to one side. "Not this time of night. I know you, though. I know you, right?"

"I work here," she said, fumbling her security pass free.

He clicked his fingers. "I do know you," he said. "You work in the post room."

". . . That's right."

"You work in the post room," he repeated. "But you shouldn't be here now."

"No, I was going home."

"Yes, miss," he said. "But you'd better come with me first. Just while we straighten this out."

2

There was a mantra for the environmentally aware: *You're not stuck in traffic, you* are *traffic.* The same was true of rush hour. To be caught in a crowd was to be the crowd, and to walk through rush hour was to drift between channels, tuning in and out of conversations poured down mobile phones. Every passing stranger was a beacon in a sea of static. The secret was not to transmit yourself: to remain mute, anonymous, unheard. Your screensaver a neutral blue. That was safest. That was Maggie Barnes's choice.

Each morning, her journey to work involved a ten-minute walk, a short bus ride, two Tubes. Maggie sat by windows when she could, and looked out on London's streets and tunnel walls, or gazed through her own reflection, or stared down at her lap. There was a rhythm to it, a tappable beat, the fingers of her right hand drumming it out on the knuckles of her left. She wore no uniform as such, but a blue jumper was provided, which she was allowed to take home. Around her neck a lanyard on which her security pass swung. While travelling—when anywhere—she tucked this out of sight. Your identity was your most valuable possession. If you lost it to a stranger, you could lose everything else.

These were the lessons that London had taught her in the months she'd been living here. That you kept your head down and your purse hidden. That when shouting broke out on public transport, you looked the other way.

The post room where she worked, in the basement of an office block south of the chartered Thames, was itself anonymous. The room was partitioned in two, with a counter carved into the dividing wall, through which she received deliveries of mail thirty, forty times a day, most of it from the hands of bicycle couriers. These were a serious bunch, who wore all-weather shorts and metal face-studs, and who, as they waited for your signature, would tell you how far they'd come, in how many minutes and seconds, but never asked how you were. From the bandolero-like holsters on their chests, their radios spat new instructions before they were out of the door. The others—the posties, some from the actual Post Office, the rest from rival firms—were friendlier, flirtier, and liked to chat, as if they saw themselves as messengers in a wider sense, bringing not only mail but fresher news, such as what the weather was doing, and who would win that evening's match. Sometimes their bulletins involved the death of a courier, another cyclist crushed beneath London's wheels, news flashes they delivered with no hint of keeping score. They themselves drove vans, or trundled along on sit-up bikes, speed not being among their priorities. But they recognised that couriers too played a role, even if one that was bound to end badly.

The mail was almost all manila-flavoured, the dull brown of officialdom, with the computer-generated addressee's details neatly centred behind a translucent window. The occasional handscrawl demanded interpretation, though, and not all letter-senders knew to include a floor number in the address. And sometimes a handwritten envelope would be cream or even blue, the recipient's name lacking a title, and the forename written in full. Stamped, not franked. The word Private underscored three times in the top left corner. Who sent letters now? Who sent personal letters to a business address? Maggie couldn't help but think that these were tokens of illicit affection, signs of the times. All those gadgets which once seemed gifts to the adulterous—mobile phones, email systems—were now links in the chains of evidence used to drag guilty parties through the divorce courts. So pens and paper were reached for instead, which she thought an improvement. An erotic email was pornographic, one more speck of dirt in the landfill of the Internet. An erotic letter you could put under your pillow, out of the reach of Googling fingers. When Maggie distributed the post, sorting the mail by floor and leaving it in the various sets of pigeonholes, she imagined the building's secret lovers loitering feverishly in her wake, eager to snatch their precious booty from the heaps of unwanted correspondence.

So much for letters. Larger packages she fed through a machine, which analysed them for dangerous content. There were instructions on the wall, telling her what to do if the machine detected anything untoward beneath the cardboard clothing, inside the sealed plastic, but Maggie had never been called upon to follow them. There was always the possibility of danger, but danger never materialised. This was true of most people's lives, and especially so in the post room.

On the other side of the counter, things piled up and disappeared again. Huge great breeze-blocks of toilet roll wrapped in cellophane. Industrial vats of liquid soap. Packing cases stuffed with sachets of instant coffee and powdered milk, with bonsaid forests of wooden stirrers. These were collected on trolleys by janitorial staff, few of whom lasted more than a couple of weeks. Maggie had no explanation for their rapid turnover. Her own colleague wasn't going anywhere. She called him Dirty Mike—he never seemed to shower, or never effectively—and mostly sat in the corner, listening to London's commercial stations, or playing Angry Birds on his smartphone. He always had a crossword on the go, but made such little progress, she was starting to think it was the same one.

Maggie worked an early shift, and finished at 3:30. For the final leg of her journey home she walked a different route, through a small park, which had a boating lake, which was a pond really, and a squadron of parakeets, who filled the trees with exotic chatter, and shellacked the paths with extravagant droppings. There was an exclusion zone round the park's café, negotiated by the park's café's dog, and Maggie would stop here for coffee, and sometimes a slice of cake, sitting outside if the weather warranted, or in the happily steamy interior when it didn't. Occasionally the café offered free refills, which could be dangerous—a second cup was "crazy coffee": too much caffeine made her hyper—and was a popular spot with local mothers, so there was usually a fleet of baby carriages clogging the doors. It would be a good place to meet with friends, Maggie often thought.

But she had no friends. She had come to London expecting to broaden her horizons, and instead had found them narrow to the width of a letterbox, the size of a cubbyhole. Her sister lived here, but they were not close, couldn't be close, not when Meredith had enjoyed all the sibling luck, bagged all the sibling gifts, commandeered all the sibling prospects. Meredith had passed exams, sailed through university, been offered the first job she applied for. She worked in the kind of office Maggie delivered mail to. She had a shiny flat, and a shiny car, and a shiny man. He had probably bought her a shiny ring by now. Trailing a few years in her wake, her adolescent potential cruelly undermined by an unwise, in every sense, boyfriend—Jezza—the best Maggie had managed had been four GCSEs, and a succession of zero-hours jobs in her home town. London had been her attempt to escape. To a degree this had worked, but only to a degree. And there were, after all, three hundred and sixty of them to navigate.

A quiet cup of coffee in a noisy park café made up the kindest minutes of her day.

London was defined by its river, it was said. London was the Thames, and had as many moods. But of London's many moods, Maggie had so far known only the moodiest. Its broadest river was the flood of strangers she found herself pressed among daily, and when she walked by the Thames itself, the only embrace it offered was equally cold. London's heart was carefully guarded. If it had a soul, she supposed it could be found in the street names that had survived fire and blitz, and now adorned prospects that would be utterly alien to the people who had dubbed them: Amen Corner, Cheapside, Paternoster Row. And whatever the opposite of a soul might be, London's lay buried beneath the barren towers of Canary Wharf.

Which was miles away from where she lived. Yet even in this unregarded corner of the city, her rent was high, her room small. It had been advertised as a space in a shared house, but she rarely saw her fellow tenants, and each bedroom door had a bracket fixed so it could be padlocked shut for security. Her trips to bathroom and kitchen were timetabled scuttles. The longest conversation she'd had involved an accusation of stealing someone's butter.

But Maggie Barnes had remained unbowed. She was learning to put feelers out, as recommended by the articles for the sad that London's freesheets recycled monthly. She was still wary of Facebook, unwilling to reactivate her account after the hateful campaign Jezza had waged, but there were other outlets. That day, the day she met Harvey Wells, she had been on Twitter. *Central Perk for coffee and cake! Nom nom!* She had seven followers, some of them bots. But it was a start.

This had been the previous autumn. It had been lightly raining, and she had sat inside, beneath the board on which local events were broadcast, and she had put her phone away and drunk her coffee and eaten her cake, and Harvey Wells had appeared in her life.

"I'm going to leave you for a few minutes, miss."

"I've told you, I work here. That's all."

"I'm sure it will be fine, miss. Everything will be fine."

But Joshua had locked the door as he left.

You can't do that!

And yet he had.

The room was one she hadn't known existed. On the third floor, not far above where she spent her working day, but not a room she'd ever noticed, and not especially memorable now she was inside it. A bare table, two plastic seats, and half a window, the other half disappearing behind a partition wall. Half a view was all it offered, and that was obscured by a Venetian blind, slicing London's nightlife into lateral fragments. There was a fire extinguisher by the door, and a fire-blanket, and a pair of glow-sticks in a plastic case, "to be used only in the event of emergency." A poster on the door was two dense columns of print, which up close translated into instructions for the evacuation of the building. The nearest safety points were across the road and in the car park round the back. A black raincoat, probably Joshua's, hung on a hook on the wall. Its cuffs were frayed, and though it had hoops to loop a belt through, it had no belt.

She wondered how long it would be before he was back, and who would be with him.

The company is not what it claims to be . . .

■ ■ ■

"Is it all right if I sit here?"

"Yes, no, that's fine."

"Thank you."

The tables weren't large, but she could hardly claim to need the entire space. The man who had joined her looked to be in his forties, with features tending towards the pig-like, too splayed across his face to be attractive in any conventional sense. He was wide shouldered, or his overcoat was, and as he sat Maggie realised she had seen him before, in the park. He'd been walking round the lake—pond—smoking, his pace delib-erate, a slow-motion strut, as if his mind were too occupied to devote itself to brisk movement. His receding hair was untidy, though he had tied a small hank of it into a back knot. It was as though he were aware that men his age could make foolish style choices, and had gone out of his way to satirise this incli-nation and satisfy it, both at once.

A reluctance to appear unfriendly kept her at the table for two minutes longer. It was when she was reaching for her coat that he spoke.

"You're Maggie Barnes, aren't you?"

". . . I'm sorry?"

She'd remember this response later, halfway between an apology for who she was, and a request for confirmation.

"You're Maggie Barnes. You work at Quilp House."

". . . Have we met?"

"Don't you know?"

"I . . . I have to go."

"There's nothing to be frightened of. My name's Harvey. Harvey Wells."

"I don't know you."

"But now you know my name."

"I'm going to go."

He had caught up with her before she had passed the children's play area, with its bobbing Olympic mascots that resembled demented sex aids.

"Maggie, I'm sorry. I didn't mean to frighten you."

"Go away."

"I'm not a stalker. I promise."

But all stalkers thought that, didn't they?

"I said go away. I'll scream."

"Jesus." He backed away, holding his hands up in surrender. "I'm sorry, Maggie. I really am."

"Go away."

Not, all things considered, an auspicious start.

Joshua would be making a phone call, seeking further instructions. He'd have no idea what really went on in this building—a living wage worker, like herself, he was well below the salary bracket for inclusion in conspiracy—but it would have been impressed upon him that if anything out of the ordinary occurred, there were numbers to call, bells to ring. The uniformed security was for show. She'd have minutes, at best, before the real thing showed up, the serious men in expensive suits.

I don't mean to frighten you, Harvey had said. *Or I do, but only so you'll be careful. You do not want to fall into the hands of these people. So extra special care, yes?*

Extra special care, Harvey. Except here she was, in a locked room, and *these people* were on their way to fetch her.

And she still had the flash drive in her pocket.

If she'd had her phone now would be the time to use it, tell him she was in trouble, but he'd made her give it to him earlier. Going dark, he'd called it. A phone was like a beacon, and as long as it was in your pocket you could never be sure you were unobserved, unnoticed. Fat lot of comfort that was now. She tried the door but it remained locked. Checked the window, but the drop was too great. She could smash it with the fire extinguisher, but she'd still be imprisoned, except with a draught. Perhaps she could smash the door with the extinguisher, come to that, but having wrestled it from its stand, she found it difficult to lift. Which didn't bode well for her chances if a fire broke out, but that wasn't top of her worry-list right now . . .

Unless there was a way of making a fire happen.

She'd smelled stale tobacco on Joshua earlier. Most smokers carried their gear with them, but if that was Joshua's raincoat on the wall . . .

Maggie went through the pockets like a professional. No cigarettes, and no matches either, but stuffed in a mystery pouch sewn into the lining, like a buttoned-up afterthought, a disposable lighter.

And on the ceiling, the winking eye of a smoke detector.

■ ■ ■

The following day, she had taken a different route home, and the day after that was her day off. But on the third day she had resumed her usual routine, and there he had been, in the café, with a rose in a twist of cellophane, its surface beaded with moisture.

"I just wanted to say I'm sorry."

No one had bought her flowers in an age. And a single flower was so much more potent, somehow.

She said, "How did you know my name?"

"May I sit down?"

"I need to know how you knew my name."

"It'll be easier to explain if I'm sitting down."

There was a scene waiting to happen, one in which she screamed at him and he fled, or at the very least backed away apologising again, but that would mean the end of her afternoon coffees, her slices of cake. She couldn't come back here to be whispered about. There was a fragility about her London life, and if she knocked away any of its supporting structures, she might never find her feet again.

"Sit, then. But if you don't tell me how you knew who I am, I'm calling the police."

"Really, you don't need to do that, Maggie."

He sat, and pushed the rose across the table to her.

"I've told you my name's Harvey Wells. And the reason I know who you are, and where you work, is because of where I work."

She had checked the building register. There was a copy in the post room.

"You don't work at Quilp House."

"No. I don't. Can I get you another coffee?"

"How did you know my name?"

"I work for the government, Maggie. I work in a . . . special department. And the reason I'm here is that we need your help."

It was surprising how swiftly it worked. She stood on a chair, held the lighter to the detector, clicked it lit, and barely had time for second thoughts before an alarm went off, a huge jangly noise, louder than during the day. Maggie climbed down. She could hear nothing but the alarm, would have been surprised if anyone in London could hear anything but the alarm, and all she could do now was drag the fire extinguisher behind her, press herself against the wall by the door and wait.

Right now, many floors above her—but also below, it occurred to her, and all around, and potentially everywhere—the bug she'd loaded into Quilp House's system was crawling into its new home, making a nest among all that data, poking around among files and folders. Whatever happened now, she'd achieved that much. But if they knew what she'd done—if they found the flash drive on her—they'd know the damage she'd wrought, and perhaps undo it. If Joshua returned, and she managed to get past him, she still couldn't be sure of leaving the building. Which meant she had to find somewhere to lose the drive, put it somewhere it wouldn't be found.

Unless Joshua didn't come at all.

But he'd just locked her in a room, and the alarm was

screaming, and how could he possibly not come and release her? It would be tantamount to murder. The flames were lapping at her ankles for all he knew. The walls hot to the touch, the floor a glowing griddle.

She thought—

But before she knew what she thought there was a scraping at the lock and the door was flung open.

"Miss—"

She rolled the extinguisher into his feet.

"Do you read the papers?"

"I . . . of course."

"The real papers. Not the freesheets."

"I see the *Financial Times* at work."

Which she did: see it. Yesterday's copies were gathered by the cleaning staff, and left in piles for recycling. You'd have expected a friendlier outlook, given its pink tint, but even its headlines seemed designed to shrivel the attention.

"Then you'll know we're going through difficult times."

This was clear enough. As far as Maggie could make out, we were always going through difficult times, and even when we weren't, things never got easier. Maybe it was different on the upper floors, where the better times pooled and set like jelly, the vaunted trickle-down somehow never coming to pass.

"You don't have to pretend," he said. "It's all right not to know these things. Life's hard enough, God knows. Just putting the food on your plate."

He glanced at the slice of cake she'd ordered.

She said, "It's a treat. I don't have many."

He waved that away. "What I'm going to tell you has to stay between us. Do you understand?"

"Aren't you going to ask me to sign something?"

"No. Because this is what we call a deniable conversation. If I asked you to sign something, there'd be a record of it. As it is, this is just between us. But it's only fair to . . . Look. If you want to go now, go. I'll pay for your, your treat. And you'll never see me again. But you'll be passing up the chance to do something special. Don't you want to do something special with your life, Maggie?"

"Maybe I already am."

"In that case, I should leave you."

He stood and buttoned his coat.

She said, "I understand."

". . . Understand what?"

"That this is just between us. I won't tell anyone." An easy promise: she had no one to tell. "What sort of something special?"

Harvey Wells unbuttoned his coat, and sat, and told her.

Maggie heard rather than saw him fall. One of those unproducible noises, unless you're in motion: a yelp of alarm that briefly eclipsed the one ringing overhead, and then was folded inside a clatter that was similarly short-lived. She was already haring for the stairwell, down which small groups of late-night workers were ambling, grumbling about the interruption, but already fishing out phones and e-cigarettes and other coffee-break tools. She tried to mould herself into their number. She was picturing Joshua climbing to his feet, shaking his head to make its carousel of birds and stars disappear.

And then he'd be after her.

The lobby was cold. The sliding glass doors that gave onto the external steps were open, so as not to impede flight from the flames. Not that anyone believed there were flames. It was just another hobgoblin of office life, an enforced evacuation at what was always the worst possible moment. At least, this time of night, there were no crowds. When drills happened during the day, the queues for the lifts took half an hour to shift.

She emerged into the lobby a second behind a tall blonde woman, articulating her discontent at a volume Maggie suspected was constant. Through the glass doors she could make out a dozen or so people, blatantly disregarding the need to head for the safety points, across the road and in the car park round the back. What she couldn't tell was whether there were serious men in expensive suits among them. Her own safety point was streets away, and consisted of Harvey Wells, waiting on a corner like a travelling salesman on a promise. He'd have his overcoat on against the cold, against the wet, but no matter how late it got he'd carry on waiting, would carry on waiting "until they damn well cart me off." All she had to do was worm her way out before Joshua recovered, before the serious men cottoned on to her, and all would be well.

But if all was not well, she still had the flash drive in her pocket.

And they mustn't find it.

I can't tell you how crucial that is . . .

She stooped by one of the lobby's pot plants and fiddled with the lace on her left trainer, before slipping her hand into her pocket and palming the drive. The plant, like those on the upper floors, was bedded in pebbles. Here was where she'd hide the drive, just plunge her fist into the stones as she rose to her feet, and bury the plastic mischief out of sight.

A hand dropped onto her shoulder.

"What are you doing?"

She looked up into the unsmiling face of a young Chinese man.

"What if I were to tell you that Quilp House is a cover for some of our nation's deadliest enemies? Not the kind who plant bombs on trains, or organise mass killings. But the kind who undermine the financial stability of the country, working to ensure that what's left of our industry, and our travel networks, and the great landmark buildings of this very city, that they all—that everything—ends up in foreign hands, under actual foreign control? Would you believe me?"

". . . Why should I?"

"Because this is serious, Maggie. What I'm telling you isn't something you'll read in the papers, and it's not something anyone who works there would ever admit. Hell, most of them don't even know. As far as they're aware they're just going about their daily jobs, managing the investments placed in their care, clocking on, clocking off, then going home and shaking their heads at the news on the telly, just like the rest of us. Never knowing that they're right there where the real news is being made."

"Mr. Wells—"

"You can call me Harvey."

"—you're obviously distraught about—about whatever it is you're distraught about, but you're not making much sense."

"I guess not. Can I trust you with a secret?"

"You already have."

"Yes, I already have. You're right. Well, here's another one. I've never actually done this before."

"Done what?"

"What I'm doing now. Having this conversation. With you."

"You've never talked to a woman before?"

This was the first time she noticed the way the tips of his incisors showed when he smiled. "I've never recruited anyone before."

"Is that what you're doing?"

"I hope so. If not, I've wasted a lot of time, and'll probably get sent to the salt mines. Joke."

It had perhaps sounded funnier in his head, Maggie thought.

He said, "Quilp House has been under investigation for some while, and what we've learned, and you'll forgive me if I put this in the simplest of terms—I'm not being patronising, Maggie, it's only when I use the simplest terms that I even understand it myself—but what we've learned is that a lot of what we thought were separate companies established by individuals, or small consortiums, for tax avoidance and investment purposes, are all part of the same huge network, and what looked at first, and even second third fourth fifth glance, to be individual trading operations with small investments in a variety of interests, from the London Underground to a steel company in . . . Bolton, to one of the largest suppliers of dialysis machines to the NHS—you name it—all fall under the control of one single company, and that all their transactions, the focal point of their operations, well, basically, Maggie, you work there."

"Quilp House," she said.

"Yes, Maggie."

"So it's run by what, some conglomeration of businesses?"

"No, Maggie," said Harvey Wells. "It's run by the Chinese government."

"I mean, don't you know there's a fire on?"

He smiled, and offered his hand.

"Oh, yes, I know. I was just doing my shoelace up."

"Very sensible. You don't want to trip. Not when you're making your way out of the towering inferno."

His hand was waiting, and if she didn't reach for it he was going to take offence. But the flash drive was in her curled fist, and she hadn't come this far to surrender it so lamely—

The alarm stopped, and a silence so sudden, so shattering, broke out that everything else stopped too.

Her knight errant looked away.

Maggie crammed her fist into the pit of stones, released the drive, pulled her hand free.

He looked back. "Well. Seems like the emergency's over." His hand was still hovering so she took it, and he pulled her upright. "Which floor are you on?"

"Isn't this ground level?"

He looked puzzled for an instant, then laughed. Nearby, someone was audibly wondering what the next move should be. Into the street, or back to their desks? The young man on reception was on his feet, in his shirtsleeves, regarding those in the lobby with an outstretched palm, as if about to deliver instruction, but had a phone wedged to his ear and was obviously still receiving such himself. A few floors overhead, Joshua was either rubbing his head, or shaking it, or letting out a mighty roar that would soon come echoing down the stairwell, unimpeded by fire alarm. And among those gathered on the pavement would be the serious men, the real security, and Maggie wasn't sure young Galahad here wasn't one of them.

"Oh, there's my friend outside—I'd better just . . ."

He still had hold of her hand.

"If you could let me go?"

"First you have to tell me which floor you work on."

". . . What if I don't want to?"

"Oh, I have plenty of time. Now that we know the building's not actually on fire." He smiled, and she saw he had very flat, even teeth, as if he took a file to them rather than a mere brush. He smelt of expensive soap. And yes, was wearing an expensive suit, though his shirt was open-necked. She imagined a rack of ties in his wardrobe, the decision not to wear one as painstaking as the choice between plain and patterned when he did. "I'll just follow you back to your desk."

She snatched her hand away.

A shadow crossed his eyes, made up of the usual male responses: surprise and hurt that she wasn't taking this in the manner intended, and the inevitable result of mixing the two, which was anger. He blinked this away. "Hey, I was only—"

"I have to meet my friend."

The receptionist was putting his phone down and explaining that everything was fine, no need to worry, but if people could just wait until the fire service had checked everything out before returning to their desks as Maggie passed through the glass doors. The air was alive with cold and damp, with the vanilla-smell of nicotine inhalers, and with whatever it is that makes night taste different to day. Among those on the pavement were other Chinese men, mostly quite young, and a pair of women in business attire which seemed to Maggie calculated to make everyone else in the postcode feel dowdy. No one gave her more than a glance. As she reached the bottom of the steps she risked a look behind, and young Galahad was by the doors, staring after her. There was, as yet, no outraged Joshua bellowing for vengeance, but this could not be long in coming. She hurried along the street, replaying in her mind the moment when she'd thrust the flash drive into the plant pot—had Galahad seen her doing this? And had her action been as slick as her memory pretended it was? A slapstick alternative wavered into view, of stones scattering across the lobby floor like marbles, and the plastic drive peeping out from the pot like an ambitious seedling.

In the background, streets away, a siren edged into hearing. Maggie walked faster, to keep time with her heart. She would not look back again, not even if she heard someone running after her. She would continue on her innocent way, her long day's work at last done. One step, another step. One of these steps went wrong, and she almost tripped at a kerb. A passer-by said "*Care*ful now," and laughed, as if he'd said something funny.

And here they came, the footsteps following.

She quickened her pace. They could not grab her on the street, no matter what they thought she'd done—this was London, and there were rules. Up ahead a bunch of lads were weaving in and out of themselves, tying their evening into one last happy knot, and she wondered what they'd do if they saw her being accosted—stand and watch or come swooping to her aid? Or take the middle way, and film it on their phones . . . The footsteps drew nearer, accompanied by thick breathing, so heavy it was a wonder he could carry it, and then he was past her, a jogger, just a stupid late-night jogger, his tracksuit banded with dayglo stripes. The group ahead parted to let him pass, and one or two shouted encouragement, unless it was derision, and Maggie didn't care either way. She looked behind, and there was nobody following. There was a police car, though, pulling up at Quilp House, its lights running somersaults up and down the nearby buildings.

The police. Of course. This was London and there were rules, but of course they'd call the police because as far as anyone knew, this was a law-abiding company, which meant that the police were on their side.

The group of lads parted for her as they had done the jogger, but with no cat-calls and no disrespect. She wanted to know if a hue and cry was starting, whether Galahad and Joshua had compared notes, and were even now pointing a policeman down the road, aiming him at her back. *Courage.* This was Harvey's voice, and it warmed through her like a welcome glass of wine. *Courage. You've done your bit. You're nearly clean away.*

She reached the corner and turned. Up ahead was dark, most of the streetlights out, and it was darker still where the railway bridge crossed the road. Her legs were starting to drag, the adrenalin draining away. In her mouth . . . She didn't know what. Something sour and acidic. This was what happened when your senses worked overtime. There was a figure under the bridge, but she only knew this because of the orange glow of its cigarette. And, too, because this was where Harvey had said he would wait. This thought brought strength back to her legs, and she started to hurry, even as the figure ahead threw the cigarette to the ground and came to meet her.

When he put his arms around her, she felt like she'd come home.

"Okay, you're okay. I've got you."

Maggie breathed in tobacco fumes and heavy wet overcoat.

"Now we're going to take you somewhere safe."

And she knew that it was all going to be all right.

Part two.

1

She had dozed off in the bath, and that's probably why she cut her finger. So she explained it to herself afterwards. She was groggy from her amniotic nap—a word from some old poem, hated at school, and a scar on her memory since—and that was why the scissors had slipped while she was trimming her fringe. It wasn't a bad cut, but finger-cuts didn't have to be. Fingertips were especially sensitive, which was obvious the more she thought about it, but the downside was that when you damaged one, you knew about it. Putting the scissors down, she held her finger under the cold tap until the smarting subsided. First a warm bath, then a cold drenching for her digit. It was as if she were having a sauna one small part at a time, to lessen the shock.

It would be something to tell Harvey about. Did Harvey want to hear about it, though? She didn't want to bore him.

Even once the hurting was done, she kept her finger where it was for a while. It was mesmerising the way water fountained off her hand, each drop reflecting light from the overhead bulb. A tiny domestic version of a palace celebration. Magnify it the right number of times, whole crowds would ooh and ah.

Afterwards, she finished trimming her fringe. A little lopsided, but it would do. If she kept trying to balance it out, she might end up bald. This was the kind of idea that itched until it was scratched, so to keep herself distracted, even once the scissors were back in the drawer, Maggie looked through her DVDs. The laptop was slow to power up, so she let it grind away while she chose what to watch. *Friends*? Maybe not again. Something funny, though. Something happy. *The Big Bang Theory*. She had two DVDs' worth of *TBBT*, from different series—seasons—but that didn't matter, because it didn't take long to work out what had happened in the characters' lives between one disc and the other. They'd met some girls and eaten some food. They were still in the same apartment, though, and still sat in the same places. One day she'd fill in the gaps, but for now she'd relive familiar moments, which was a way of trampolining into a different reality, one in which she shared their jokes, their endless takeaway meals, their absurdly spacious living room.

Her apartment too—the word didn't really fit—was mostly one room. It was a basement flat, a converted cellar, and dark, because the few windows were at ceiling level, and only let in low-down light, the kind that gathers in pools on pavements. Besides, Harvey had covered them with black bin liners, for security. The street she couldn't see outside was quiet. It was a cul-de-sac, so the only traffic noises were locals, parking their cars, and the occasional motorbike or scooter able to swerve around the concrete bollards. Maggie could identify the odd footfall, though. Someone wore high heels, regardless of the weather. She heard them in the evening, two or three times a week. It was like a code being tapped out, a message meant only for her.

There was a kitchen, but without a door, just a beaded curtain, like a prop from the 1970s, and a tiny bathroom. And a bedroom, which wasn't much bigger. Barely contained the bed, in fact, which was crammed against a wall, but still didn't allow room for the wardrobe to open fully. Sometimes on waking she'd haul the duvet through and lie on the sofa and continue dozing while thin daylight struggled to make its presence felt. Everything seemed on hold then, as if she'd found a way not of stopping time, but of slipping outside its compass. Otherwise it either dragged interminably or sputtered in fits and starts, like now, when eight episodes of *The Big Bang Theory* had zipped past without touching the sides, as Jezza used to say about drinking too fast. She ejected the DVD and put it on the bottom of the pile.

Her finger felt warm, the one she'd cut. She wondered if it were infected, and what she'd do if it were, and took a paracetamol because that was all there was. It still felt warm, though that might have been because she was thinking about it too much. But if it were actually infected then that would remain the case whether she was thinking about it or not. She held it under the cold tap some more, but couldn't determine whether this was helping or making it worse. Various scenarios suggested themselves, up to and including her having to perform an auto-amputation, slicing the finger off to save her hand, her arm, her life. There was a carving knife which might do the job. What surprised her was how calmly she was contemplating the possibility. How calm she would remain if push came to shove—or knife to bone—was another story entirely.

Meanwhile, she'd eaten three biscuits, and the packet was still on the table. Before she could succumb to temptation, she hid it in a cupboard. Hiding wasn't the word—she kept thinking of words that weren't the word—because finding it again would be easy, but out of sight out of mind. Too many biscuits lately. *Podge.*

And what she could do with was an exercise bike. She was sure there were foldaway types available, and it could live behind the sofa when not in use. And she needed something, because her jeans felt tighter. Everything did. She thought: I could do the stairs for a bit. The stairs didn't lead anywhere except to the door, but they'd be exercise. Fifteen of them going up, same number coming down. Obviously. Thoughts like that kept tripping her—thoughts which, if she heard someone else say out loud, she'd wonder if they were simple. Meredith had a look she used to give her when she'd said something daft, and remembering the look, Maggie wondered how many daft thoughts she'd had—simple ones—she hadn't caught herself having. Was that one of the ways you fell mad? It was like the bar had been taken away. You needed to be around other people to know what was normal. When your company was mostly yourself, standards frayed.

But not being around other people was the point, of course. She was safe here precisely because of that. She was safe. Here, in the safe house.

This little queendom, bounded by damp shadows.

Their early meetings had taken place in the park, when she'd stop on her way home for coffee, sometimes cake, and he'd be pacing round the pond in his slow, contemplative way, usually smoking.

He worked for the Secret Service.

"We just call it Five."

She'd never met a spy before.

"How would you know?" he'd asked, with a twisted smile that cast his face into that of a friendly goblin.

(Ugly but not in a bad way, she'd found herself thinking. Ugly, but she was getting used to it.)

But he was right, how would she know? She'd told him she just would. But what she mostly meant was, she hadn't met anyone she could imagine being a spy before now. Nobody interesting enough. Though they were probably trained not to seem that way.

"How long have you . . . had an eye on me?"

"I don't want you to feel you've been targeted."

"Except I obviously have."

"But only because of where you work."

Quilp House.

"Is it really some kind of . . . base?"

"Does the roof open, you mean, so a space rocket can be launched? Does it have an alligator pool in the basement?"

"I think I'd have noticed."

"Yes, well, good, because no, it's not a base as such. It's one of several . . . locations we're keeping an eye on. And you working there is a boon."

"It's only the post room."

Harvey said, "Which is ideal. You deliver the mail to every floor, right?"

"Yes."

"So you have access."

He made it sound as if this were the Holy Grail.

"Tell me again what they do there."

So he'd told her again what they did.

At first he had wanted her to "keep an ear to the ground"—nothing more.

"You're on the premises. You're on site. We call that human intelligence, and it's worth its weight in rubies."

"I thought that was an honest woman."

"Which is what you are, Maggie. Our honest woman. Our woman in place."

So many of the things he said meant more to him than they did to her, as if he were speaking a code to which she didn't have the key.

"And what does keeping my ear to the ground mean anyway? Not the expression. I know what the expression means. What exactly do you want me to do, I mean."

"Nothing dangerous."

"I'm already not doing anything dangerous. That's not telling me enough."

"What I want is that if you see anything unusual, anything out of the ordinary, you let me know. That's all, really. And I pass it on to . . . well. You don't need to know. Chain of command."

He couldn't smoke in the café, of course. He'd sit across from her, and she'd be able to smell the tobacco on his clothes, his breath. This was unpleasant, and yet, like his ill-fitting features, it was swallowed by the intensity of his presence. For all the slowness of his movements, the calculated way he paced around the pond, there was something urgent wrapped inside him, something tightly bandaged up.

(Jezza had been like that, towards the end. Constantly near the boil, rage never far from the surface. When she tried to get him to talk, there was a string of reasons: her ceaseless nagging, his dead-end job . . . Anything but the truth.)

"What do you mean by unusual? All I see is people doing their jobs. Sitting at computers. Making cups of tea."

"Just . . . unexpected activity. The sort of thing, when it happens, you think, that's not happened before."

"I'm mostly in the post room."

"I wouldn't be asking if it weren't important."

"What do you think is going to happen?" she had asked.

"I think we're going through a period of change. There are . . . complications. It's a difficult situation."

Newspapers had told her that much.

She said, "You need to give me more than that. You're asking me to, well. To break the law."

"There's nothing illegal about what I'm asking you to do."

"But you want me to be a spy."

"I think—*we* think, we think some kind of attack is being planned." He raised a hand as if to silence whatever reaction she was about to make. In fact, Maggie hadn't been about to react. She was too stunned. An attack. "But not the kind you're thinking of."

She was thinking what everybody thought. Bombs in the Underground. Automatic weapons spray painting the walls in shopping centres.

"We think there's going to be an economic shift. That there'll be a concerted attempt to bring a number of UK-based companies under Chinese control. At the same time as . . . Look. All I can really tell you is that it's important. And that we need your help."

He had looked at her hands, which were on the table in front of her, forming a protective circle around her mug. She wondered if he was going to reach out and take them in his own, and it was possible that he was giving thought to this, but if so, he decided against it.

Maggie was glad. It would have seemed too obvious a ploy, something planned in advance.

She said, "Okay."

"... Okay?"

"Okay. I'll do it. I'll be your ear on the ground."

If she'd been expecting this to produce another of his crooked smiles, she'd have been disappointed. He simply looked down at her hands once more, and nodded, as if a weight had been removed from him, only to be immediately replaced by another, equally burdensome one. Maggie found herself wanting to comfort him, though was aware how absurd this was.

At last he said, "Thank you, Maggie." And then, "We'll need to talk more. I'll see you tomorrow."

When he left the café, he was deep in thought. He didn't even look up when ducks started fighting on the lake, beating their wings against the water, screaming their duck throats sore with avian hatred. Maggie watched him until he was out of sight, and when she returned to her coffee, it had gone cold.

Had she known then that he'd eventually ask more of her, had intended to do so from the start? She supposed she must have done. The tales she had brought him from Quilp House, her *reports*, had been of all-day meetings and unexpectedly heavy mail deliveries, and can't have meant anything, though he always pretended her intelligence was gold. But mail was only mail. And she had no idea who the people at the meetings were, no idea what they were about. It was a company. It occupied the entire building. There were always meetings, because that was what companies did. Without meetings, nothing would happen.

Months of that, until he had brought her the flash drive.

Whatever happens, you mustn't let this fall into their hands.

Anyway. Now she was here.

Because she knew he'd arrive soon, she did what she always did, which was pace the basement, taking deep breaths, gauging whether it smelled bad. There was a fan above the oven, which was supposed to draw odours out, or suck them in, whatever, but it was difficult to tell how well it worked. When you stayed anywhere, you grew accustomed to what it was like. So she couldn't tell whether, coming in from outside, you were entering soupy air, breathing in smells of tinned food and pasta, and the foggy residue of her bath, and—worse—whatever noxious odours drifted from her toilet, unconquered by the scented candles arrayed around the place.

Thinking this, she lit another. The dead match scribbled its oily signature on the air.

Stop it, she thought. There are worse things to worry about. You're safe here. Maggie's safe.

But when he arrived, glad as she was to see him, there was a complicated undercurrent to her greeting.

"You're just out the bath, aren't you?" he said, after they'd embraced.

So she smelled clean, which was good. But did that mean she didn't always?

Harvey flung his coat onto the wooden chair which sat in a corner, devoid of any purpose other than being his hanger.

He had brought a bottle of red, and offered it to her as if she were his hostess in a perfectly usual setting. She gave a little bob as she accepted it, to make him laugh, though he didn't notice. He had had his hair cut, she thought, and then decided he hadn't. It had simply become tighter on his scalp, which happened when it went unwashed too long.

"Shall I open this now or . . ."

"Or?"

"Afterwards?"

"Afterwards," he said. "Oh, definitely. Afterwards."

Afterwards, they sat up in bed and drank wine, her head on his shoulder. Maggie had not asked him for news, because if there was any he would tell her soon enough, and besides, the news was always bad, and she didn't want to hear bad news.

"This is nice," she said.

"Uh-huh."

"Have you missed me?"

"I always miss you, Maggie." He lowered his head, so it was resting on hers. "You know that."

She cried for a while, and he made soothing noises.

"You've cut your fringe," he said, when she was quiet again.

"Yes."

"I like it. It's nice."

"I cut my finger too."

"Not on purpose?"

"No. The scissors slipped."

He held her tighter. There was a pungency about him tonight, a new acidity, but she decided it was the wine, either the effect it was having on her or the effect it was having on him, its flavour seeping through his skin.

She said, "I was thinking—"

"Uh-oh."

"Ha ha. I was thinking about what you said last week, about how important it is I get enough exercise."

(He had said something, she refused to bring to mind the exact sentence, but it had included the word "podge"—they had been lying like this and he had poked her in the tummy. *Podge*. She had pretended not to mind. What else could she have done? Stormed out?)

"The stairs," he said. "Run up and down the stairs a hundred times a day. That should do it."

"A hundred?"

"Or a hundred and twenty. I don't know. You'll find your limit. You just need to stick with a regime, that's all."

"But it's boring just going up and down the stairs and it's not safe. Up at the top you have to bend your neck else you'll hit the ceiling, you know you do, and that can't be safe, or good for your neck. My neck." She wasn't sure how this had got to be about his neck. "I don't want to knock myself out and fall down the stairs. What would happen then?"

She had a sudden memory, a starburst image, of the damage that could be done inside a moment. Of rolling the fire extinguisher at Joshua's feet, and being through the door before witnessing his crash.

"You're not going to hurt yourself. Stop worrying."

She let her head drop back onto his shoulder. "No, well," she said, her voice muffled, but not so much he couldn't hear. "What I was thinking, it would make more sense to get one of those exercise machines. Like a stationary bike? You can get quite small ones, I think. It wouldn't take up much room."

He shifted position.

"Harvey? Could you not ask them to get me an exercise bike?"

"Can we talk about this some other time? I can't stay long."

"Why not?"

"I just can't."

"Well it won't take long to talk about, all you have to do is say you'll do it. Ask them to get me an exercise bike. It's hardly a huge demand, is it?"

She could hear herself getting louder.

"Harvey? Please?"

"I don't know, Mags."

"Why not?"

"It would attract attention."

"How?"

"Just, bringing it in. Collecting it from the shop. We could hardly have it delivered, could we?"

"Why not?"

"It's a safe house. It's supposed to be secure. You know?"

"But—"

"And they're probably pretty expensive. Bound to be."

"So what? They can afford it, can't they? *Five?*"

"Yeah, but—"

"So just go buy one. And then put in a chitty, or whatever you call it. Claim it on expenses. It's a legitimate expense, isn't it? I was your spy. That's why I'm here."

"Maggie—"

"So you're *supposed* to look *after* me!"

"Maggie, the thing is. Something's happened."

He had used this phrase before. *Something's happened.* It was never followed by anything good.

If she could wind back the conversation, and stop it at the point when he'd suggested she use the stairs—*run up and down the stairs a hundred times a day. That should do it*—she would do so. That way she might never have to hear what he was about to say now. Like everything else, it was all her fault.

"What's happened?" she said.

"Don't get mad."

"How can I get mad? I don't even know what you're going to tell me."

"Yeah, but when I do—"

"Harvey, just tell me, okay? Just tell me."

"It's Five. The Service."

"What about them?"

"It's an operational thing, and I argued and argued, but—"

"Just. Tell me."

"They've cut the strings."

"What does that mean? I don't even know what that means."

"It means they're no longer funding the operation. They say it was over a long time ago, and it failed, and they're saying—they're saying you were never officially recruited. Because of the way I approached you. They're saying it wasn't orthodox, and they're not liable. And they have no responsibility for you and your—our—situation."

She blinked. The room about her shifted, without becoming larger or brighter.

"Maggie?"

"Is it because of Joshua?"

"No."

"Because if they're going to turn me over—"

"Nobody's going to turn you over, Maggie. Not to the police. Not to anyone."

"I didn't mean to kill him."

"I know."

"It was an accident."

"I know."

"And it's been two years."

"I know," said Harvey.

Something's happened.

Lots of things had happened.

In the two years since that night at Quilp House when she'd killed Joshua the security guard, the world had changed. Of course it had. In the two years before then it had changed too, in ways Maggie hadn't noticed, or had only noticed once. When did people start watching TV on the Underground? That used to be science fiction. And then suddenly it was something to do over someone's shoulder, like reading their book, and just as normal. When did video ads appear at bus stops? You looked away, and when you looked back things were different. It had always been like that. It hadn't stopped just because she was in the safe house.

So. Here were some of the things that had happened, while she was living her cutaway life in the basement:

The economy had folded. Not gone into recession, the way it had the last time, and the time before that, but folded. This was the phrase Harvey used.

It was the high street banks, he had told her. Those immutable, pedigreed institutions, with their venerable logos and their permanent presence. Those bywords for stability. All gone.

Had just one gone shaky, the government would have stepped in. But as soon as the fault lines showed in one structure, the people—everyone—scared—rushed all of them.

"It was madness."

The banks, themselves desperate, called in debts and foreclosed on mortgages. It was like a giant closing-down sale, happening everywhere, at once.

"There were families on the streets, all their possessions in bin liners. It was like some kind of . . ."

Harvey hadn't been able to say what it was like. Because nothing like it had happened before, or not *here*. Not to *us*.

They called it the tsunami effect.

Businesses, unable to pay wages, crumbled overnight.

Public transport vanished.

Power supplies became intermittent, with whole cities blacked out for up to thirteen hours a day.

The army patrolled high streets, stood guard at depots housing food supplies. Established a perimeter around Parliament and the palace, facing outwards, and similar cordons around prisons, facing in.

The BBC ceased transmission. Other news outlets began broadcasting contradictory reports, and calls for calm that provoked increased panic.

All within ten days—that was how long it had taken. From a peaceful, functioning society to a hooligan mess, and it had only taken ten days.

"They say Liverpool city centre was razed to the ground. Not two bricks left standing."

Maggie had never been to Liverpool, but still. It touched a nerve.

"They must have been so frightened," she said.

"Who?"

"Everybody."

And then the Chinese government had stepped in to bail the country out.

She said, "I thought you said they were the enemy. The Chinese."

"They are."

"Then why did they—"

"Maggie. Ask yourself this. Why did the banks fail, all at the same time? Why did other governments, other foreign institutions, withdraw their funding and sell stock in British companies overnight? You think they did that off their own bats? What did they have to gain, seeing the UK go down the tubes?"

They were dancing to a Chinese tune. The Chinese economy, the dragon in full roar, was wrapping its scaly tail round the country, and flapping its terrible wings.

But the buses were back on the streets again. The lights were on, most of the time. If once-familiar high-street supermarkets were no more, a new chain, Sunrise Stores, was starting to appear, and most of its shelves were usually full.

An armed presence remained visible at hot spots round the country, but the flag flew over Buckingham Palace, making the Queen's presence plain for all to see.

There was a price to pay, of course, because there always was. The benefits system was an X-ray of its former self, with unemployment and disability payments cut to below subsistence levels, and while the state pension was still being paid, it too had been substantially reduced, and the national retirement age increased to 70. The NHS continued under that name, but it cost £32.50 to register with a GP, and two thirds of the hospitals in the UK had closed their doors. After the Collapse, as it had become known, conscription had been introduced for under-22s, partly to tackle the near 100 per cent unemployment in this age group, and partly because an increased army was useful at times of national stress. There was talk of raising the age to 25.

"Austerity" was looked back on with ironic fondness, by those still capable of irony. "Stern measures" was the phrase now in use.

"Was it because of what we did? I did?"

"No."

"But you were running an operation against one of their—"

"I know. I know. Look." While he talked, his hand crept to the nape of his neck, and he tugged at the lock of hair there, bound in place by a rubber band. "It would have happened anyway. That's the truth of it. But it's possible, yes, that because of what we did, what *I* did, that it all happened sooner than it might have done. We both have to live with that."

And while the country had started to heal itself, at least outwardly, the hunt for Maggie Barnes continued.

Two years. She had no phone, no TV set, no radio.

"They can track you, Maggie. Your phone would be a beacon."

And there were other ways of pinning her down, other electronic giveaways.

"The security services remain independent, at least in name. But Chinese intelligence has a presence in this country, and while both governments maintain that's not so, I guarantee you it is. There's a private firm, it's called New Dawn, and it came into being not quite a year ago. Out of nowhere, it's taken over all Civil Service security contracts, including at GCHQ. It's the biggest Trojan horse in history, and we're supposed to pretend it's above board, but it isn't. The Chinese might not be running Britain's surveillance outfit, but they're getting first view of its product."

She remembered how he had slumped when telling her this, as if something inside him was draining away.

"And nobody's supposed to be living here, Maggie. I'm sorry. It's too risky. No Internet, no TV. Nothing. I'm sorry. It's just not secure."

She couldn't remember, though, whether he had cried. She knew she had.

Two years could bring hundreds of changes.

She would not know the world, she thought, if she were in it now.

But of all the things that had happened, the worst was Joshua being dead.

"How? How can he be dead?"

"Tell me again what you did."

"I didn't mean to—"

"I know. I know. But tell me what happened. Once you were in his room."

Already it seemed like something she'd seen on TV. When she recalled it, she was hovering behind her own shoulder, an uninvolved spectator.

"I rolled the fire extinguisher at him."

"It was on the ground?"

"*Rolled*, yes, it was on the ground!"

"Please, Mags. I'm just trying to determine—"

"I rolled the fire extinguisher at him. And then I escaped through the open door."

"And you didn't see what happened next?"

"I was running away! I was doing what you told me to do!"

"Shush now. Shush."

He'd put his arms round her.

The safe house—the basement flat—was new to her then. It was her first day there, hot on the heels of her first night. For twenty-four hours her heart had been hammering, at first for the excitement of a job well done—she was a spook now, a spy, an *asset*. This was the word he had taught her. Nobody had ever thought of Maggie Barnes as being an asset before. She had heard herself called a liability more than once—usually by her sister—but never an asset.

And her heart had thumped too when he had taken her to bed that night, though that wasn't really the way it had happened. She had taken him, that was the truth of it. There was no way she wasn't having a man that night. Not after what she'd been through.

But then it was the evening of the next day, and Harvey had been gone for hours, and when he had come back, this was the news he had brought her, that Joshua, the security guard at Quilp House, was dead.

"You've heard of eggshell-skull syndrome?"

"No! No! I never have!"

But it wasn't something, once you had heard about it, that required much explanation.

All the time she had been awaiting Joshua's angry voice, his sudden reappearance, he had been lying dead on the floor instead, with empty eyes, the blood no longer moving within him.

"What's going to happen to me?"

"Shush now. Nothing. Nothing's going to happen."

"They'll be looking for me!"

"But they're not going to find you. You're safe here."

Nobody was ever safe. Nobody was ever safe anywhere. Was he really trying to tell her any different?

"I was just trying to do what you said."

"I know."

"I didn't mean to hurt him."

"I know."

"What about the police?"

"What about them?"

"Should we go there? Explain it all?"

"Maggie. Listen."

She had been sitting on the sofa. Not all of her memories were as pristine as this. Some had faded like hopscotch grids in wet weather, and others never rose to the surface of her mind at all, but this conversation, the one about Joshua, the one where he was dead for the very first time, felt like something she could replay in its entirety whenever she wanted. And sometimes when she didn't.

"Listen. We're not going to the police. We can't go to the police."

"But—"

"Because nobody can know what you were doing there last night."

"People already know! You know!"

"I'm Service. I'm Five. Remember? We know, of course we do. But nobody else can. Or else . . ."

That was the first of his *or elses* that she could recall. The first time he had dropped any hint of the other things that were coming their way, the other somethings that would happen.

"Maggie, listen. Joshua's dead, and it wasn't your fault, nobody thinks that, but all the same you've got to stay hidden for a while. Just for a while, until things get sorted out. You're a hero, you know that? You're not a villain, you're a hero. It's not your fault he died, and if anyone's to blame it's Joshua himself, because he was on the wrong side in all of this. You're one of the angels, Maggie. That's all there is to it. We know that. Everyone at Five knows that."

". . . So I just stay here?"

"For a while. Not for long."

"But they'll notice I'm not there at work. They'll know I've gone and they'll put two and two—"

"No. No, it'll be all right. I'll make sure a letter's sent, saying you've been called away, saying you've had to go home for a family emergency. Nobody's going to put those two things together. Nobody saw you there, did they?"

First you have to tell me which floor you work on.

"There was the man. Right at the end. Remember?"

"Oh. Right."

"That's why I had to hide the flash drive . . ."

"And he was Chinese."

"Yes."

He said nothing.

"They'll find me, won't they?"

"We'll work something out," he said. "I promise."

And here they were still, two years later.

"Will I have to move?"

It felt like hours had passed, but they hadn't. Time was doing what it always did, and playing tricks. It was no more than three minutes since Harvey had told her Five were cutting the strings, but three minutes was enough to have your foundations threatened. When you didn't know where you'd be three minutes from now, that three minutes dropped away like an abyss. Any second of the hundred and eighty on offer could see you slip and fall, and you'd be gone before the clock caught up with you.

". . . No."

"But if they're not paying—"

"We'll manage. For now. Don't worry."

"And they won't give me up? Won't turn me in?"

"No. They wouldn't do that. This isn't about wanting to turn you in . . . It's about resources, Maggie. Like everybody, like all of us, the Service has got to tighten its belt. It's been pared to the bone as it is."

He had been pared down too, she thought. He no longer had that tiny pigtail. She wondered if that had been part of his cover, an image he'd been trying to project, but had never asked, worried that his answer would be yes, and that the Harvey Wells she had first met was not a real man, but a character assumed in order to recruit her. But that was not the only difference. His hair was greyer, his eyes flecked with worry, and his cuffs and collars frayed. The newest thing he wore was the scarf she'd given him. Often he arrived with the smell of cigarettes in his wake, as if he had stubbed one out on the doorstep. Once, when she complained about this, he had snapped at her, and she never dared mention it again.

For now, though, he held her in his arms, and she felt safe. The world outside had grown alien and hostile. Here, at least, things continued as she had come to know them.

Harvey said, "I'm sorry about the exercise bike."

"It's okay."

"No, it's not, it's . . . I'm sorry. Maybe some time. But not yet."

"It's okay," she said again, and then: "I'll do what you said. I'll run up and down the stairs."

"Good girl."

But I hope I don't hit my head at the top, she thought. I hope I don't fall and break my neck. No ambulances screaming through the streets any more. The only sirens were police cars, imposing stern measures. They'd find her eventually, if she died in here, and carry her out in a plastic bag. Chinese men in suits and dark glasses would watch her shovelled into a car boot. They'd know what she'd done, or tried to do. They'd know she'd had a mission, and failed it.

If Joshua hadn't died. If that hadn't alerted them to Harvey's operation . . .

It was too late. This is what happened. There was no changing that now.

Harvey grunted, and she realised he'd fallen asleep. That meant he would stay a little longer, which was a good thing.

As she lay breathing quietly, not to wake him, she felt her finger throbbing again, and thought once more about taking a knife to it, if that was what the situation demanded. *Cut the finger off to save the hand.* Could she do that?

She would do what was needed, she thought.

After a while, she slept too.

2

London was full of memorials, of statues to the famous dead. There were plaques fixed to houses where genius once lodged, and words carved into pavements where brilliance walked. Anonymous souls had their monuments too. Unknown soldiers were remembered in granite and marble, and husbands and wives, parents and children, in brass plates fixed to benches in parks and on riversides. Ghost bikes—haunted white cycles—were left near the sites of fatal accidents, and bunches of flowers tied to railings marked spots where lives had ended. Even the homeless were granted epitaphs, in scrawled notes pinned above nooks where they'd spread their blankets. In London, it would be easy to think you were walking over bones every step you took, each of them carefully labelled. A city erected on the remains of its own inhabitants, with every street corner a cenotaph.

But plenty went unmourned, and these were the ones Maggie thought about. There were stories that never got told, questions that went unanswered. How many people get lost in the city? Die under bridges, and aren't ever found? She remembered walking past bleak shapes huddled under cardboard in shop doorways, so many of them they were rendered invisible, but what about those who went home and closed the door and became lost in their own tiny rooms? Wasn't there someone who died surrounded by Christmas presents, and slowly mummified as the days weeks months went by? How come nobody rang her bell? She must have had a life—who had she bought those presents for?—and still she'd fallen through a crack she can't have known was there. How could you drop out of life like that? Why didn't bailiffs turn up? This last thought nagged at Maggie, wouldn't go away. You'd have thought the woman owed somebody something, enough to get them banging on her door. When your credit card debt didn't matter—was there a clearer indication that you'd failed to leave a mark?

Her own traces would have been obliterated by now. Somewhere in the city, at an address she was starting to forget, the remains of her old life must have mouldered into nothing. The padlock she'd fixed to her door would have been broken, her possessions dumped in the street. Someone else would be living there now. Maggie wondered if they ever thought about her, the phantom previous occupant, who had left for work one morning and slipped into oblivion. Though perhaps, in this strange new world everybody else was living in, such disappearances were ever more common.

She sat at the foot of the stairs leading up to the door she'd only been through once, and wondered what London felt like now.

■ ■ ■

Sometimes she found herself making lists of things she was frightened she'd never see again—sunsets, dogs in parks, children playing hopscotch. But the habit came to seem unreal. Were these actual memories, or was her mind playing with words and images? A sunset happened whether you noticed it or not. And she wasn't sure children played hopscotch any more, unless there was an app available. There probably was.

Memory should be easy, she thought. In films it came so completely: flashback scenes iridescent with detail. In books, whole pages of dialogue were rendered intact. In real life, there was not much. The occasional detail. But mostly she was still here, on the bottom step.

She determined that eighty was the maximum number of times she could do the stairs. Eighty, meaning forty up and forty down. After that, she had to rest until her legs unjellied. The first time, she'd nearly been sick.

If there was a way of rolling back time, she wondered how far she would go.

It did not matter that the wardrobe door wouldn't open fully, because there was little inside it. Maggie had few clothes. Her jeans were the ones she'd been wearing the day she arrived, and the sweatshirt she had on now was one of Harvey's. He'd brought her other gifts, including a tracksuit she'd hated at first but now wore most days, and some underwear she found scratchy, but she liked the sweatshirt best. It hadn't really been meant as a gift, he had simply forgotten to take it away with him, and he hadn't understood at first when she explained that it was now hers. But he'd got the message eventually. It looked better on Maggie anyway.

Besides, such appropriation rendered the sweatshirt a boyfriend garment, and thus far removed from the hand-me-downs of her pre-teen years, one of the inescapable indignities that being a younger sibling involved. In time, she'd reappraised Meredith's taste, and frequently borrowed items without permission. A dark blue jacket with a zip she'd managed to break, to her sister's fury. A yellow scarf, which she'd so successfully pilfered it had become hers, and had survived even her translation into the safe house, because she'd given it to Harvey some months before. It had been an impulse gesture, a thank you of sorts. After Jezza, she hadn't thought she'd ever trust a man again. Harvey had proved her wrong. And like the best of kindnesses it had proved its own reward, because there it still sometimes was, around his neck, a reminder of a different life.

Anyway, clothes. Laundry was a chore. She washed things by hand in the bath, and left them to drip dry. Her jeans took two or three days to recover, and felt stiff as cardboard afterwards, as if new again. That was a treat, in a small way. New clothes had been a rarity even before the safe house. Her wages were so small, her rent so high, she'd had to save for everything, and only ever made one purchase at a time. This should have had the effect of making each new item feel finer, but somehow the opposite was true. Nothing took the shine off new boots faster than having to wear them with shabby jeans. Her trainers, though, the ones on her feet now, they were lasting a good while. They'd seen little wear and tear, after all.

But just because the wardrobe wasn't packed full of clothing didn't mean it wasn't useful storage space. Harvey had brought her a handful of DVDs the previous day, perhaps as compensation for there being no exercise bicycle—not now, not ever—and to maximise their novelty, and prevent herself gorging on them, Maggie decided to hide some at the back of the wardrobe, an emergency supply. In forgetting what they were, she'd be storing up a surprise for some future week. There were half a dozen of them, bundled together with elastic bands and bought as a job lot from Oxfam—there were no new films available, and Amazon no longer operated in the UK—and as she reached to place them on the low shelf at the back of the wardrobe, her fingers encountered something, a piece of laminated plastic the size of a credit card, though that's not what it was. Brought into the light, it turned out to be a library card instead.

And that was how she discovered Dickon Broom.

When Harvey arrived the following day, she had questions.

"Am I the first person who's lived here?"

"It's an old house. A hundred years old. How could you be the first person to live here?"

"I meant, live like this. Am I the first person who's used it as a safe house?"

He was taking his coat off. It was raining, and droplets shone on its collar and sleeves. Wet overcoats had their own peculiar smell, one borrowed from the outside world and brought indoors. Harvey's coat was better travelled than she was.

"Why do you need to know? Why are you asking me this now?"

He sounded tired and worn, and sometimes when he was like this it ended in argument, or in her crying about something, and him having to hold her a little longer than usual afterwards, though once or twice he had simply left, and there had been no afterwards. Maggie didn't want any of that to happen, but still. Her story had bumped into somebody else's, and she wanted to know whether the edges fitted together. At the same time, she wanted to keep Dickon Broom to herself. It was so long since she'd had anything of her own, that hadn't been brought to her by Harvey.

"I've just been thinking, that's all. Wondering who's lived here before me."

And what happened to them, she didn't add. Where did you go after being at a safe house? Somewhere safer? And what did that look like?

Now he was taking his shoes off. They were black, and scuffed. The expression "down at heel" was probably called for. He didn't keep slippers here, just padded about in his socks, and these, too, were past their best. Nothing was new. Nothing would ever be new.

"Make some tea?"

She put the kettle on, and he came up behind her while

she was dropping a teabag into a cup and put his arms round her. He had been smoking. She worried what the air was like in here, what odours he was letting himself into when he came through the door, but he brought more than enough with him.

He said, "I can't tell you, Maggie. I'm sorry. You know I can't."

"Why not? It's not like I'm going to tell anyone, is it?"

"Mags—"

"I mean, it's not like I have people dropping in, not like I'm gossiping on the phone all day. Who do you think I'll tell, the woodlice? You know there are woodlice, don't you? I keep saying we've got woodlice, and you never do anything."

"Are you finished?"

"Who am I going to tell, Harvey? I never see anyone."

"And what happens if you're caught?"

She wriggled free of his embrace. The kettle was shuddering to a climax, steam ploughing into the air.

"I shouldn't have said that. I'm sorry. You're not going to be caught. You're safe here."

"How do you know?"

"I just do."

She reached for the kettle, but instead of pouring the water into the teacup, she poured it down the sink. More steam billowed, plastering itself to the taps and the surfaces of the saucepans.

"Because it's tried and tested, okay? It's a tried and tested safe house. So yes, there've been people here before. But I can't tell you any more than that, and you're not to ask, all right?"

"Nothing's safe forever though. Is it?"

For a moment she thought he was going to lie to her, as he had done so many times on similar subjects, but instead he simply nodded. Meaning yes, he agreed with her. That nothing was safe forever. He was past pretending that it was.

"The fact that they've not found us yet doesn't mean they never will," she said.

"I'm working on a plan."

"What kind of plan?"

"About getting you away from here. Somewhere where there's more room, somewhere you can go outside. Out in the country. Far from the cities. They're not good places now."

It was odd, but the first thing she felt on hearing this was a splinter of fear. The country. The country was packed full of open spaces, so many of them that they crowded up against each other, barely held in check by raggedy hedges. You could be seen for miles, out in the country.

And then the thought of sunshine took hold of her, and of warm air touching her skin. She thought of walking up a hill to the top, and looking back, and seeing the tracks she'd left in the wet grass.

"When?" she said.

"Soon."

"How soon?"

"We'll need a car. These things take time."

Maggie was still holding the kettle. She felt ridiculous now, having poured the hot water away. She turned the tap on, and started over.

"It'll be okay," Harvey said. "You'll see."

She wasn't a real spy. She had fallen into the role, and then into this half-life, by accident. There were no books about people like her, and no films either. But Dickon Broom was different. For Dickon Broom, the safe house must have been a necessary bolt-hole after a whirlwind escapade. Dickon Broom would have chosen this career for its adventurous possibilities.

Harvey had left. She was alone again, and unsleeping. Sleep was difficult. She had to lure it into her bed with stories.

How long had Dickon Broom lived here? And who had he been hiding from? Dickon Broom, anyway, what kind of name was that? Not a heroic one—something about its rhythm fell wrong—but that only contrived to make it realer. He was flesh and blood, not a celluloid fantasy, and to have arrived in the safe house, he must have placed himself in harm's way. And not for him, she thought, the accidental assassination of a minimum-wage security guard. He must have really got up somebody's nose—Maggie wondered whose. Who were the global villains back then? Russian mafia types and Islamist extremists? The US President? Or perhaps it was the Establishment he'd crossed swords with, uncovering some nasty secret about a powerful individual. All those possibilities swept away by the Collapse, as simplifying as a landslide.

Her hand closed around the library card. She had placed it

under her pillow, as if it were a love token, or a guarantor of pleasant dreams. What else did you use a library card for, if not to borrow stories? Some of which might have a happy ending.

He'd have been trained in all the things she knew nothing about, in the art of scaling walls and dodging bullets. She pictured him silhouetted against London's skyline, a sleek shape in tight black clothing, evading faceless guards on rooftops, abseiling through windows. He'd been here in the safe house before the Collapse, but she couldn't help thinking he'd fought against it, nevertheless. Had perhaps staved it off, preventing it from happening years before it did. Had been sent by Harvey Wells on missions more dangerous than her own, and had returned victorious but wounded, in need of sanctuary. Thinking these thoughts, she felt the basement flat become roomier. He had slept in this bed, laid his head on this pillow. Wherever he was now, those experiences were part of his baggage. The safe house had been one stop on his journey elsewhere, and this meant that she too might move on some day. Just as soon as Harvey got his plan together, and managed to get hold of a car. Things weren't as easy as they used to be. When Harvey said "car," he also meant petrol. All those things we used to take for granted.

Her bed was cold, and the sheets slightly damp. The laminated card had sharp edges. She knew that when she woke—if she slept—her palm would retain the dents its corners made. Even ideas could do this, leave marks behind by being gripped too firmly. And now that she had met Dickon Broom—now that he was part of her life in the safe house—she wondered how long it would take him to make an appearance. This seemed the logical next step. He would somehow find out about her—was he still one of Harvey's agents? His assets?—and come to her rescue. Harvey was a desk man at heart. He pulled strings and cast shadows, but essentially he was one for paperwork, for assigning tasks others would carry out. He was not precisely a coward, and had shown this by standing by her even while Five abandoned its responsibilities, but even so, he had become worn where the outside world had rubbed against him. The Collapse had left him tarnished and afraid, and while he was surely doing his best, this might not be enough to save her. Not any more.

"I need a hero," she murmured, and though the words were indistinct even to her own ears, she felt them a kind of prayer nevertheless. She did not expect God to be paying attention. But if they could slip through the night-time quiet, and somehow find their way into Dickon Broom's heart, they might yet prove her salvation. So thinking, she slept at last.

Mornings were difficult. If she was expecting Harvey there was much to do, including having a bath, and thinking of things to say. It mattered to her that she could still be interesting. And on days when she wasn't certain he'd be there, much of the same routine prevailed. It would be awful if he arrived unexpectedly, and she was unbathed, with a head full of empty thoughts. This had happened more than once, and always ended in tears.

Today was a Harvey day, so she began it with her new regime, forty times up the stairs, forty times down. Her mind found a rhythm while her body was doing this, and the train of thought she'd stepped off last time picked her up again now. If there was a way of rolling back time, how far back she would go? To before she killed Joshua, of course, but having reached that point, there seemed little sense stopping. No, she would travel on backwards through the days, living dusk to dawn, all those journeys from and to Quilp House, all those afternoon breaks in the park before the day's work began. Maggie had been lonely then, and a little frightened that her life would never change, but as things had turned out, change had not been the answer. Change had wrought havoc. It had erased her from the normal.

Would she go as far back as Jezza, she wondered—to before his deceits had unwound her life? His treachery had been commonplace enough: he had had someone else. But the someone else was pregnant, and that was not. The first Maggie had known of it, Jezza was married. She had thought herself a girlfriend, and suddenly she was the other woman, an identity foisted upon her without warning. She had become un-personed. The life she had thought she'd been living had been erased, and she herself had become a blank.

Her heart was pounding. Forget Jezza. Up the stairs, down the stairs. Up the stairs, down the stairs. She put her hand to her stomach as she climbed, imagining it diminishing beneath her palm—*Podge!*—and would have laughed at herself had there been anything to laugh at. Sweat was gathering in the usual places. The air would be swimmy with it soon, and she would have to light more candles, and flap a towel to make it scurry into corners, and have all its molecules swap places.

How far back would she have to go to change everybody's future? To make all the molecules swap places, everywhere, and make things utterly different?

She remembered the café where she'd spent so many afternoons, with its view of the park, and the pond on which ducks swam. That was where she'd first laid eyes on Harvey Wells. She could even recall the specific afternoon, one on which she'd been feeling optimistic. She'd sent a tweet, her eleventh? *Central Perk for coffee and cake! Nom nom!* How many followers had she had—nine? Seven? Some ludicrous number. Did they wonder what had happened to her? Were they anxious to know how many more cups of coffee, slices of cake, she'd enjoyed since then? Did they tweet amongst themselves, *Where's Maggie?* I always liked her. It's a shame she slipped off the map.

One hundred and forty characters. That was how many you were allowed in a tweet. One hundred and forty characters, like a hugely-cast soap opera. No one knew that many people. Not in London, anyway. In a village, perhaps, but not in London. London was far too full of people to know that many.

She had lost count of her ascents, her descents, but she knew she was nearing the end because her legs felt about to give way. She wondered how many of these Dickon Broom had managed. She thought probably two hundred. At least. A man like Dickon Broom would keep himself in shape. His life was one of constant training, with emergencies waiting round every corner.

Seventy-nine, she decided. Eighty. And that was that.

Maggie sat on the bottom step, her body quivering as if in anticipation. She recalled weather like this, the moments before a storm, when the very air felt wet with rain that hadn't begun to fall. But she hadn't seen weather in a long time, and might have been misremembering.

Later, she bathed and dressed. It was in the bath that the idea first came to her, and grew like a seed from stony ground. Was that biblical? It sounded biblical. You would never expect it to have taken root, let alone put forth a stem. And this reminded her of something . . . It was the plants at Quilp House she was thinking of, their pots brimful of smooth pebbles. Those plants had grown healthy, their leaves the size of dinner plates. Stony ground had something going for it.

The idea was this: she wanted to go out.

When she'd first arrived in the safe house, that was all she'd wanted. Or all she'd wanted after the first few days, anyway, days during which she'd been too shocked by what had happened, Joshua dying, to want anything. While absorbing that grief she mostly lay in bed, hoping no one would find her, but it was astonishing—frightening—how life asserted itself, and made fresh demands. The same way roots clung to life among the stones: always this need for survival, always. So after a few days she had wanted to go out, to breathe proper air, but by then the Collapse had begun, and Harvey had had to explain that it wasn't safe. That if she were discovered while things were so lawless, there'd be little he could do to protect her.

"But Five—"

"Five are propping up the country," he'd said. "Five are making contingency plans in case the bottom drops out. And we go into free fall."

She had tried to imagine what that was like, a country in free fall. It would involve high winds, trees bending low and buildings becoming loose. But Harvey had a bleaker frame of reference:

"Like Germany between the wars. You remember those stories, how it took a basketful of currency to buy a loaf of bread? And if you got robbed, it was the basket they were after. The money had no value."

"Things can't get that bad."

"Can't they?"

We're only ever three meals away from anarchy, he said. Think of the happiest family you know, the most secure, the most well-balanced. Now remove food and warmth and shelter, and picture how they'd cope.

"And that's just the backdrop." He put his hands on her shoulders, but not to embrace her. He wanted her to be looking into his eyes while he spoke. "They're after you, Mags. The people whose job it was to protect the company we tried to hack into."

"The Chinese secret service," she'd said, her voice a whisper, nearly a lisp.

"You're safe here. Trust me. But you can't leave. Not yet."

And so she hadn't.

But things had calmed down, hadn't they? Things weren't as bad as during the police strike. She couldn't remember when that had been, exactly—spring of last year?—but it was long finished now. And the streets here had never boiled over anyway, one or two nights of loud brawling aside, which could as easily have been pub overspill. Even under the new dispensation, with foreign hands twitching Westminster's threads, people would still fight for stupid reasons. It didn't matter that clever ones had become available.

The idea wormed away within her all afternoon. She made a new kind of meal from the contents of the same old tins, and all the while she was preparing it, the idea was fastening its grip.

She would tell him, she decided. As soon as he turned up. Tonight. She would tell him:

"I want to go out."

Harvey laughed. "Good idea. Where shall we go? A movie? A pub?"

"I'm not joking."

"You think you're not joking. But you don't know what it's like out there." He put an arm round her. "Come on, Mags. We've talked about this. You're safe—*we're* safe—as long as we're careful. And being careful means staying in here."

"You go out."

"Of course I do. It would be more suspicious if I disappeared. That happens, they'd come looking for me."

"Do they know you're a spy?"

"They?"

"The Chinese."

It sounded ridiculous, put like that. The Chinese. As if they thought with one mind, moved to one heartbeat. What was that old fable, that if everyone in China jumped up and down at the same time, there'd be earthquakes our side of the world? That didn't happen. Not all of them jumped, and the earthquakes weren't physical. Anyway, Harvey knew what she meant. She meant the Chinese.

He said, "Yes. I have to assume so."

"Why?"

"Because that's the safest way." He reached for his cigarettes, which he'd put on the arm of the sofa, and she tapped his hand. It was bad enough him smelling of stale smoke. "Okay, okay. I was just moving them."

"Why is it safest?"

"Mags, they have eyes everywhere. I already told you about GCHQ. If they're getting their info from the world's most effective listening post, then yes, you can assume they've got the names and addresses of everyone who works for Five. Why do you think I keep such a low profile? I'd be here all the time if I could be certain I wasn't being watched."

That made her eyes sting. When Harvey said such things she felt warm and wanted, though at the same time as if she were very far away—watching what was happening, and weeping.

He slipped his arm around her, and fondled her breast.

But if this continued, there'd be no time left for conversation. They would go to bed, and afterwards she'd doze a little, and when she was awake again, and ready to talk some more, he'd be gone, or going. So she shrugged his arm away, and moved apart.

"What's the matter now?"

"I've told you. I want to go out."

As she said the words again, she realised she was no longer sure that was actually true. Stepping outside, feeling her feet on the pavement, the air on her skin, these ideas were frightening. But . . . She didn't want to back down. She needed Harvey to take her seriously, to recognise that what she wanted mattered. That she couldn't be diverted by a hand on her breast.

"Maggie—"

"No. I don't want to hear you say *Maggie*. I just want to hear you say yes."

"You don't know what you're asking."

"Of course I do! If I didn't, I couldn't bloody well ask it, could I!"

"Oh, for Christ's sake."

He pushed himself off the sofa. His face had gone black, thundery, and she'd never seen him like this before.

She grabbed his arm. "You can't go!"

"Get off!" He pulled himself free and reached for his coat. "You stupid bitch. You really want to put us both in danger? You know what they'll do to us if we're caught? To me, as well as you?"

"I don't care!"

"Well you bloody will! You bloody will when you're on a plane heading straight to Beijing!"

"They can't do that. I'm a UK citizen—"

He slapped her.

He'd never hit her before.

She was too stunned to cry.

He spoke quietly, viciously. "You don't get it, do you? You still don't bloody get it. You're still too bloody stupid. *They are in charge now*. Is that clear enough for you? *They are in charge*. The world you used to know, it's gone. It's not like that any more. It might look the same, but it isn't. The rules have changed. They're in charge and they can do what they like. Because they can pull the plug any time they want, and we know what'll happen if they do. We're back to anarchy. We're back to . . . fucking basics."

"You hit me."

"I'm sorry."

Now she started to cry.

"Maggie? I'm sorry."

She leaned into him and he put his arms around her. "I'm sorry I'm sorry I'm sorry."

His arms felt like protection, and his voice was soft again.

After a while she relaxed, and let the tears flow freely. Her shoulders heaved and Harvey patted them comfortingly, whispering calm sounds into her ear, being tender, being gentle. Her cheek stung where he'd hit her, and her finger throbbed where she'd cut it the other day. The palm of her hand, too, sent out a thin white signal where she'd clutched the library ticket that belonged to Dickon Broom.

"It'll be okay," Harvey was telling her. "It'll all be okay."

"You hit me," Maggie whispered again, and then she said, "I'm sorry."

It was dark and she'd been sleeping when he shook her by the shoulder.

"Come on."

". . . Wha'?"

"Quickly. Get dressed."

". . . What for?"

"Why do you think? We're going out."

Maggie felt something clutch her from inside. Like being told it was Christmas when she hadn't been expecting it. A frightening kind of Christmas, with savage reindeer.

"It's the middle of the night."

"Best time. Come on."

I don't want to go, she almost said. I want to stay in here.

But Harvey had his trousers on, and was pulling his sweater over his head.

She emerged from the duvet, limbs still heavy with dreams. Meredith had been inside her head, making big-sister noises, *I-told-you-so*s. She hadn't seen Meredith since the funeral. The dream dissipated, and she reached for her clothes. Harvey was watching, his mouth set in a thin smile. He seemed grey around the edges, but she felt that way herself. The middle of the night. Everyone was grey when the day was still unhatched.

She climbed the stairs in his wake. Fifteen up, and none down. That had never happened before. Harvey had the key in his hand, and unlocked the door with a practised gesture. It swung open. Harvey stepped through it, and Maggie followed.

A hallway, dark. The floor was wooden. Her hip bumped something, and she yelped.

"Careful."

A table. A hall table.

Harvey took her by the elbow. "It's not far."

And then he was opening another door, the front door, and the world reached out for Maggie, and drew her back into its embrace.

The street was quiet, the air damp. It held a touch of mist, enough to fuzz the streetlights and moisten her face.

So much air. So much of it, and all of it here at once.

Maggie raised her hand, tried to grasp a fistful.

"What are you doing?"

"Nothing. Nothing. I'm just . . ."

"We'll go to the corner. Come on, we can't dawdle. Someone might see us."

The ground was hard under her feet, sturdy and reliable. Little shockwaves shivered up her calves with each step.

"Hurry, now," he said.

A neat queue of cars lined the kerb. These were the vehicles she heard arriving and departing most days, emblems of a mode of life in which travel was part of the bargain. Others moved around the city, the way she'd once done herself. They stretched the borders of each day to allow for more geography. She looked with wonder down at her feet, at how much distance they were covering. All these things that used to be normal.

"What are you doing?"

"I'm just—nothing. I'm just walking."

She heard a squeak enter her voice, somewhere between excitement and fear.

"We're nearly there."

The houses had narrow windows, which gave them a stern appearance. When Maggie looked up, past the rooftops, she saw nothing but cloud, a great grey mass of it boiling in place. It made her dizzy.

Harvey kept a tight hold on her elbow.

"Watch where you're going. Don't slip."

She didn't intend to slip. She was more worried she might float away.

At the corner, Harvey stopped, almost jerking Maggie off her feet.

"Here. This is far enough."

But everything seemed quiet to Maggie. She didn't see why they couldn't go further.

"Please?"

"Maggie, this is already dangerous. If anyone came . . ."

But there was nobody coming. They were all alone.

Distantly, there were noises, traffic. She'd been on this junction before, but wasn't used to seeing it from this corner. So she turned, and across the road were trees, great dark galleons shifting uneasily in the night air. A park. And as the trees shivered again, scratching at nothing, Maggie realised it was *her* park, the park where she'd stop for her afternoon coffee, her afternoon cake. Here was where it had all begun. She hadn't realised the safe house was so close. The night she had arrived at the flat she'd been quickly bundled out of a cab, and had no real idea where she was. And ever since she'd been at the centre of her own blank map, its contours an imagined array of familiar London sights, as if the Gherkin, the Eye, Big Ben, the Globe, were lined up in a neat row, the way they were on tourist T-shirts. But now she'd stepped back into the real, and across the road was her park, its black railings less a barrier to those without than a promise of delights within.

"Please?" she said again.

In the park there was grass and winding footpaths. A pond—the boating "lake"—with tethered boats and sleepy ducks. There was a squadron of parakeets nesting in those trees. There were benches with memorial plaques screwed into them, reminding those who sat there that beloved individuals had enjoyed this peaceful place, and that the place, in turn, had not forgotten them.

"I've told you, it's not safe. You wanted to come out, and

we've come out. But we have to go back now, before anyone sees us."

This made sense. It would be stupid to throw it away, this precarious version of safety they'd constructed. But before his grip on her elbow could tighten, she heard a phantom whisper—might have been her sister, might have been Dickon Broom—and while she couldn't make out the words, its message was clear enough. So she ran. Harvey's grip was easily broken. The road was easily crossed. Or was until the last two yards, when a car erupted out of nowhere—came racing round the corner, its headlights twin dragons.

It screamed when it saw Maggie. She screamed too, and Harvey shouted, and the car shuddered to a halt, steam or smoke or something spouting from its frame. Noises erupted everywhere at once, car alarms piping up. Maggie was on her knees, and wasn't sure how she'd got there. All the breath had been knocked out of her. The car door opened, and she was sure a man in a suit, a Chinese man with hostile eyes, would emerge, but he didn't. Instead there was a young woman, her face split into two kinds of furious, the kind where she'd just had an awful shock, and the kind where it was at least partly her fault. She swore at Maggie, loudly and without stopping. To Maggie's ears, she might as well have been using Mandarin.

Harvey was gathering her up, gripping her arms, hauling her vertical.

"You're not hurt, you're not hurt. It didn't hit you. Just gave you a scare."

The young woman was still shouting. Lights were flickering on in nearby windows.

Harvey said, "Excuse me. Excuse me? You were going far too fast. *Far* too fast. So get back in your car and fuck off, right?"

Maggie thought her knees might liquefy. All those stairs, up and down, up and down, she should be made of sterner stuff by now. But her knees felt about to collapse. She said to Harvey, "I want to go home."

"We're going."

"I want to go *now*."

"We're going. Fuck *off*!" This to the woman.

And then they were heading back along the road the way they'd come, and the young woman was climbing back into her angry car, and driving it away past the park, the big trees waving them goodbye. Harvey was muttering something, but Maggie couldn't tell what. Her body was all sixes and sevens, or eights and nines. None of the numbers added up. She wanted to go home. She wanted to be safe, away from sudden lights and noises. And before much time had passed, she was.

Later, after Harvey had gone, and daylight had begun its morning creep across the ceiling, slyly wending through small tears in the plastic sheeting, Maggie thought about the park again, and its pond, and its dog and its parakeets, and those benches with memorial plates screwed into their slats. The thought that these things had been so near all this time served to remove them even further from her orbit. It was as if the London she had known had been set at a tilt, and she would never find a foothold in it again. It would carry on without her, adjusting itself to its strange new realities, and the only memorial to her it would allow would be a lungful of expelled air, in one place for a single moment, and then everywhere, or nowhere, it didn't matter which.

When she was up, she put the library card back where she'd found it, on the shelf in the wardrobe. It was no use as a talisman or anything else. She didn't want to think about Dickon Broom any more. All she wanted was to be safe.

Part three.

1

"So, Mr. Broom. You have experience in this field."

"Well, I think my CV speaks for itself. I've been teaching in various capacities for more than twenty years, and English as a foreign language has always been my special area of expertise."

"You taught at Cambridge, I see."

"As a post-grad. I can't recall exactly for how long—sorry, the information will be on the sheet there."

The woman, he'd forgotten her name—Mrs. Aldridge?—glanced down at the paper in front of her and nodded.

"And for the past few years, you've been giving private lessons."

"And the occasional adult education class, yes."

It was going well.

The job wasn't one you'd chew anyone's arm off for, a language school off the Edgware Road, but it was what he knew, and came with a wage. Not a huge amount, but enough to cover living expenses and pay off some of the debt he'd been accumulating. A few new shirts wouldn't hurt either. A proper haircut, one where they teased what you had into perfection, rather than just shortening it according to the number on the blade. Dinner somewhere nice. Three times now he'd bought Sue coffee, and it was starting to look odd that he hadn't escalated. He was pretty sure she was waiting for the next step.

You couldn't tell Dickon Broom he didn't know what a woman wanted.

This woman, now, Mrs. Aldridge—if that was her name—was looking towards her colleague, who hadn't spoken yet, beyond introducing himself. Mr. Patterson. Mr. Patterson was tall, and looked to be in his thirties, younger than Broom, with one of those beards which couldn't decide whether that's what it actually was or just the result of a few days' not shaving. He'd spent the interview so far either making notes or doodling patterns. What he'd do now, Broom thought, was pick up the slack and ask about Broom's outside interests, the full range of his professional development. Broom had practised this part too. He was nearly home and dry.

A new Italian restaurant had opened locally, and chances were good it involved actual Italians. It wasn't expensive, and would give him the chance to show off his language skills. Sue would be impressed, though he knew she'd hide it. She wasn't the sort of woman to let you know what marks you were getting.

Early evening meal, not too heavy on the garlic. A bottle of wine back home in the fridge. The attic flat, with its view of London rooftops. If he picked a night with a good moon, that was half the job done right there.

"Yes, about your CV," Mr. Patterson said.

When he left the building, exiting through a glass-panelled door which gave onto an alleyway, Dickon Broom paused before rejoining the street. He brushed the sleeves of his jacket, though they showed no obvious signs of having picked up dust. Then curled his right hand into a fist.

"Fuckingfuckingfuckingfucking*cunt*."

He punched the wall once, twice, and again. Hard enough, if it had been Mr. Patterson's face, he'd have leaked blood and teeth down that scraggly mess of a beard. But not quite hard enough to damage Broom's actual hand.

And then he went to the pub.

He sat at a table looking out on the street. It wasn't lunchtime yet, so the place was quiet. He took a long draught of beer, then placed his wallet on the table next to his glass. After a while, he picked it up again, and leafed through its contents. Fifty-five pounds. Four tens, three fives. There was change in the coin compartment, but it didn't feel heavy enough to amount to much. He took another mouthful of beer. He didn't know what the matter with people was. There was enough on his CV to satisfy any interviewer. Patterson should have just given him the fucking job. But instead he thought he had the right to go poking around in Broom's life, looking for the lies other people had told about him.

The lies Lin Hua had told.

Broom shook his head. It was pointless floating back into the past, when there was so much present to contend with. Bills that were coming in, and kept coming in regardless. There ought to be a way you could just keep very still, not breathe almost, and it wouldn't cost you anything—they would all just leave you alone. A little respite while you planned your next move. But it didn't matter what you did, it always ended up costing more than you expected. Thank God rent wasn't an issue, or he'd be up the creek. But to have a regular job slip through his hands like that—his job, he'd already started thinking it—was worse than never getting near it in the first place.

A couple walked past, breaking his line of vision, the man in an immaculate suit, light grey, the woman in darker clothes, but with a bright pink scarf. As he watched, they climbed into a car that was hugging the road, so low it was, so sporty, cool and green. This was the trouble with London. Everywhere you looked, there was someone with the life you deserved. Broom had always worked hard. Had always had ambition. But circumstances contrived to fail him, and leave him here, drinking beer by the window, while that couple there motored off into a prosperous afternoon . . .

And he could be rich. That was the absolute truth of it: He. Could. Be. Rich. Not as a long-term prospect, either, but something that could be accomplished in less than a week, even. And if he were free to make that happen, if there were just some way he could put the Situation to bed and get on with life the way it was supposed to be, then he could have the low-slung car, the immaculate suit and all the rest of it. That new Italian place: screw that. He'd take Sue into the West End, dine her in style. All those self-help courses you saw adverts on the Tube for, the ones that encouraged you to be The Best You You Can Be? That would be him. The best Dickon Broom available, and all it would cost was money.

In the meantime, even a small amount would help. Something to tide him over, that was all.

But oh no. Apparently no.

That cunt Patterson . . .

"You've taught at City University, I see. One of their evening classes."

"Yes. A politics course. Not to a very high level, you understand. I mean, my own degree—"

"The thing is, Mr. Broom, there's a list of tutors on CU's website, and your name doesn't appear on it."

"Ah, no, it wouldn't. I taught as a freelance. I was covering for one of the course tutors who was off sick that term? So I was never actually part of the faculty."

"I see. And how about the Open University? Were you also teaching as a stand-in when you taught, let's see." Mr. Patterson's finger ran down the sheet in front of him and stopped at the entry he was looking for. "GCSE Italian?"

"That's right. Teaching cover is, well, ha! Another of my areas of expertise, you might say."

"Which is why you don't appear on the Open University's list of accredited tutors either."

"That's right."

He realised he was twining his fingers round themselves, and forced himself to stop. To let his hands rest flat upon his knees.

"But English as a foreign language is your particular speciality."

"Yes. Which is why I applied for this post. The Lonsdale School is one of the most respected—"

"And I understand you taught for some years at the Marylebone Intensive School of English."

". . . I'm sorry?"

"I understand you taught for some years at the Marylebone Intensive School of English."

"Oh, yes, right, I'm sorry. I misheard. Yes, I did."

"But that doesn't appear on your CV. Why is that, Mr. Broom?"

". . . It doesn't . . . ?"

"It doesn't appear on your CV. The only reason I know you taught there is that I have a friend on the staff, and she happened to mention it."

It seemed to Dickon Broom that there was a sudden rise in temperature.

He said, "Ah, I see what must have happened. Yes. You see I recently applied for another role, not a teaching role, so I sent them a version of my CV which didn't have that job on it. It wasn't relevant, so it didn't seem worth including."

"Didn't seem worth including."

"No. Not for this other role I was applying for. And what must have happened, I must have sent you that version instead of the fuller one. I'm sorry about that. A simple mistake."

"You are aware, Mr. Broom, of what a CV is? It's a record of your employment career. Not the edited highlights."

"Yes, well, I suppose we have different—"

"And that doesn't explain why this . . . redacted version includes your other teaching roles. Be that as it may, now that it's on the record, would you like to explain why you ceased teaching at the Marylebone Intensive School of English?"

"Why I ceased?"

"Why you're no longer teaching there, yes. Given that you're now applying for a role very similar to that one. Identical, really."

"Well, it's just that, at the time, I was planning a change of career. Hence the other role that I applied for recently."

"I see."

"Only I've since revised my view on that. Teaching is—"

"Mr. Broom, is it or is it not true that you were fired from the Marylebone Intensive School of English after a student complained of a number of acts of sexual harassment and stalking? And that's why you've airbrushed it from your CV?"

Broom blinked twice. "I don't understand."

"It's quite simple. Were you or were you not—"

"No, I mean, I understand what you're saying, I just don't

understand where you got your information from. It's a complete fabrication."

"You're saying it's not true."

"I'm saying it's a complete and utter lie."

"I see."

"I left that teaching role because I had other plans, which didn't in the end work out. And the only reason it's not on my CV—"

"I see."

"—is an oversight for which I've already apologised."

Mr. Patterson stared at him for what felt like a full minute before speaking again. "Well, in that case I have no other questions. Ms. Alderton?"

She smiled uncertainly. "Thank you, Mr. Broom. We'll let you know."

Fuckingfuckingfuckingfucking*cunt*.

Broom left the pub. He wanted another beer, but knew that if he had one, he'd want another, and that would be it for the day—pop would go the weasel.

Starting to drizzle. Ah, London. Always ready to take your mood and underwrite it with the weather.

He caught the Tube, a particularly rattly stretch of track, and while it bucketed along set about adjusting his outlook. Earlier, he'd had a new job in prospect, and everything that brought with it: money, new routines, new people. Now he was back to where he'd been when he got out of bed this morning. But this wasn't the end of the world. That was what he told himself, scanning the ads above the benches, none of which encouraged him to become The Best Him He Could Be. It was almost as if they were prepared for him to continue being The Him He Currently Was.

Besides, students. Being around students all the time. A lot of them from overseas, obviously, because that was the nature of the job, and overseas students were the best kind, true—they had a level of respect for their teachers that the homegrown variety had dispensed with—but even so, even with the more deferential ones, who knew precisely how much their education was costing their parents, even so: students. Sooner or later, they let you know you were just another paid functionary.

At the Marylebone School, he'd had some good years. There was a social element to being a tutor—theatre outings, cinema trips—that Broom had enjoyed. Being around young people, especially when they were mostly young women, with the curated good looks moneyed backgrounds provide, was a sweet gig. He'd made friends, made connections. He was older but they'd accepted him as one of their own, a little wiser, a little more experienced, but someone you could have a good time with nonetheless, someone who got the jokes, got the cultural references, came to the parties. He could prove all this, too. He'd worn a collection of friendship bands on his wrist, which had been a thing then, and all were genuine, gifted by students who wanted him to remember them when they'd moved on, returned to their home countries to build their adult lives. And the friendship bands in turn served as a character reference to the next year's intake, who saw what he'd meant to their predecessors.

When he'd first met Lin Hua, he'd felt a familiar stirring. Nineteen, Chinese, drop-dead beautiful—he'd had a number of Chinese students over the years, but she was taller than the norm, a little sturdier too, in an athletic way. He could imagine her on a sports field. The meeting happened in a bar near what the students fondly called the campus—Marylebone Intensive School of English occupied a three-storey building—on a Friday evening, when everyone was there. Strictly speaking, Broom shouldn't have been. There were lines you weren't supposed to cross, and a lot of them involved alcohol, but as far as he was concerned they were all adults, which was how come they were in a bar in the first place. And the lines tended to blur even when alcohol wasn't a factor. Take the first law of teaching young adults. The prime directive, the tutors called it, and what it was was this: don't fuck the students. This was serious and unbreakable but it was also unwritten, since writing it would have been an acknowledgement that such situations had to be legislated for, because yes, sometimes, tutors fucked the students. Broom had, once or twice. They were adults. Who got hurt?

It was easy to start talking to someone, with everyone part of the same big group. He'd bought her a drink, chatted about her course, her family, her home. She was already fluent in English, was on the School's "pre-University" module, and was living not far off, sharing a house with others from the college. He could tell she liked him because she kept touching her hair, and her shoes pointed directly at him while they spoke. They were always flattered when you singled them out. Attracting their own age group was like scoring a four or a five. Older men were a different proposition entirely.

On his way back from the bar with a second drink he found she'd moved seats and was talking to a boy. She hadn't noticed him approaching. "Have you seen his collection of bands?" she was saying. "How old is he, fifty? He should get a proper job."

Students.

It was his stop. He left the carriage, took the stairs to street level, and found himself back in the rain.

He needed stuff. He'd made a list. The high street was mostly fast food and bookies, but there was a new supermarket, Sunrise Stores, and a few traditional shops, including a hardware place and a grocer's. Broom believed in supporting local tradespeople, but you could get most things cheaper in Sunrise. While he was collecting a basket a man walked past who looked familiar, though Broom couldn't think why. He gave a brief nod anyway, covering his bets, but the man looked straight through him. Sod you, then. Basket in hand, he found the list in his back pocket. He'd have upscaled it if he'd passed the interview, but now—again—he'd have to go for the no-frills options, the cheap alternatives. The goods reduced because they'd hit their sell-by dates.

Lin Hua. It was her fault he'd not been given the job. Her fault he'd lost the last one. Happy enough to drink free drinks, simper, cross her legs in that microdress. When they talked, she'd lean close and touch his arm. She was the worst kind of cocktease, the kind who'd open her eyes wide at the suggestion she was anything of the sort.

Vegetables. Onions, courgettes, calabrese, carrots. Not leeks. Too often, you got a slimy one, a layer coated with gunk. He hated that.

Maybe he should offer to cook for Sue. Explain that he couldn't afford restaurants, his job situation what it was—but was that wise? Would that make her think him a loser? On the other hand, not having a job didn't make him unemployed. He was between positions was all. Planning a change of career, like he'd told Patterson.

Cans—different kinds of pulses. Kidney beans, black-eyed beans, borlottis. In the past these came dry in little sacks, and you had to soak them overnight and cook them three hours straight. They still came out indigestible. Cans were simpler all round, not to mention costing less.

Baked beans too, of course. And chicken breasts, pasta, eggs.

What was it Patterson had said—he had a friend at the Marylebone School? Was that even legal? Not the having a friend bit—that was simply unlikely—but relying on hearsay, gossip, to prevent Broom getting a job. There'd been a lot of gossip spread by Lin Hua and her cronies, the girls who sucked up to her because she was pretty and rich, the boys who wanted to get into her pants. Most of them succeeded, probably. She'd actually stood there, said she was prepared to take her allegations to the police if they—the School—didn't sack him. Broom. He should have called her bluff. See how her lies withstood official investigation.

Tampons. He'd better get a bumper-sized box. Soap too. He thought he had toothpaste.

But it could have backfired, he knew. There were too many people prepared to lie on her behalf. One of her housemates had invented a story about finding Broom outside their front door after midnight, *lurking* was the word he used—lurking! He hadn't been fucking lurking. As he'd explained at the time, he'd made up a new reading list for Lin's course, and, knowing he'd be passing this way after his evening out, had brought it with him to push through her letterbox.

So where is it, the young man had asked. He'd opened the door, and was gazing down at an undisturbed doormat.

Well, Broom had said, that was the funny thing. He'd only just realised he didn't have the reading list with him after all. He must have left it in his other jacket.

A perfectly reasonable explanation—*two* perfectly reasonable explanations, and still the man had looked at him with open suspicion, open hostility. He was Chinese too, of course. The idea was to integrate into the host country, but they always settled in groups.

And what could you do, if that was their approach? All of them backing her up, nobody taking Broom's side? He'd worked there for years. The last time there'd been a complaint it was over before it started: an agreement that there'd been misunderstandings, and then everyone got on with things.

It was because Lin Hua was rich. Trust the rich to put themselves always in the right, as if it were a property they'd paid a deposit on. And the rest of us are just squatters.

It was still drizzling when he left the supermarket. He cut through the park, and kept an eye out for the parakeets, but they were hiding from the rain. Even the dog was quiet. One of his carrier bags developed a tear and nearly scattered cans and a pint of milk across the road, but he set it down in time, and redistributed the weight. Disaster averted.

All those moments when you set a chain of events in motion, started a wheel that you couldn't then stop. This one hadn't happened. Sooner it had, though, than some of the others he was still chasing after.

Back in his kitchen, he unpacked most of the groceries, repacked the rest in the untorn carrier bag, then looked out of the window, across the rooftops. Even when there wasn't much to see—like now, with the sky a grey bucket upturned over London—there was still pleasure in the view. It held him for a few minutes, until at last he picked up the bag, left the flat, and trod quietly down the stairs.

In the hallway, sliding his key into the lock, he realised who the man had been, the one he'd thought he recognised earlier. It had been whatsisname, Joshua, the security guard from

Quilp House. The one he'd told Maggie she'd killed. That was a problem solved, then. Only about a million to go.

He sighed, turned the key, and stepped inside the basement flat to face the Situation.

It had all got out of hand.

After being sacked by the Marylebone School, scalding with fury, he'd paced afternoons away, stalking the streets in ever-increasing circles, the epicentre of which was his mother's house. He'd still thought of it that way, his mother just three months dead. He remembered telling Lin Hua about this. They had been in a pub near the School, a jazz venue. Broom didn't like jazz but it was popular with the students. He'd wedged himself into a corner near Lin Hua to tell her about his mother's death, and she had put her hand on his arm. *I'm so sorry.* That was the kind of memory he'd had fizzing in his head, the hypocrisy of her, her cruel lies.

The local park was in his orbit. He'd circle the pond, watching the idiot ducks. Imagine skewering them one by one, and roasting them over an open fire.

Women were treacherous, would happily slice your feet to ribbons and abandon you on a salty beach.

One of them showed up most afternoons, and sat eating cake at a table by herself.

That one, of course, turned out to be Maggie, and she greeted him now with her usual litany of complaint. He'd barely handed her the bag of groceries, the tampons he'd remembered without being asked, when she was off.

"Harvey, why don't you ever bring me a newspaper?"

"I've told you." He was always patient with her, and the few times he wasn't, he could hardly be blamed. She had a way of resurrecting questions that had been dealt with time and again. "There are hardly any newspapers left. The ones that haven't closed down don't print proper news. They're just mouthpieces. They get told what to print."

"I don't care. I just want some idea what's going on."

"They'll tell you nothing, Mags. They're full of pointless shit. Buying one's an act of treachery. They peddle Chinese lies." She pouted. He hated it when she did that. "Anyway. I thought last week's little trip put you off the outside world."

He could still hardly believe he'd let her talk him into that. For two nights afterwards he'd barely slept a wink, all the different endings that might have happened hammering away like a heartbeat. He'd been too soft on her. Making up for hitting her, when that had been her fault.

"I get lonely."

"I know. Is there any wine left?"

She shook her head. "Didn't you bring any?"

A wave of anger pulsed through him. Did she think he was made of money? "I thought there was enough. You want to watch how much you're drinking."

"Well it's not like I'm buying it in secret."

They ate a meal Maggie put together out of what he'd

brought with him, and a few things she had in cupboards. Afterwards they sat on the sofa.

"Tell me about your day."

He invented a meeting he'd had with some senior agents. Said it was early days, but there was some movement afoot, some negotiation going on. A handing back of a certain degree of control.

"In exchange for what?" she asked.

"I can't talk about that. You know I can't."

"But will we get our country back?"

This, he'd told her long ago, was the phrase on everyone's lips. When will we get our country back?

"It could happen," he told her. "And then all this will be over."

She cuddled into him, making what he thought was a happy sigh.

Women. Even when on their own, they were making trouble for someone. This one—the one who would be Maggie—sat at her table, tapping at her phone. She'd be emailing, tweeting, blogging, sowing lies about some man or other, burying a seed of rumour that would grow and spread and flourish, wrap him in its queasy tendrils, make sure the poor bastard never took another unclumsy step.

Lose him his job, cut him adrift.

That afternoon, two and a half years ago, Broom had sat drinking coffee, surrounded by mothers with their offspring, a hipster engrossed in a laptop, and watched the woman take a photo of her cake. He had walked a long way, anger boiling his blood. Lin Hua had called him a stalker—made him sound like a fucking predator, when he was the victim here. And they'd all lined up behind her, the student body, the staff, the College President. The prick actually called himself that—the College President, as if the Marylebone School were an Oxford institution, not a threadbare scam, gulling rich foreigners into forking out for so-called degrees.

Your position is untenable, Broom had been told. Reputation to think of. Lucky not to have police involved.

One thing Broom was glad about, that he'd had the presence of mind to tell the College President he was a worthless fuck.

But he was out of a job, and couldn't count on a reference from the Marylebone School. He'd altered his CV to fit, blurred some dates, boosted a few part-time teaching jobs so they ate away at the huge hole at its centre, but he'd worked at MISE for seven years. How was he supposed to cover that? His life had had the air let out of it.

The woman had put her phone down, and was separating her cake into parts. It looked to Broom like she was collecting the icing into one big forkful. On a whim, he took his own phone out. The café was one of a couple of thousand in the world called Central Perk, and Google listed most of them. On Twitter, though, this actual one had been tagged a minute ago. *Central Perk for coffee and cake! Nom nom!* The Twitter handle was @maggiebarnes92.

He clicked on her feed.

It was only her ninth tweet. Previous stunning bulletins included *Sunny day! Bet it won't last!* and *First day at work! Quilp House!*

Getting to his feet, Broom thought, Jesus. Had nobody ever explained to her how easy it would be? Just to take a few shards of information and use the jagged ends to prise apart her life?

She was sitting under the bulletin board with its collection of flyers for local events, craft shops, gardening services, handymen. A poet called John Harvey was giving a reading in the local library. Sadler's Wells was premiering a new ballet.

He said, "Is it all right if I sit here?"

He had sex with her on the sofa. It was getting more and more difficult to summon up interest, but if he made her keep most of her clothes on, and didn't let her lure him into bed, he could pretend she was a stranger who'd invited him in off the street. To make himself come, he tried to remember other women he'd fucked in this flat. He'd lived here while his mother was alive. The middle flat, the one on the ground floor, had been occupied by a middle-aged couple. They'd moved out when their lease expired weeks after his mother's death. The estate was then in the hands of her lawyers, and they hadn't been able to renew.

"You're hurting me."

He'd been jobless, then, but waiting to inherit property. A flat of his own and two to let, each worth four times the rent his mother had charged.

"Please, Harvey . . ."

A man of assets. Fuck Lin Hua and her lying friends, because he didn't need the Marylebone job any more. And now here he was, more than two years later, and he wouldn't need the job he'd applied for this morning, either, except . . .

"Please . . ."

Except for Maggie.

Except for what happened with Maggie.

It had all got out of hand. He'd planned to frighten her, that was all, knowing her name, where she worked, and if she hadn't scuttled away like a mouse he'd have had a bit of a laugh with her, probably warned her about using social media in public, and that would have been that. But the way she ran made her unfinished business. So he'd returned, and returned again, until he encountered her once more.

What's the most fun you can have with a woman?

Making her do what you tell her.

My name's Harvey Wells. I work for the government, Maggie. I work in a . . . special department. And the reason I'm here is that we need your help.

She was new in London, and had no friends. He knew what loneliness looked like, was used to seeing it in the faces of students every year, freshly arrived in a big foreign city, scared and exhilarated both at once. Expecting adventure, but not sure what form it would take. Ripe for plucking.

Don't you want to do something special with your life, Maggie?

Just getting her into bed wasn't enough, would have been a waste, so he'd decided to play a game with her. See if he could get her to do something.

What I want is that if you see anything unusual, anything out of the ordinary, you let me know. That's all, really.

And it would have been, if she hadn't been so pliable. At least once a week she'd turn up with some titbit he'd pretend significant. A meeting? In an office block? I'll alert MI5. Someone working on the lift? A double agent. I'll pass it on. It was pathetic and funny at the same time. He could have fucked her months before he did, but he was enjoying watching her cream herself into a lather. Meanwhile, the lawyers were working through his mother's estate. Eventually, eventually, papers were signed and boxes ticked. The keys were in his hand. He'd cleared out of the basement flat and moved upstairs.

In celebration of this event, he'd upped the stakes and given her the memory stick.

By then, she'd have abseiled down the building if he'd asked. She was so sure what she was doing was preserving our democracy.

It will install a surveillance program into the company's network.

It was a fucking memory stick. It cost £3.99.

It will allow us to monitor their internal communications.

He'd actually cased Quilp House by this time. It was an ordinary, ordinary building, full of ordinary people doing ordinary things. A couple of guys in dark suits manned the lobby, one a big black guy with a name badge, Joshua. Maggie was there every day, had worked there for months, and still she swallowed every story he told her, still she believed she was surrounded by villains.

Whatever happens, you mustn't let it fall into their hands.

And in celebration of a mission well done, he'd taken her back to the empty basement flat—"the safe house"—and let her take him to bed.

Job done.

Tonight, once he'd finished, she cried, which had long since been normal. Broom sat for a while, but wanted a cigarette, and she wouldn't let him smoke—he couldn't even smoke in his own damn flat—so he pretended to leave, locking the door behind him, then creeping up the stairs to the top floor. This was what it had come to. He couldn't move about his own house normally, because she was there in the basement, always, and there was nothing he could do about it.

The middle flat still vacant, unlettable. How much had it cost him, keeping that place empty? He shuddered to think.

In part, he was to blame. Telling Maggie Joshua was dead—picking up her story and running with it—had been, in retrospect, a mistake. At first, it had simply been another loop in the knot he'd tied, and it was only later that he realised how tight that loop had pulled, so tight he couldn't *un*pull it. Two days later, maybe. Three? By then he'd started telling her the outside world was falling apart. It had seemed a brilliant game, a psychological experiment, and if he ever wrote it up, it would make for sorry reading. She was so fucking gullible, you could weep. Everything he told her, she gulped down whole. The "Collapse." The end of banks and the BBC. The way the Chinese Secret Service was hunting her down. If she had any kind of filter on her brain, it had rotted from disuse.

But now, and for two years already, she had him in her power. Because now he'd told her all this stuff he couldn't let her go. If he did, it would look like he'd kidnapped her, kept her prisoner in his basement. Even by the third day, even by the second, it could have been made to look evil. And with people like Lin Hua around, and fools like the President of the fucking Marylebone Intensive School of English, all ready to paint him black, he could wind up in serious trouble. "Stalker" they'd called him last time, more of their fucking lies. They'd say there was a pattern of behaviour. They'd make it look like it was all his fault.

But now here he was, two years on, and still no income from his property. How could he let the ground floor flat without Maggie hearing noises above her head, without new tenants wondering who was in the basement? And how could he release Maggie into a normal, unCollapsed world?

He smoked, looking out of the window. Property prices in London meant he could put the house on the market and walk away inside a week two million richer. He'd never need a job again. He could wine and dine Sue seven evenings a week, and Mr. bloody Patterson could kiss his arse.

If not for the Maggie Situation.

While smoke rose and clouded the air, tinting the ceiling grey and blue, Dickon Broom sat and thought: *If only something could happen to Maggie.*

2

The important thing was to have the right sort of cleaver.

Next morning, Dickon Broom executed a half-formed plan—he rang Sue and invited her to supper.

"At your flat?"

"Yes."

"Just the two of us?"

"Yes."

A long silence, during which his insides grew sticky—*stupid bitch, why have you been leading me on?*

"That would be nice," she said. "I'd like that. Thanks."

The inner voice quietened.

"I was thinking tomorrow," he said. "If you're free?"

"Tomorrow's fine, yes. Tomorrow would be lovely."

After disconnecting he lay on the sofa. Two floors below, Maggie would be watching a DVD or eating biscuits—she'd been getting fatter lately, and her skin pastier. When she ran up and down the stairs, he could hear them complain about her weight. If she were no longer there, if a way could be found to make her just *go away*, then Broom's future would unroll before him like a stretch of carpet. The only good thing about her presence in his house was, he never thought about Lin Hua any more.

Other good things, though. Think about other good things. He thought about Sue, and how pleasant it would be to have an attractive, intelligent woman in his life. What should he cook? Something Italian. His mother had had a healthy collection of cookbooks, and from one of them he now learned about Pork Valdostana, a northern Italian dish involving pork chops, prosciutto, fontina cheese, Marsala. Broom cast a mental eye over his bank account. A cheque would clear today, two lessons' money. A sullen, acne-ridden teenager in Highgate who was falling behind in French. His mother was a narrow-faced blonde with a mole at the corner of her mouth. A good tutor was hard to find, she had told Broom, and he had agreed with her, smiling, but had had the feeling they were approaching the subject from different angles, and she had not yet rung to book another lesson.

Be that as it may, her money was good. He scribbled a list and went shopping.

A saw, too, needs to be carefully chosen. It has to have the right sort of teeth to deal with meat.

■ ■ ■

What he still couldn't quite believe, even after all this time, was that nobody had come looking.

Maggie Barnes had dropped off the surface of the planet, and no one had batted an eye.

A week after the Situation had developed, he had walked past her old address, a bedsit in a crumbling Victorian. By this time, the irrevocability of what he had done had sunk home, and Broom had half-expected to find a police car outside, perhaps a phalanx of press photographers. Except there had been nothing in the papers, or nothing he had seen. And the house, too, seemed free of official intrusion. Three, four times he walked up and down the road, and nothing happened except that a young woman left the house, slamming the door behind her. She had dark, eastern European features, exactly the kind of girl he'd expect to find living somewhere like this. Broom knocked on the door. Nobody answered, and he went away thinking, well, okay, that's that.

But it wasn't, quite. He left it a month, by which time the Situation had started to take on the aspect of ordinary life. Still there had been nothing in the press, not even one of those boxes in the free papers, with an out-of-date photo and a plea for contact using precisely the wording of every other plea made in every similar box. This time he had visited in the early evening, and when nobody answered his knock he had knocked again. At length a timid woman, not the one he'd seen previously, answered. He asked if there were rooms available. She shook her head. He asked if a Maggie Barnes lived there. She disappeared, and came back with a handful of mail. Almost before he'd taken it, she was closing the door.

It was junk. Letters from charities, from credit card companies, from network providers. Some of it didn't even specify Maggie, but simply The Occupier. It was as if the woman who'd handed it to him hadn't cared to differentiate between Maggie and any other figure who might shelter behind that door, herself included.

She must have had clothes, books, a radio, cutlery. At least one plate. At least one mug. He imagined all of it, all of her legacy, piled into a bin liner and left on the kerb. Two square feet of landfill. Not much less than would accommodate a body. And all it took was one rubbish collection to erase it from existence.

He had dumped the mail in a bin before reaching home. Return to sender, he thought.

Sunrise Stores didn't stock fontina cheese, it turned out. Nor Marsala. Broom walked through the park, heading for a deli on the far side, one of a row of shops which put a spring in the step of local estate agents.

Near the far exit, where several paths met, a man stood on an upturned crate, hectoring anyone within earshot. This currently included a young couple standing side by side, his right arm round her shoulders, her left hand tucked into the back pocket of his jeans, and a man whose dog was truffling in a pile of leaves, and who might just have been waiting for it to finish. Broom slowed to hear the speaker's pitch.

"Welcome, sir, I'm glad to have you join us. Can I ask if you've taken the red pill?"

Broom had come to a halt beside the young couple, and he glanced at the woman, in case she offered any clues.

"Oh, you need her permission to listen, sir?"

"I've no idea what you're talking about," Broom said.

"I'm talking about Men Going Their Own Way," the man said. He was short, and in the way of such things, standing on his crate made him look that much smaller. His nose had a curious dent in its tip, and his mouth was narrow, though not so narrow it wasn't able to shape capital letters. Men Going Their Own Way. He was evidently working up to the world's clumsiest acronym. "I'm talking about waking up to the way the world really is, and resisting the matriarchy which blights men's lives. Your life, sir. My life."

"What about mine?" the young man asked, his grip on his companion's shoulder tightening a notch, an audible smirk in his voice.

"Oh, yes, you're very proud of saying what she wants to hear, aren't you, sir? Can I ask if you're married? Living together?"

The couple looked at each other and smiled.

"Because if you're either of those things, sir, have you ever examined your payslip at the end of the month? And worked out how much of your earnings goes into her purse?"

The woman laughed. "Fat chance!"

"Have you ever considered how your taxes pay for women's maternity leave?"

The man with the dog shook his head, a movement allowing for a wide range of interpretation.

"What about the divorce figures, young man? Do you fancy spending the rest of your life paying your girlfriend's bills there, even if she kicks you out twelve months after the wedding?"

"You're seriously in need of a blow job, aren't you?" the young man said, and his girlfriend dissolved into hysteria.

They moved on. So did Broom, but not before hearing a few more opinions from the man on the crate. Men Going Their Own Way—*Mug-Tow*—wouldn't be silenced. Men Going Their Own Way were turning their backs on a society which demanded men kowtow to women every day of their lives, providing them with food, providing them with shelter, and all of this indentured servitude hastening their own paths to the grave. Was it any wonder women lived longer? Was it any surprise—

A passing lorry obliterated the remainder.

Broom fingered the shopping list in his pocket, though he had its contents memorised. MGTOW, he thought. Mug-Tow—he'd come across the name before, a growing band of self-identified victims, who insisted that their shortcomings had been foisted upon them by women. The red pill business, now he thought about it, was a reference to *The Matrix*, in which the red pill allowed those who took it to see unfiltered reality, while the blue pill left its users wallowing in imagined comfort. A bunch of crackpots, although. Broom waited for the traffic to ease, then crossed the road. They claimed to have been brought low by a system which methodically prioritised the needs of women at the expense of men, which any sane person knew was ridiculous, except. The deli was the third along in the row of shops, and he hovered outside for a moment, checking out the window display. They were delusional, they were crackpots, but.

But.

He entered the shop, and bought most of the items on his list.

Next to the deli was a butcher's, and Broom stood and watched through the window while a man dismantled a pig's carcass at the rear of the shop, on a huge wooden block. He worked evenly, methodically, putting one tool down halfway through his task and reaching for another. His body knew what weight to apply. His shoulders grew taut beneath his bloodied white apron.

The important thing was to have the right sort of cleaver, Broom noted. One that would hack through a joint in two blows at most. A saw, too, needed to be carefully chosen. It had to have the right sort of teeth to deal with meat. If the teeth were too small they would clog up, becoming raggy with flesh.

This wasn't knowledge he especially required, but it was useful to know how things worked.

With his plastic shopping bag swinging by his side he walked on, deciding not to go back the way he'd come, but to wander the streets for a while. He had nothing urgent to carry him home. London always offered something for the active mind to chew on, and Broom prided himself on his active mind. Others might plod through life in a stupor, the city's stimuli wasted on them, but his own brain teemed with overlapping themes. He had planned to write a book once—a novella. It had been perfect in his head, all night long. A crumbling villa in rural Italy, and the story behind its ruin. For hours he had lain unsleeping, holding the thing entire in his mind, and he had understood completely, absolutely, how it was that books came to be written. Which was all he wanted, just to write it. He had no greater ambition. Simply to write it and know he had done such a thing, and then maybe get it published. That was all he wanted. To see it on a shelf, or on one of those tables they had in Waterstones, with his name on it, and lines from glittering reviews on its cover. He imagined accepting a prize, knowing his face would be in the papers, seen by people who had slighted him in the past, by Lin Hua. But in the morning, when he tried to put the story on his laptop, something jammed. What had felt like seamless prose in his head became insubstantial, nothing more than a series of whispered suggestions. He had lost his novella in the few short hours of sleep that had claimed him at dawn.

He sometimes thought of this lost book while walking London's streets, and when he did so he knew that it was still there inside him, still reachable. All that was needed was relief from other pressures. If the Situation were to resolve itself, his novella was one of the futures that awaited him.

His blogs had at least made it onto the ether. These had been written in the wake of his book's stillbirth, and having learned from that misstep, he had set himself a schedule: one a week. They would slowly accrue readership, gather noise, be commented on, awaited, quoted widely. Whole careers had sprouted from the web, most of them attached to narrower talents than his. One a week: he had kept this up for two weeks, then gaps appeared. He had managed four in all. There was a box for readers' comments, but it stayed empty.

The problem with ambition, with talent, was that people were always ready to tear you down.

Broom suspected that this was a fate that mostly befell men.

He stopped for a beer in a cramped little pub with photographs of boxers on the walls, and leafed through a newspaper someone had left behind. A picture of Canary Wharf graced its front page. Canary Wharf was foreign territory to Dickon Broom, a mini-Manhattan on the skyline, and he resented the way it drew no nearer. While he had never desired to enter the world of commerce it embodied, he nevertheless felt excluded from its wealth. He had a Cambridge degree, had come this close—and with the phrase he conjured up a minimal distance, the space between two digits—to earning a PhD in philosophy, and none of that even took into account his gift for languages. By rights, he should be among the garlanded, but education had somehow contrived to wash him up on the margins. Society had no time for the merely brilliant. He was overqualified, doomed to accept second best as a direct consequence of being first rate.

You use your cleverness as a crutch.

Out of nowhere, his mother's words.

She had never truly valued him either.

He sipped bitter, and contemplated the following evening. Pork Valdostana as a main course. Something for a starter, salad, a dessert. Details. He'd figure them out. Sue was in her early thirties, worked in advertising, was a shoulder-length brunette with long legs. Wore glasses about half the time, with no obvious correlation between what she happened to be doing and whether she was wearing them or not. They had met, of all places, in the same café where he'd met Maggie.

She'd been sitting at the table next to his, gazing through the window at something, a flock of somethings, which were dipping and wheeling and gathering in one ever-changing shape above the duck pond, before scattering into the trees.

"Parakeets," he told her. "You just saw parakeets."

She had looked at him uncertainly.

So he had explained that a long time ago, person or persons unknown had released into the park a number of parakeets—the exact number was unclear, but more than two, that was for definite—and they had been a feature ever since.

"Oh. I didn't know that." She looked happy to have discovered it, though. Everyone liked parakeets, until one of them crapped on you. "I'm new to the area."

He thought about asking where she was living, but knew that might come across as creepy. A stranger, asking for an address. Some men behaved that way, but not Broom.

"One of our many local attractions," he said.

They had chatted for a while—local amenities, house prices,

a poster for a street fair. Broom had bought her a refill—crazy coffee—and they had ended up sharing a table. So it went.

He finished his beer.

Tomorrow evening, he thought as he left the pub, he would have to make sure Sue was quiet when entering the house, that she followed him up the stairs without a sound. Up in his flat, no problem. He could play music at a volume that wouldn't reach Maggie, and even if she started gallumphing about at her exercise, it wouldn't disturb them. But in order to get up there, in order to have the ground-floor buffer, he'd have to tell Sue—what? That there was a madwoman in the basement? Too schlocky. Besides, the problem wasn't Sue hearing someone downstairs, it was Maggie hearing noises from above.

Maggie, Maggie.

What was he to do with her?

Maybe she'd get sick.

That was a worry, actually. If she got sick, doctor-type sick rather than just a cold or whatever, he wasn't sure what he'd do. He kept her supplied with paracetamol, but beyond that he had no expertise. He couldn't diagnose. He didn't visit her every day—this was too much of a burden—and he sometimes wondered what would happen if she simply—well—*died* in his absence. If he turned up to find she had passed away, or succumbed to some other gentle euphemism: slipped off, gone to her everlasting, left the building . . . Leaving the building was key. Once she was out of the building, Broom's life could get back on track.

Of course, there would be the problem of disposal. But if she passed from natural causes—sorrow or loneliness or whatever—then the simple thing would be to cart her off in the watches of the night. He could leave her on a park bench, to be found come daylight by a dog walker or jogger. There would be mystery and speculation, but in the end it would be just another London story: one of the lost, who had wandered unseen for a few years, and now was done. Kind strangers would leave flowers on the bench. It would be over.

But he knew that he was painting this in the best possible light. The fact was, removing her from the flat would be a nightmare. There were always people around, never a time when London was empty. He'd be stopped and questioned and all sorts of wrong conclusions would be drawn. No, it would require more thought, though it was undeniable that these things were managed—that some people managed them. Otherwise where would they come from, all those bodies that turned up in canals? Perhaps there was a procedure he was unaware of, an inverse bridal rite. Stepping over the threshold backwards, with the corpse in a fireman's lift. If he invoked the right procedures, appeased the right gods, he could throw Maggie over his shoulder and waltz her through the darkness to the land of the parakeets, unseen.

Where was he now, anyway?

He'd been walking in a reverie, he realised, turning corners he hadn't intended to turn. His immediate surroundings were unfamiliar, a short street of terraced houses which looked like they hadn't changed since the 1950s. For a moment he had the feeling, brilliant and frightening at once, that he'd stepped through some invisible shimmy in the air, and landed in a different time. But it wasn't so. The world hadn't done him that favour, it had simply blinked, and allowed him to lose his way.

Which was a temporary loss. He turned and realised what he must have done, made a left at that last junction instead of heading straight on towards the park. An easy mistake for one freighted with thought. He stopped, set his bag down, and knelt to tie his shoelace. He was by the front wheel of a red car, a Japanese model, one which positively sang the delights of being a woman about town. On its rear shelf lay a glamour magazine, and on the back seat one of those boxy paper bags with rope handles, a designer name embossed on its side. Broom had the feeling that this car's owner spent more on shoes than Broom paid in tax, more on soap than Broom did on food. Before he could change his mind, he grasped the car's wing mirror, and pulled on it savagely as he rose. It broke, not coming away in his hand, but falling limply against the flank of the car, held in place by the wiring that allowed for its automatic adjustment. No alarms went off, no fuss ensued. Broom collected his shopping and walked back the way he'd come, a little calmer for this adventure, despite the heightened beating of his heart.

Later that night, two in the morning by his bedside clock, he woke reliving the event. By now the woman would have found her car, and would have cursed some passing vandal, which of course Broom wasn't. But what mostly interested him was the way there had been no consequence. Why was it that, with London stuffed so full of CCTV cameras, so much went on that nobody noticed?

He rose and poured a glass of water. The flat looked different in the dark, taking on its previous guise as his mother's realm. No amount of rearrangement seemed able to fix this. He sat, stared into nothing, sipped from his glass. There'd been a woman, hadn't there, who had died in her own flat, surrounded by freshly wrapped gifts. And there her body had lain, softly mummifying, and nobody had known, and nobody had come knocking. If that could happen, what couldn't? If London let you slide away like that, what wouldn't it allow?

There was no actual moment when you took a red pill, not here in the real world. No actual moment when you took a blue one. There was just the life you were living and the choices you made. And Men Going Their Own Way were a bunch of deluded idiots, neither at ease with themselves nor at one with the opposite sex, but . . .

Having no pill, Broom didn't take one, but finished his water and returned to bed. As he lay there, drifting back to sleep, another thought swam past, a thought about all those bodies that turned up in canals.

They weren't usually in one piece.

"Why can't you stay longer?"

"Because I can't."

"But you hardly ever stay any more—you just disappear, that's all you ever do!"

He suppressed a sigh. "What is it you want, Maggie?"

"I want to go out."

"We tried that, remember? You didn't like it. It scared you."

"Yes, but—"

"Yes, but nothing. What do you think's going to happen if we try again? We were lucky, you realise that? We were lucky the only person we saw was some stupid cow in a car. Else we could both be under arrest now. You for murder, and me for hiding you."

"Yes, well, you'd be okay, wouldn't you? You'd have *Five* to back you up. You'd have *Five* making sure nothing bad happened to you."

Broom said, "Working for Five isn't going to cut much ice with the Chinese authorities. Precisely the opposite, you want to know the truth."

Mags put a finger in her mouth and sucked it briefly. She'd been doing that a lot lately. She said, "You'd think there'd be more of them."

"Who would think there'd be more of what?"

"*I* and *you* and *everybody else* would think there'd be more Chinese people out on the streets. Even late at night. If they're so all powerful these days."

He said, "If?"

"You know what I mean."

"No. Really. Tell me what you mean."

"I just meant it didn't seem any different outside than before. Back when things were normal."

"So why were you scared?"

"Because I just was, okay? Because I've been here so long. You don't just walk outside and not feel nervous. Not after two years."

"So what are you saying, eh? What are you saying? You're saying you think everything's normal out there, and I've just been, what, making up stories? You think that's what I've been doing?"

". . . No."

"You don't sound very sure."

"I am."

"Because if you really want, you can go. Just waltz out there and see how long you last. But you want to know something? Once you do, there's no coming back. Once you're in a cell being raped by a gang of Chinky thugs, you can't say you've changed your mind and want to go back to your safe house. Because it'll be too late. Once you're out of here, there's nowhere else to go."

She was crying now. "I'm sorry."

"You're what?"

"I'm sorry."

"I can't hear you."

"I said I'm sorry, Harvey. I'm sorry I'm sorry I'm sorry."

"That's fine. That's well and good. But saying sorry's no fucking use unless you act it, is it?"

She shook her head.

"I still can't hear you."

Whatever Maggie Barnes said next was also inaudible,

but it didn't matter, because she got down on her knees anyway.

He made his escape at last, later than he'd intended. Despite Maggie's apologetic ministrations, which should have had a relaxing effect, he could feel a knot growing in his stomach, if that even happened. Knots growing, he meant. Her whining had taken on a new pitch, and the tone of her complaint was calculated to make Broom's life difficult. Today should have been uncomplicated. He had to buy the chops, prepare the supper, tidy up a bit, and then get ready for Sue. It was a long time since he'd had the prospect of a quiet evening with a pleasant companion, but Maggie couldn't even allow him the peace of mind to enjoy it. *If.* What did she mean, if? *If they're so powerful these days.* As if she were beginning to doubt the very thing that had kept them together so long.

Proper chops, not supermarket-packaged. He'd push the boat out for Sue. At the butcher's, waiting to be served, he eyed up the tools on the rack next to the cold room. Whole sides of meat were carried from there and rearranged into portable cuts inside minutes—practice made it seem effortless, but the first time you actually wielded the cleaver, he supposed, it would be more difficult than it looked. Not just the physical action, but the sensation it surely imparted through your hand, up your arm, into your organs, as the blade made gristly contact. But in the end, it was only meat. The major part of the process had already taken place.

The chops seemed heavy, industrial, as they were wrapped in greaseproof paper. The illustration accompanying the recipe had made the finished dish look graceful and fat-free, a sophisticated choice. These babies looked more suited to a greasy spoon. He just had to hope that, trimmed and prosciutto-wrapped, they acquired the appropriate air. Lamb might have been better. But too late now.

He hadn't been going to drink this lunchtime, but a quick one couldn't hurt. He wanted a cigarette, too. He hadn't smoked in Sue's presence, suspected that she was probably anti-, so he'd better get his ration in now. There was a yard round back of the Fox which they had the nerve to call a garden, and he sat there with a pint, and smoked for a while, and considered his options.

Maggie probably wasn't going to die of loneliness or sorrow.

You could argue that this was the fault of the times. Back in the day—for these purposes, call it the mid-nineteenth century—the evidence suggested that damsels dropped like mayflies when stricken by heartbreak or whatever. Country churchyards were stuffed to the boundaries with young virgins, who died from being sad. That didn't happen any more. These days, women's sense of entitlement acted as a dynamo, keeping them going when they ought to just give up. All those magazines, all that media attention, constantly drip-feeding the notion that they deserved it all, so even when life looked like a colossal fuck-up, and the sane thing would be to make a graceful exit, they got angry instead, and stamped their feet, and demanded that things improve. The list of things that they wouldn't put up with had probably sounded reasonable when they were marching for equal rights, but was starting to look plain greedy. Why should their load be lighter than men's? Who had more to complain about, when you got down to it? So no, Maggie wasn't going to fade away. She'd remain in place, a drain on his resources, growing fatter and less attractive and preventing him from moving on.

Broom realised he had lit a second cigarette. See? See what effect she was having? He finished it miserably, staring down into his diminishing pint, his thoughts as grey and prone to buffeting as the smoke uncurling from his cigarette's tip, as the bad air he exhaled.

Going through the front door quietly, as usual. Tiptoeing upstairs without a sound. Being careful not to breathe too loud, being careful not to cough. It was like having a baby in the house. Except with a baby things were presumably going to improve, eventually.

Safe in the upstairs flat, with the door shut, he placed his parcel of meat on the kitchen counter and studied the recipe again. Trim the chops by cutting around the lower part of the bone, scraping off the fat. Okay, he could do that. Then trim off the fat surrounding the loin. He supposed, left to themselves, chops weren't as elegant as they might be. Flatten the meat gently with a meat mallet or the end of a rolling pin.

He was pretty sure he didn't have a meat mallet.

And it turned out he didn't have a rolling pin either, though he thought he'd seen one somewhere. He went through all the drawers, and found a number of implements he had no name for—how often had his mother used these things?—but a rolling pin was not among them. Broom closed his eyes, tried to calm his sudden rage. Why did everything always grow more complicated? Why did it *always* get more expensive?

Out on the streets again, he was always out on the streets. He was always being quiet on the staircase, and he was always out on the streets. The hardware shop was his destination, and loose change jangled in his pocket. A red car went past, its onside wing mirror fixed in place with silver tape. The driver had jet black hair and an angry profile. Lin Hua—it was Lin Hua. And then it wasn't, or at least, and then it only might have been. He couldn't tell. The car had disappeared halfway down the road, and Broom was standing outside the hardware shop, its window display a dusty collection of boxed sets of screwdrivers, lengths of extension cord, and an optimistic array of garden chairs.

The kitchen department, such as it was, was at the ground-floor rear. Most of it was electrical gadgetry or sets of kitchen knives, and he had no interest in the one and was already equipped with the other. Rolling pins did not appear to be in stock either. They were, come to think of it, a peculiarly old-fashioned implement, so much so it took him a moment to recall their precise use. Pastry, was it? As far as Broom was aware, most people bought pastry in ready-rolled packets these days. Their other function, if his recipe was anything to go by, was simply as blunt object. Anyway. No rolling pins, but the shop did have two meat mallets, chunky wooden objects with a cubic head, one side of which was rounded at the corners, and the opposite crosshatched into grooves, like little rows of rooftops. That was for tenderising, he realised, or perhaps recalled. There was something familiar about its heft, something comforting. The two mallets looked identical, but one was priced at £3.50 and the other at £4.50, so he took the cheaper.

Before paying, he went downstairs. Wouldn't do any harm to look. Here was more electrical stuff, not gadgets but components, and all sorts of different ways of making things stick to walls. And tools—power tools and the other sort.

Broom stood for a while before an array of saws, all different sizes, different gauges. Some would take two men to wield, so were obviously out of the question. But one in particular looked to his eye roughly the size of the one the butcher had used. That would get the job done, he thought. He reached out and ever so gently laid his finger against its teeth. Sharp, but not only sharp—sharp and rugged. Sharp would do for flesh. For bone, you'd need rugged.

He checked the price, winced a little, then took his meat mallet upstairs to the till.

There were so many places in London. So many nooks. So many crannies.

How many times did you pass a rubbish bin, stuffed with knotted carrier bags which might have held anything?

How many alleyways did you pass that reeked of garbage? In whose unlit corners who knew what might have been left?

And besides, besides, besides. There was always the river.

Dickon Broom, carrying a meat mallet in a paper bag, let himself quietly into his house, and padded softly upstairs.

Part four.

1

"Sue."

"Hello, Dickon."

"Thought I'd better come out to meet you—the doorbell's broken."

Which must be why she hadn't heard it ring. "Well I hope you've not been waiting long." She was ten minutes late. "Bit cold for lurking on the doorstep."

It was another grey evening. The streetlights wore soft, mizzy haloes, and the traffic criss-crossing the end of the cul de sac sounded more guttural than usual, as if it were coming down with a cold.

Dickon Broom was in a checked shirt and jeans, and was not long out of the shower. He put a finger to his lips. "Sorry about this. Another reason I didn't want you knocking on the door."

". . . Yes?"

"The couple in the basement flat, they have a baby? Only it's not been sleeping well, and—"

"Of course."

"Only they'd be up all night, and I'd feel bad."

He swung the door open, and waved her in, pointing towards the staircase.

The hallway was dark, as if the sleeping baby were sensitive to light as well as noise, but there was a glow from above, falling through an open door. Quietly, conscious that Dickon was close behind her, she made her way up two flights. He didn't speak until he'd also entered the flat.

"Welcome," he said.

"Thank you."

She handed him the bottle of wine she'd brought, and he paused to examine the label.

"Looks very nice! Thank you!"

"Oh, it's only—"

"No. It looks really good."

"—just an ordinary red."

He leaned forward and kissed her cheek. "I'll let it breathe."

She followed him into his kitchen.

They were on the top floor. Through the window she could see, because of an incline, the rooftops of houses that were actually no shorter than this one. Distant roads showed as red and white ribbons, each colour blurring and fading then coming to life again, as the cars that made them disappeared, and new ones took their place.

Dickon was removing the wine bottle's seal with the business end of a corkscrew.

"I think it's a screwtop," she said.

"It's what? Oh. So it is." He put the corkscrew down, and completed the job with his bare hand. "Ta-dah!"

"Where should I leave this?" She meant her coat.

"Oh, God, sorry. Anywhere. Put it anywhere. No, wait, let me take it." Placing the bottle on the counter, he made a bit of a mess of easing her raincoat from her shoulders. "I'll hang it in the hall."

She was alone for no more than four seconds.

When he returned, she said, "What sort of baby is it?"

"What sort . . . ?"

"Boy or girl?"

"Oh. Oh. Girl."

"Sweet." She wasn't sure why she'd said that, or at least, wasn't sure what she'd have said if it had been a boy. Sweet, probably. Babies were babies.

The kitchen smelt of sage and uncooked meat. An open recipe book lay next to the stove, and a wooden mallet sat atop a marble chopping board.

"Here. I think it's breathed enough, don't you?"

He had produced two wine glasses, and was handing one to her.

"Wouldn't want the oxygen to go to its head," he said. "It'll get the bends."

He poured a generous slug of wine into each glass, and then said: "Why are we in the kitchen? No, why are *you* in the kitchen? Guests belong in the sitting room."

Which was large enough, but made smaller by the heaviness of the furniture. There was a sofa—dark green, with tasseled cushions—that looked as if it had spent most of its life wrapped in the protective covering it arrived in, and a matching armchair which was more worn, with a faintly shiny patch around a small person's head height. Between these sat a coffee table, punctuated with coasters. There was a desk in a corner. At the room's other end, a dining table, flanked by just two chairs, indicated they'd be eating in here.

"Please. The sofa."

She sat. It offered a little resistance at first, but then seemed determined to accept and quite possibly keep her. She placed her handbag on the floor.

Dickon put his wine down and pulled one of the dining table chairs nearer. He sat. "So. And how is the world of advertising?"

"Oh, you know. What you see is what you get."

He looked puzzled.

"Sorry. In-joke," she said. "Actually, I'm not working at the moment. I'm taking a break."

"Uh-huh?"

"You know how it is. Things not exactly light and bubbly in the commercial sphere."

"Oh, tell me about it. Not everything's happy in my . . . sector, either. Teaching, you know?"

"I didn't realise they were closing schools down."

"Ha! But no, I don't teach in school, not a . . . state school. Language schools mostly. And private tuition."

"Right. You said. I should imagine private tuition's taken a bit of a battering. The current climate."

She took a sip of wine. It was all right, actually. Most wine is, when you need it.

Dickon said something else about work, and how he too wasn't fully engaged in that world at the moment, and she nodded and continued her internal assessment of her surroundings. There was a tint in the air, a citrussy something, as if a freshener had been sprayed not long ago, and underlying that a deader, sick aroma. She'd been a smoker herself way back, stupid days, and was attuned to the smell. Dickon Broom hadn't smoked when they'd had coffee in the park, but she'd recognised the habit's afterburn. It never leaves the clothes.

Now he was talking about the different ways London looked, the different cloaks it wore throughout the year, and she found herself telling him about something she'd seen that morning, a hugely fat man, not so much riding a bicycle as sitting astride one, feet on the ground, propelling himself forward very slowly. Steering with one hand, he had held a pie in the other, and was eating it as he moved. Flakes of pastry littered his wake, as if he were Hansel, all grown up, but still mapping his way back home. By the time she got to the end of this tale, it no longer seemed to have much to do with whatever it was Dickon had been saying, and she confessed as much, and they both laughed. It was all London, wasn't it? Their stories had that common root.

"I should get on with preparing supper," he said. "Excuse me if I bob in and out of the kitchen. It shouldn't take long. Put some music on if you like."

"Thanks."

Dickon left, and very shortly afterwards she heard a fridge door opening then closing, followed by a variety of other noises.

As quietly as she could, she rose from the sofa and searched the room.

"Pork Valdostana."

"It's nice," she said. "Lovely. Italian?"

"Northern Italy."

It was in fact nice, or might have been, if prepared a little more cleverly. But the pork was cut too thick, and required a fair bit of chewing. This she did, and drank wine too, and listened to Broom, who, somehow, had started explaining the PhD he hadn't finished yet, but planned to. Lots of doors would open, he said, once he had his doctorate. She calculated his age at mid-forties, *late* mid-forties, and wondered how many doors he thought might yet be ajar for him, given how few he'd so far come through. Education, obviously, he had a fair amount of that. But what she, perhaps unfairly, thought of as real-world achievement: well. When the subject of Italy re-emerged, she latched onto it.

"Do you go there often?"

"Italy? Not as often as I'd like." He switched to that language, and uttered three or four swift sentences, only a word or two of which she caught. Something about very pretty—and possibly kind?—people?

"I'm sorry, I don't really—"

"Oh, I was just showing off."

He leaned across and refilled her glass.

Behind him were bookshelves, their contents a curious medley, leather-bound book club editions mingling with Penguin Modern Classics, and text books on philosophy. On the far wall, behind the sofa, was a mantelpiece containing none of the detritus you'd expect, no candlestick holders or cards from friends, no ornaments or souvenirs. Instead, outlines in the paintwork showed where such things had probably stood. She had seen these close up, while he'd been in the kitchen.

"Have you lived here long?"

". . . In this flat?"

"Well, yes."

"Sorry, I thought you might have meant London. In this flat, yes, a couple of years now. You're new to the area though, I think you said?"

"Uh-huh." He seemed to expect more, so she added, "Just a few months. I'm in temporary accommodation. But looking to buy."

"Around here?"

"Yes. Yes, I might do."

He nodded, as if he'd extracted a promise, and said, "Let me clear these plates away."

He wanted to walk her home, but she was equally insistent he shouldn't.

"It's silly. And I can manage by myself, you know. Most women can."

"Well at least to the end of the road."

She compromised on that because he already had his coat on.

They took the stairs quietly once more, and he eased the front door shut with his key, so as not to make a noise. It was damp outside, not actually raining. Their footsteps were muffled. A branch had fallen from one of the trees lining the kerb, and had been propped against its trunk, as if the tree were using its own limb as a crutch.

Broom said, "Sue? I really enjoyed this evening. Thank you for coming."

"Thank you for having me. That was a nice supper."

"My life—things are a bit tricky at the moment. I'm really glad I've met you."

"Good. Here—really. There's no need to come further."

He was reluctant, but her tone brooked no opposition, so he nodded and said, "I hope I see you again soon," and kissed her cheek. She gave him a brief hug in return, said, "Me too," and headed off down the road briskly.

When she was sure he was no longer watching, she hailed a taxi.

Dickon Broom.

She wondered what she was getting herself into.

Dickon Broom.

It was possible he was just a bit odd.

She had Googled him, obviously, and established the basic facts: that he was available to teach foreign languages—Italian, French, Spanish—at reasonable rates, both to businessmen and students. His LinkedIn page proclaimed that his "work" existed at "the interface of business and education," and she had read enough CVs to recognise this for the vacuous bullshit it was. Mediocrity was tricky to plaster over. Jargon was the usual camouflage. And Broom's list of interests resembled something you'd come up with if you were inventing a human. Animal welfare, the environment, politics—he was deeply concerned, in an utterly non-specific way. Or perhaps just knew what he was supposed to be concerned about.

There was a blogsite too, a short-lived flurry of activity. His postings were a mixture of the pretentious and the bland. Littered with references to once-hip names—"as Lacan says"—they stuttered into banality when shorn of borrowed thought. In our treatment of the environment, *we should be really careful for the sake of the future.* Another, on the criminalisation of drug users, ventured that the system treated poor people more harshly than the rich. And his thoughts on historical sex abuse pussyfooted so timidly round their subject, they'd been barely worth writing down. *Such allegations cause real grief. They can damage people's lives.*

But if all this spoke to shallowness of thought, it didn't necessarily speak to character. It was possible he was just a bit . . . useless.

The taxi dropped her at her apartment block, some miles

from Broom's flat. She paid, let herself in, and took the lift to the seventh floor. Once in her apartment, she shucked her shoes off, hung her coat, and poured another glass of wine. It wasn't desperately late—not quite eleven—and she wasn't yet ready to power down. Sitting, she took from her handbag the bank statement she'd stolen from Broom's desk drawer. There had been a stack of them, and the one she had purloined had been three or four from the top: fairly recent, but she had few qualms about its absence being noticed. And even if it were, he'd assume he'd misplaced it. Why imagine she had taken it? She wasn't entirely sure why she had done so herself. But probably the need for something concrete. With numbers on, anyway, which amounted to the same thing.

It told her nothing, though, or nothing of use. Broom did not have a huge amount of outgoings, or much in the way of income. Two cheques had been deposited in his account that month, neither substantial. He had the usual debits: gas, electricity, water, Council Tax. This last seemed particularly large. Ah, London, she thought. It's a wonder anyone survives it long. She studied the numbers a while, noted how they wobbled around a fixed point, several hundred pounds below zero, and then cast the statement aside. It had nothing to tell her, or nothing that answered important questions.

Dickon Broom.

Maybe you're just an odd duck

She sipped her wine, closed her eyes. It was quiet here, one of the blessings of good insulation. She wondered what it was like at Broom's, when the infant downstairs started wailing.

Did the cries drift up through ceilings and floors? Did Broom lie with his head beneath his pillow, cursing someone else's baby?

Things are a bit tricky at the moment.

They always were. What made him think otherwise?

He had approached her in a café in a park. She'd been watching through the window while a flock of birds performed a casual miracle of flight above the pond, winding and unwinding around an invisible spool, then scattering into the nearby trees. Like a magician's handkerchief, she had thought—something to do with their appearance out of nowhere, and there being more of them than at first seemed—and it had only slowly dawned on her that they were greener than birds had a right to be.

"Parakeets," he had said. He'd been sitting at the next table, watching her while pretending not to. He had been wearing a yellow scarf. "Parakeets," he repeated, "one of our many local attractions," and went on to tell her the story behind their colony in the park, which was no more and no less than she might have conjectured for herself. More interesting to her at that precise moment was the fact that he was there, doing this—talking to her, moving a little nearer, at length shifting his chair so they were at the same table, buying her a coffee, probing her for information under the guise of discussing the area, its advantages and disadvantages, its property prices. There was, true, nothing especially out of the ordinary about this, and similar things happened everywhere, all the time. And yet and yet and yet. That it was happening here, of all places . . .

And that he was wearing that scarf.

It's a foolish notion I'm having, she had thought, as she sat drinking the coffee he had paid for. But is it?

She still didn't know, a few weeks later.

Dickon Broom.

We know you like chatting up women in the park.

Dickon Broom, wondered Meredith Barnes.

Did you take my sister?

"Take," meaning take away, remove from circulation. The way a conjuror removes a card from a pack, say. The card is still there. You just can't see it any more.

Or "take," the way a fox takes a duck. And then the duck is nowhere. Then the duck is dead.

But she wouldn't allow herself to think that. She was looking for a living sister, not a dead one. Whatever she found—if she found anything at all—it was important to remember that. That the Maggie she was looking for was still alive. That Maggie was still among the living.

Because for as long as she could believe that true, there might still be room for the happy ending.

The last time they had spoken had been at their parents' funeral. What kind of sisters row at their parents' funeral? Meredith didn't know, or wished she didn't. *Us*. How did things reach that pitch? Their father, their mother, had died in the same moment. You'd think such closeness would have acted as reproach.

But a crash, its juddering impact, sends shockwaves spreading outwards. It fractures, splits and rips things apart. Long-buried resentments and hand-me-down grudges had wriggled into the light. They had always been different, in looks, in temperament, and were leading very different lives by then, Meredith gradually accruing the capital that went with being a Somebody, Maggie seemingly exploring how low expectations could scrape along the bottom before running aground. Her boyfriend had been to blame, Meredith thought, looming like a wrecker, luring Maggie into the shallows. Meredith had tried to warn her, with as much success as that usually has. You'd have thought she was the one encouraging Maggie to forget about college, forget about qualifications, to go for cash-in-hand jobs and a life without responsibility.

The estate had been settled quickly. There hadn't been much money. For several years, Meredith had been supporting her parents, though she didn't think Maggie had known this. The car in which they had died, for instance, Meredith had paid for. Even now this kept her awake, once, twice a year. So after the funeral she had returned to London, to her career, to her fiancé, and Maggie had—had what, exactly? Had floundered. Had made her way to London too, eventually, having ditched the evil boyfriend, but then what? She found a job and somewhere to live. Meredith had received a postcard informing her of these things. It had felt like one of those notifications you get when someone you've traded with moves premises. She had filed it in a drawer, ignoring the hollow feeling it carved inside her. Maggie had made her choices. That she resented those that Meredith had made, and the lifestyle they had brought her, was hardly Meredith's fault.

She opened her eyes. The room had grown dark, but a familiar sort of dark, freighted with the shapes of known objects. London could be frightening when you first arrived. Exciting, but frightening. It took a while before you knew where you stood in relation to it. And her own arrival had been cushioned: she had come as an intern, to work in a bank for a summer before heading off to university. Big enough—scary enough—but a long way removed from turning up on your own, and having to work out for yourself what things looked like in the dark. She remembered talking about this with Maggie, before the fall. Before Maggie's awful boyfriend, and run of poor choices.

"I thought an intern was a sort of doctor."

"It is. But it's also not. It's a name for when you're just trying out for a job, seeing whether it's suitable or not. Or whether you are."

Maggie had been fourteen, and had started borrowing Meredith's clothes without permission. There had been a yellow scarf. This had been on Meredith's mind when she bought one, not long ago, from Issey Miyake. The colour of spring, and certainly fifty, possibly nearer one hundred, times the price of that long-ago favourite.

"Where will you live?"

"In a flat. In a place called Islington."

"Is it nice?"

"The flat? Or—"

"All of it, " Maggie had asked.

"I hope so," Meredith had said.

And it had been: nice. But then, people had been nice to her. She was young, attractive, had somewhere to be each day. There were places to eat and shops to explore. At the same time, it had been impossible not to catch glimpses of what London could be like when left to its own devices, the way it could reduce people to outlines. Anonymity was one of its favourite fates, and it pretended an even-handedness in its disposal. Identity could be obliterated when you were poor. When you were rich, it could be redacted.

"Can I come visit?"

"Of course," Meredith said, but for one reason or another, this had never happened.

That topic had not been raised at the funeral, it occurred to her now—Meredith's promise of a visit that never transpired. But it was probably buried there somewhere, finding expression in one of the other million grievances Maggie had unearthed. Meredith, it seemed, had had all the luck, all the advantages. It was difficult to refute such charges when you hadn't even known you'd be expected to present evidence. But still, this one Meredith wouldn't have been able to shrug off. She had been excited by London and the future it was painting for her, and too busy to make time for her little sister.

When they were small, both under ten, their mother had had a one-size-fits-both instruction, *don't let go of your sister's hand*. For use when going to the shops, or crossing a road. Don't let go of your sister's hand. When had that stopped?

Her glass was empty. Now, perhaps, would be a good time to take advantage of the dark, and crawl into bed and let sleep perform its magic. But it was difficult to disentangle yourself from a string of thoughts that demanded unravelling.

So Maggie and Meredith were in the same city, but inhabiting different Londons. Meredith's flat was on the seventh floor, and had big windows. A fridge the size of a coffin graced her kitchen, but she ate out most nights. These things didn't register on her consciousness often, but were simply the way things were, the inevitable accoutrements of the life she'd chosen. Banking wasn't a career anyone with an ounce of sense yearned for as a child, but at this level, it certainly rewarded those who'd put childhood's dreams behind them. So of course there was a flat with a big fridge, and of course she didn't spend time counting her blessings. Had it occurred to her to do so, she would anyway have scrupulously balanced them against the outlay involved. Presumably Maggie had had her own arithmetic by which to account for her situation. But the numbers would have been smaller, and the final tally a disappointment.

And that was how the equation might have remained, with Maggie's postcard forgotten in a drawer and Meredith continuing to build her life, if other numbers hadn't come into play. There was a rule about things happening in threes, one of those rules everyone points out when life observes it, but rarely mentions the rest of the time. Last year, in short order,

Meredith broke up with her fiancé and was made redundant. That these were bad things was open to argument. The split with Sean had been coming for a while, the pain of its arrival mitigated by a sense of relief that the waiting was over. As for the job: once the country had made its decision to leave Europe, anyone with sense knew that bad times were coming. But the redundancy settlement was generous, and there were worse prospects than the opportunity to spend a year, two if she were careful, considering her options. So they were not, perhaps, entirely bad things, but that they were things was indisputable, and there were only two of them. So what was the third?

How long could you carry an answer around before you realised that's what the weight was?

The last time they had spoken had been at their parents' funeral.

But that had not been the last time Meredith had seen Maggie.

A little more than two years ago, she had been sitting in a coffee shop in Canary Wharf when Maggie walked past the window. She didn't recognise her at first. Maggie had looked tired and poor, in that category of people who arrive to clean and polish the area and serve its busy people, and then disappear to far-flung corners of the capital to lick their wounds until the next round begins. There goes my sister. She remembered the thought as clearly as if she'd had it again just now. *There goes my sister.*

Crowds swirled and gathered and broke apart, like flocks of parakeets scattering into trees. There was no finding someone if you let a minute go by. And it must have been two minutes, possibly three, before Meredith abandoned her coffee and left the shop, ran in the direction Maggie had been heading. This was the Tube station, the Jubilee line. During the day's trigger points it was horribly crowded, less so mid-morning, but even so, there were shoppers arriving and dispersing, groups of students, business people. Of Maggie, she saw no sign. That evening she had dug the postcard from its drawer, but it contained no telephone number. She had pinned it to her fridge, and allowed herself to forget it again. *There goes my sister.* It was another two years before she went looking.

And of all the outcomes Meredith might have expected when she at last knocked on her sister's door, the simple anticlimax of finding her gone was way down the list. In retrospect, it was obvious. Years had passed. London was in flux, constantly, and rising rents and a fierce job market kept those on lower incomes on the move. But she had geared herself up for an emotional showdown, and the uncomprehending stare of the woman who opened the door was a poor substitute. No. No young white woman. No Maggie Barnes. No.

As to dates, or forwarding addresses, or any outcome other than the plain negative, she had nothing to offer. No.

Meredith tracked down the house's letting agency, and spoke to a woman who'd worked there for years.

"That's confidential information, I'm afraid. Data protection."

The phrase, like "health and safety," acted as a verbal checkpoint. Beyond here, no one could tread without the proper papers.

"It's my sister. I'm trying to find her."

"I'm really sorry. I wish I could help."

When she called again, she spoke to a man, and declared herself a lawyer. Her imaginary firm's title contained five surnames, and simply reciting them felt like an act of assault with a briefcase.

"This is going to sound like an old movie," she said.

"You're trying to trace someone who's been left a million pounds?"

"Not quite that much."

But it wouldn't have mattered if it had been twice that amount. "I'll speak to my supervisor and get back to you," he'd promised, but never did.

The third time, it was a medical emergency.

"Yes, she used to date my brother? A few years ago?"

It was a big letting agency, but even so, she was relieved to encounter another new voice.

"And he's just been diagnosed."

"Oh no."

Meredith had allowed a trace of a sob to enter her voice. "He's having difficulty adjusting. But it's crucial that he speaks to ex-partners. I mean, she's almost certainly clear, but—"

"I shouldn't really. But in the circumstances." His own voice dropped to a whisper. "I've had friends in that boat. If you know what I mean."

Down the line, Meredith had heard the clacking of keys, the opening of virtual doors. "Barnes, M., did you say?"

She did.

"I'm afraid there's no forwarding. She just left without a word—missed a month's rent, didn't collect her deposit." More clacking. "Her belongings were disposed of, it says here." He sounded apologetic. "That's perfectly legal. It's all in the terms of the lease."

But Meredith had turned cold inside. "When was this?"

Almost two years.

There goes my sister, and around her London grew large and wild once more, and full of things she wouldn't recognise in the dark.

But how worried should she be? This was the rational side of Meredith asking, the career woman used to analysing facts, and drawing firm conclusions. How worried, really? That Maggie was not where she used to be did not mean the very worst. It was possible that she had simply grown sick of the life she was living, and had walked away without a backward glance. Why not? She had been living in a bolt-hole for the transient. It was in the nature of such places that you would leave as soon as you were able, and even abandon all you'd brought there, the better to start anew. No wonder the disposal of possessions was in the terms of the lease. It must happen all the time.

Still, though. Still.

This didn't stop Meredith growing cold inside.

She had done the due diligence, as the lawyers would have it. She had ticked every box she could find. Maggie's phone contract had lapsed more than two years ago, which might mean she had moved onto a cheaper alternative—pay as you go?—or might mean something worse, of the kind Meredith wasn't allowing herself to think about. The lawyer who had settled their parents' estate had had no dealings with Maggie since. And on a frazzled, fraught week back in the town they'd grown up in, with its concrete outlook and its rained-on low-rise estates, Meredith had found that Maggie's presence there had healed over, the way a minor wound might, leaving no scar. She even sought out Jezza, the one-time evil influence. In her imagination, he had swollen with possibility, become a possible abductor, a grimacing devil. But in the here and now, while he had indeed leered at her while leaning through his front door—its missing pane of glass taped over with cardboard—he reeked of inertia, and grubby misdeeds. There filtered past him the sounds of domestic unhappiness, high-volume profanity and slapped limbs. She could see him spending the childrens' birthday money on beer and scratch cards, yes. But any greater wickedness surely required more effort than he was capable of. An instant judgement, but her own, and who else could she rely on?

And meanwhile, Maggie was still missing.

■ ■ ■

So the next stop was the police, and the massed forces of official indifference. The officer who took her statement seemed to have had all human interest leeched out of her about two Home Secretaries back.

"And how long ago did she leave this address?"

Heart sinking, Meredith told her.

"Can't have missed her much."

"What?"

"And she hasn't been in touch?"

Meredith said, "That's what missing means."

"If you'll just fill in this form."

Meredith did.

"And this one."

Paperwork, paperwork. Maybe they could use it for a big paper boat, and float all the lost down the Thames, dropping them off at bridges and jetties.

There were tears in her eyes as she made her way home. Maggie had been missing for years, and she had only just come to know it. So many things could have happened to her, so many unseen objects might have tripped her in the dark. There were predators out there too, monsters in unmarked cars. Life was full of them.

She felt as if a loss she had been carrying for years, almost unnoticed, had grown sharp edges. As if all of Maggie's accusations—the buried resentments and bitter complaints—had hit home at last, and this time were true. And the thought that they might be past repair came close to undoing her. But she wiped her eyes dry. Not yet, she thought. Not yet.

The police officer had said *We'll let you know*, as if it were simply a matter of them deciding whether or not to return Maggie. But Meredith couldn't wait that long. *There goes my sister*, she thought again. And now I'm coming after you.

Facebook was a dead end, but there was a Twitter feed she was sure was Maggie's. Barnes wasn't an uncommon name, but the handle included Maggie's birth year, and its discontinuation around the time of Maggie's disappearance was suggestive. The tweets themselves were bland, the tenuous offerings of someone who wasn't sure anyone was listening. *Sunny day! Bet it won't last!* Well, of course it hadn't. No day did. Meredith's heart bled, a little, but there was more useful information to be gleaned.

First day at work! Quilp House!

The hard time she'd been given at the letting agency, and by the police, was mitigated a little by her reception at Quilp House. The block was twenty-seven storeys high, and her heart sank when she saw it. Maggie could have worked on any floor: How was she to determine which? But of course, the workforce Maggie had been part of was rarely allocated floor space: it worked on every storey, or none in particular, vacuuming floors, emptying bins, cleaning lavatories. Or, in Maggie's case, below ground, in the post room.

The young woman at the reception desk was alert to the possibility of losing one's sister.

"Our Tiffany was always running away. Proper running away, like, not the kind where you hide at your mate's all weekend. Got as far as Manchester once." She reached for the phone. "If she worked here, I'll tell you who'll know. Jazz."

Who belonged to the company who supplied the support staff, and happened to be in the building that afternoon.

"Oh, she wasn't one of ours, love, but I do know who you mean. Used to work in the mailroom, didn't she? With Old Mike." Jazz leaned forward, conspiratorially. "He's Dirty Mike, really, but not for the reason you're thinking. Just, not so keen on the personal hygiene."

"Maggie who?" Dirty Mike had a folded-open newspaper in front of him, and had been about to start a crossword, by the look of it. "We've had all sorts in here."

But memory fired, perhaps triggered by Meredith's presence.

"Was she the one who just never turned up one day?"

The question was like a slap in the face. But "Yes," was all Meredith said. "That would be her."

"Oh. Well. She just never turned up one day." He reached for his newspaper. "I think Joshua knew her. Or had some story about her or other. But it was a long time ago."

"Who's Joshua? Does he still work here?"

He regarded her as if she were mad. "Well of course he does. Why wouldn't he?"

■ ■ ■

Meredith found Joshua on the third floor. The girl on the desk had allowed her up: it wasn't strictly allowed. But a missing sister.

Joshua was a big black man with a bald head, a uniform gone shiny at the elbows, and kind eyes. The girl had phoned to let him know Meredith was coming, and he didn't need prompting to tell her about the evening he'd caught Maggie Barnes creeping in the stairwell, gone midnight. And how he'd brought her to this very room.

"I don't know, man." He rubbed his big head. "We have orders to apprehend anyone who shouldn't be in the building—that's the word it says, apprehend. And I don't even know if that's legal. Anyway, I locked her in here, and then there was a fire alarm. I keep thinking how badly that could have turned out, you know? If I'd had her locked in a room and the building burned down?"

"Was there a fire?"

"False alarm. I came to unlock her soon as it went off, man, I hadn't even reported the incident yet. And when I came through the door, I tripped over the fire extinguisher! She must have moved it, getting ready to fight the flames or something."

Meredith glanced around. There it was, the fire extinguisher. There was a fire blanket too, and a pair of glow-sticks in a plastic case.

He said, "I went arse over teakettle, I don't mind telling you. Your little sister, she just ran. Never did find her after that. She never came back to work. Must have been scared she'd get in trouble, but man, I'd already decided I wasn't going to report her or nothing. I don't know what she was doing, but I don't think it was anything bad. And I shouldn't have locked her in here. That was wrong."

"Thank you for telling me this."

"I've got married since, Miss, and I have a little girl. It changes your perspective. I hope you find your sister. I'm sure she wasn't doing any harm. I didn't mean to frighten her."

Which meant this much: that if Maggie had stepped into an unmarked car, it hadn't been an isolated event. Something had happened, something that had caused her to steal about Quilp House in the middle of the night, when she had no business being there. And on being discovered—caught—to flee without returning home for her things.

Joshua hadn't thought she'd been doing anything bad, but it seemed as if Maggie had thought she was.

A man, Meredith thought. Maggie had history when it came to bad choices with men.

She felt like the big sister who fell asleep in the long grass, and awoke to find Alice gone. Off down a hole in the ground, chasing after a white rabbit who would turn out to have teeth.

Follow-up calls to the police had produced the expected bromide: *A twenty-six-year-old decides to move on? It happens.*

With the unspoken corollary, *If she was really missing, don't you think you'd have noticed that two years ago?*

Where next, though?

Where next was back to Twitter.

Central Perk for coffee and cake! Nom nom!

Something shifted in Meredith's world, back in the here and now, and she realised she had let the empty wine glass slip from her grasp. It was time for bed. Her unravelling of time had brought her back to where she was, in her apartment, some weeks after she first visited the café in the park.

None of whose staff remembered Maggie. None of them had worked there for more than a couple of months.

But Meredith had sat anyway, where Maggie had once sat, and drank the same coffee and ate the same cake. There was a dog that belonged there, and every so often it would run a circuit outside, barking at ducks, and chasing the birds that swam overhead . . .

"Parakeets."

And thus had Dickon Broom offered himself up as a suspect.

It was the scarf that grabbed her attention. He had been wearing a yellow scarf, the colour of spring, like the one Maggie had borrowed, never to return. Which in itself meant nothing, but what else did she have? It was the scarf, and the fact that he was here, where Maggie had been, where her trail ran cold. *A smile, a kindly word, a dangerous stranger . . .*

It wasn't much, Meredith knew, was almost nothing at all, but still, it left her with needles under the skin. Because, scarf aside, there was something off about Broom, off enough that she hadn't given him her name on first meeting, and had provided a false one on the next. Women did this in the city, when they felt the need to be careful. At clubs, yes, and on dating sites. But also, it turned out, at little cafés like this one.

Dickon Broom.

We know you like chatting up women in the park.

Dickon Broom.

Did you take my sister?

Rising from the sofa in the dark, Meredith bent to retrieve her fallen wine glass, along with the purloined bank statement that had drifted to the carpet too. And as she did so, it struck her what was missing from its documented outgoings, its meagre income. There were sums that weren't there. Broom paid no rent. He paid no mortgage. He owned the flat he lived in.

In fact, judging by the amount of Council Tax he paid, Broom owned the entire house.

2

From a pile of worn-once accessories—mistakes—collected in her wardrobe, she plucked a woollen cap that could be pulled over her hair. Her reversible mackintosh, too: she'd forgotten about that. Black one side, grey the other. With several pairs of trainers to choose from, she opted for the most neutral: grey again, with a silver flash. She wore dark jeans, and a matching roll-neck top with a zipper up the front. It was as if she'd long been outfitting for a sortie like this, hitting the streets in a muted version of herself, one that couldn't be picked from a crowd.

She found a cream tote bag, with green writing on—an independent bookshop—into which she put another bag, a heavy-duty plastic one, and a small umbrella and two scarves, one red, the other sky-blue. From the drawer where she kept her discarded spectacles, she chose two unfortunate errors, one hipsterish pair with thick black arms, and the other—purchased in an ironic moment, surely—large and square and, of all things, pink. These too went into the tote bag.

Am I really going to do this, she wondered.

And then: yes. I'm really going to do this.

Meredith took the Tube to the stop nearest Broom's flat, and spent a while walking the streets, noting her reflection in shop windows. With her hair out of sight, and different glasses, she didn't look her daily self. But did she still look like Meredith Barnes? It was a lot of effort to have gone to, if its effect was to make her look like herself being odd.

But it was the best she could do. She walked down Dickon Broom's street. His house had no lights on, or none she could see. At the corner she turned, walked round the block and came down the street again, on the opposite pavement. While out of sight she had put her red scarf on, and tucked her tote bag, and all it carried, into the plastic carrier. Quick-change artist, she thought, feeling ridiculous all the same. And not unlike a spy.

And what were her objectives here? To get to know him better, she thought, without his realising it. To take a look at him while his back was turned. Did he approach other women in the park, or anywhere else? What were his secrets, what were his lies? And the house, too. If he owned the house, why had he not told her so? He'd been trying to impress her, that was for sure: his nearly-PhD, his languages. He wanted her to think he carried weight. Owning a London property outright would do the trick, nine times out of ten. So why keep that hidden? What was going on in the rest of the house?

Maybe she should talk to the people in the basement flat.

Round the block once more. The house remained unlit, and though to her mind it seemed charged and fizzy, as if powered by an unseen battery, the reality was that nothing was happening. Behind its locked door, any manner of activity might be brewing, but to the outside world it maintained the same impassive aspect as its neighbours. Ordinary houses on an ordinary street. Undramatic was the word. She did another circuit, then walked to the park where she'd first encountered Broom. It was growing dark, the afternoon surrendering its grasp on the day. The café's dog was nowhere to be seen. In the far corner, where the footpaths met at the gate, a man was picking up a crate, and leaving.

Meredith was starting to discover the main difficulty involved in following somebody, which was finding out where they were in the first place. She had the look and she had the time. What she didn't have was her quarry. She made one circuit of the park, then caught the Tube home.

For the next two days she repeated this routine, the first time in the morning, the second in the early afternoon. She didn't lay eyes on Broom on either occasion, though once she was sure a light dimmed in his upstairs flat, and she tensed, ready for his appearance on the street. But that didn't happen.

On the evening of the second day it rained heavily, and she sat in her living room and watched the weather beat against her windows. What was she trying to accomplish, she wondered. Suppose Broom left his house while she was watching, suppose she followed him unobserved—what then? What difference would it make? She thought once more about the yellow scarf, a little worn, a little faded, just like hers would be by now. Would she know it for her own if she held it in her hands? She thought she probably would. She could not at this distance in time recall the label, but knew she would recognise it if she saw it. Maybe that was what she should aim for: to get inside his house, to find the scarf, Maggie's scarf. And if she were unable to manage that on her own, well, there were detectives for hire in the city. There would be some among them, she had no doubt, prepared to break into houses, rustle up knowledge by illegal means. Her own legal, if embarrassing, attempts had yielded nothing. All it would take was money. She could afford that.

But it mattered that she do this herself. She had let go of her sister's hand. It was up to her to take hold of it again, not pay someone else to do so. If Maggie's hand were even solid enough to take. It had been two years since the world had marked her presence, longer since Meredith had laid eyes on her. *There goes my sister.*

Perhaps, too, she could not face explaining to another stranger how it was that she had allowed her sister to stray.

On an impulse, she picked up her phone. It rang twice, three times. Her window blurred as the rain came down.

"Dickon Broom," he said.

"It's Sue."

". . . Sue! Hi. I was hoping you'd ring."

"Any special reason?"

"No—no. Just, you know. I was hoping you'd get in touch."

It occurred to her that her number was forever lodged now in his phone's memory. She'd have to remember to answer with *Sue* whenever his name appeared on her screen. And what if he called from a different phone? A hairline fracture appeared in her defences.

"Sue?"

". . . Yeah, sorry. How are you?"

"Fine, fine. Just . . . you know. Keeping on keeping on. How about you?"

She was fine too. Everything was fine, except the weather. Was he busy? Getting out much? What, in fact, did he do with himself during the days?

"A lot of questions! Let's see . . . I've been doing a bit of teaching up at the community centre. It's part of a third-age education programme . . . Other than that, not a lot. How about you? Enjoying your break from the advertising world?"

This gave her brief pause: she had forgotten she'd told him she'd worked in advertising. There was more to being a spy than just wearing strange glasses and a reversible coat. There was remembering your cover story too.

"It's good not to be in an office," she said.

"It must be."

"We should meet for coffee soon," she said. "In the park?"

"I'm free tomorrow morning."

They agreed on eleven. She wished him goodnight, and sat a while longer, wondering if the rain would ever cease, if she'd ever see her sister again, if Broom was in fact no more than he appeared to be, one of London's also-rans, and all her vaulting suspicions simply the product of her own guilt. Well, she would find out. One way or another.

The rain had stopped by morning. She was in the park by 10:45, on a bench with half a view of the café door, a few hundred yards distant. Of the tables arrayed outside, only one was occupied, a middle-aged woman with a Kindle and a lapdog, the former taking all her attention, the latter winding its leash round a table-leg. Meredith wore her raincoat grey-side out and her hair inside the woollen cap. Her phone was in her hand and she pretended to study it, but her eyes were on the café. When Broom arrived, three minutes before the hour, she sent him a text:

Hope this catches you. Really sorry. Something came up. Will be in touch soon.

She twice erased this final letter, but in the end let it be:

x

He was fishing his phone from his pocket as he pushed open the door and disappeared. A moment later he was outside again, and incredibly—unbelievably—he stamped his foot. The woman with the Kindle looked up, then down again. Perhaps he'd said something. Meredith was too far away to hear.

A moment later, her phone trembled.

No problem. Call me when you're free? xx

Upping the stakes, she noted. But stamping his foot? A grown man? She wondered.

She sat, phone in hand, while he lit a cigarette and wandered towards the duck pond. A number of its denizens glided to greet him, barely even pretending they cared about anything other than bread. He wasn't looking round, seemed mostly to be studying his own smoke. If he turns this way, she thought, will he recognise me? No hair on view, thick-framed glasses? It occurred to her that in his eyes she wouldn't be wearing an unfamiliar coat, because every coat of hers was unfamiliar to him save the only one he'd seen her wearing. How did spies manage this? Really?

But he didn't turn. He paced a little, slowly, methodically, and at length tossed his cigarette into the water. The ducks made brief idiots of themselves over it, then swam away embarrassed. Broom went into the café.

Two minutes later her phone thrummed in her hand once more. *Having coffee anyway. Wish you were here. x.*

She gathered herself together and left the park.

Though the rain was still holding off, she unfurled her umbrella for extra cover. The street leading back to Broom's was largely empty of pedestrians, an old man with a shopping bag the sole exception, and he had his back to her, was approaching the bollards at the far end. Meredith walked swiftly, a pulse in her neck keeping time with her feet. But there was no need for an adrenalin rush. Broom was drinking coffee, back in the park.

And even if he weren't, even if he changed his plan and headed home this minute—what was the harm? She was knocking on his door. Had found herself in a muddle, and this was its outcome. A disguise? No—her usual midweek outfit. She reached his house. Its path was two strides long. She climbed the steps and surveyed the doorbells, three of them. One for each floor.

Thought I'd better come out to meet you—the doorbell's broken.

She pressed his bell first anyway, just to make sure he didn't answer—that there weren't two of him, one in the park, the other upstairs. After a minute she stepped back, and looked at the windows. The ground floor had its curtains drawn, and no light showed behind them. Had he mentioned anyone living in that flat? She didn't think so. The windows below—what could be seen of them—seemed to be covered from the inside, but not with curtains. Plastic sheeting? A curtain substitute, Meredith thought. They weren't full-length windows, were little more than a foot deep, three feet wide, down below the steps leading up to the door. The basements here would be converted cellars. In their previous versions, they'd have had no need of light. In their current, they were ill-shaped for conventional drapes.

There was a story, a threadbare fiction, and she rehearsed it now. A friend of Dickon's—just missed him—she needed to leave him a note. Could she just pop up the stairs? Then what she didn't know, except that she would be inside . . . And the tenants, besides, the couple with the baby, might be a source of information. Had they noticed a young woman visiting

Dickon at all? She imagined secrets spilling out, with simple pressure on a button, but when she pressed their doorbell, she didn't hear it ring. Was this broken too? She tried again, and waited a full minute. Now, her adrenalin rush seemed more pertinent. How long would Broom linger over a solo coffee? When she stepped back into the road, would he be heading towards her, cigarette in hand, puzzled recognition on his face?

Again she pressed the bell, and stepped back to look down at the covered-over windows. No sign of movement, but why would there be? There had been no baby carriage in the hall, it occurred to her. Would a couple with a baby hoick its transport down the stairs every time they returned home? But maybe she was mistaken about that: it had, after all, been dark in the hallway. Which itself seemed odd—why keep a hallway dark, when welcoming a guest? She pressed a finger to the buzzer one last time, and got one last nothing in response. Then she left.

Plan B having come to nothing, she reverted to Plan A: follow him. In the park again, she took up her previous station and checked her phone. There were no further texts from Broom. And she hadn't replied to his *Wish you were here*, but why would she? She was busy—something had come up. Meanwhile, she grew a little colder. The parakeets had made themselves scarce. The café door opened and out came Broom, heading directly towards her.

Oh shit, she thought. Do I get up and walk away?

But if she did, it would draw his attention. Besides, he wasn't looking at her but simply walking, with his eyes open, as people do. Meredith raised a finger to her brow as if concentrating, and only accidentally obscuring her face. The phone in her hand was chock-full of absorbing information. He grew nearer. She couldn't look. Her hair, surely, was escaping from her cap. Her coat was turning itself inside out, grey to black to grey. He was nearly upon her, and then he was, and he glanced at her in passing, but all her attention was sealed on her little device, and she didn't even tremble, and then he was gone, a whiff of cigarette smells trailing in his wake. Back at the pond, the ducks were kicking off again.

When she looked up, he was nearly at the gate where the footpaths met.

A man had established himself there in her absence, the same one—she thought—she'd seen the other day. He was standing on his crate, and was midway through a harangue. Religion, she assumed, but the words that came floating towards her didn't include the usual holy syllables: Jesus, Mary, Allah. Something, instead, about a red pill, about the persecution of the male. Four times more likely to commit suicide. Broom seemed interested. Hands in pockets, he leaned to one side slightly, and she couldn't tell if that was his usual posture—at an angle to the world—or the result of close attention.

"For far too long, brother, we've let ourselves be ground underfoot. It has to stop. It must stop."

She couldn't tell whether Broom responded.

"I'm not advocating rebellion. I'm not advocating resistance. My message is a simple one, brother, and it's this. Walk away.

Just walk away. We can't hope to win this war. All we can hope is that one small band of us can survive the matriarchal genocide of our sex."

Oh, right, yes, thought Meredith. Genocide. I knew there was something I should be getting on with.

"Men Going Their Own Way. Remember that name, brother. You'll have cause to be glad of us in the days to come."

Broom either nodded or didn't, made his farewell or kept his mouth shut. It was all the same to Meredith, with only a view of his back. But he moved on, anyway, out of the park on the opposite side to his house. After a moment, Meredith tucked her phone into her pocket, made sure her hair remained beneath her cap, and followed.

She was wearing her blue scarf now, her tote bag over her shoulder. Broom was some distance ahead, maintaining a medium pace, neither hurrying nor ever slowing down . . . It hadn't escaped her that what she was engaged in was at least partly what she suspected him of doing. Stalking. Had he targeted her sister in the park, tracked her through her daily travels? Had he worn down the outer shell of her life, and helped himself to the softness within? Stalkers were only half a rung up from rapists, though in their own eyes, probably, half a rung down. But no, that was glib. Stalkers denied their nature. They imagined themselves more sinned against. It must be like having spiders in your head.

But was her own any freer of creeping, crawling thoughts?

She lost sight of him momentarily, and realised he had taken a path down to the canal. It would be tricky to follow him there, the towpath being long and straight. He only had to glance over his shoulder to see her on his trail. Once, she might get away with. Twice, and she'd start to look familiar.

There didn't, though, seem any alternative. She took the same turning to find the towpath, where she joined it, made narrow by the weeds and bushes sprouting from the high brick wall which ran alongside it. The land on the other side banked sharply and steel railings lined the roadside. She couldn't see Broom for the curve of the canal. Unless he were crouched in this undergrowth, of course, ready to spring out as she passed.

The notion gave her pause, but only for a moment. In a short while the path straightened, and there he was, way ahead, moving at his usual pace, and smoking again. He was just passing under a bridge, over which a bus rumbled as he stepped into shadow. When she too reached that point her nerve failed her, and she took the path up to the bridge. Once there she crossed the road and gazed down the towpath at his diminishing figure. He was simply going for a walk. People did that. The towpath was gloomy, especially in the damp, but there was no law requiring cheerfulness.

As she watched, he reached some kind of opening to his left, and he stepped off the path and out of her sight.

Meredith waited. But Broom did not reappear.

She told herself she was being ridiculous. He was a perfectly ordinary man, his only crime to chat her up in a café from where her sister had once tweeted. This proved nothing. Or proved only that things had to happen somewhere, and often chose the same place to do it in.

But he was the nearest thing she had to a suspect, and he lurked in parks and loitered round dreary towpaths. He wore—had worn—a yellow scarf, like the one Maggie had pilfered so long ago.

At the very least, he was a man who threw cigarette ends into a duck pond.

A woman with a dog walked down the towpath towards her, and looked up warily, as if worried Meredith might choose that moment to launch herself off the bridge, and flatten her dog in the act. She looked visibly relieved as she passed without this happening.

Meredith took her phone out again, and stared at it. No more texts, no calls. She thought about ringing him. *Hi. Where are you now? What are you up to?* Then was glad she hadn't, because he reappeared on the path at last, heading back towards her.

She put the phone to her ear as if taking a call, and walked out of his line of vision. Then recrossed the road and stood by the path leading down to the canal. Like the towpath itself, this stretch of tarmac was obscured by an urban version of pastoral: the gnarled and knotty branches of stunted trees, one waving a blue plastic bag. After a moment Broom passed into view, or his body did, his coat, his feet. She couldn't see his head. The rest of him, though, moved with his usual premeditated unhurried strut, and as he vanished from her sight a shudder ran through her. It didn't matter, she thought. Didn't matter that she had no proof of anything, nothing but the vaguest suspicions. The man was wrong. He was out of true. He moved like a predator nursing a secret joke, its punchline being that he was king of all creation, and nobody knew it but himself. Like any psychopath, he thought he was divine.

The feeling left her as soon as it occurred.

After giving Broom time to move on she descended onto the towpath, taking the direction he had come from. The air here felt very still after the trafficky bustle of the road. The water was calm, dark green and slick in patches, where an oily sheen glazed its surface. Rivers flowed and bustled, eager to get from one place to the next. Canals were workhorses, and would get you where you needed to go, but saw no reason to hurry.

The high wall to her left was becoming flaky. Bricks had dropped from it, sometimes onto the towpath, and a reddish dust coated the rubble in its lee. It was losing height, too, and in a few broken places she could see over it to a sprawling mess of metal barrels, stacked car tyres, and a smoke-blackened industrial building with brooding angry windows. Then the wall built up again, continued for a hundred yards, and came to an abrupt halt about where Broom had stepped off the towpath.

There had been a factory here once. There still was, partly, but it was now dead, and whatever it had pumped out—glassware or ceramics or bricks or steel or paper, something, anyway, there was a pressing need for, and the desire for which kept furnaces burning and wheels turning and barges full of cargo—was nothing more than a memory soaked into what remained of its structure. It was now a shell, a half-formed thought. Two walls were mostly standing, and a third had only recently tumbled, judging by the freshness of the wounds, but there was no roof, and the beams that had once kept it in place were charred stumps on an ash-strewn ground. There were scorched circles where fires had been lit, and cans and empty bottles and broken sticks littered round them. A raggy mess might have been a coat once. For a horrible second it had been a body, but even Maggie's would have had more shape than this. Even after all this time.

Meredith stepped off the towpath, as Broom had done before her, and walked gingerly into the ruin. There was nobody around. Even the remnants of possession, the abandoned trophies of a night's drinking and smoking, looked ancient, as if this drunkards' Camelot had long been abandoned for pastures more solid, offering overhead shelter. The ground beneath her feet was rough, unready. She trod on something slithery, and before she could stop herself looked to see what it was: a pile of tiny glassine envelopes, stamped with a marijuana-leaf design. Everything's branded now, she thought. Deadheads to breadheads in two generations. Empty cigarette packets had been stomped into the ground, as if their emptiness were a failing to be punished, and plastic lighters, too, had been taught the meaning of disposable. It was a sorry, desperate place, and just being here made her feel she'd put on weight.

But what had drawn Broom here? Had he arranged to meet someone? Except, if all had gone to plan—his plan, not hers—he'd be sitting with Meredith now, in the park café. Was this where he came for inspiration? To contemplate the fate of others, and think there-but-for-the-grace-of-whatever? She couldn't delve into his mind, but she could at least poke around his haunts.

She walked to what remained of the back wall. There were smoothed out patches in the ash there, where boxes had been dismantled and used as mattresses. The odours were what you might expect: damp vegetation, and a sooty residue released from the ground by her movement. Urine, of course, and excrement. She traced the wall to where it forgot itself, and became less than the sum of its parts, a pile of rubble giving way to scattered bricks. On the other side, nature was pushing. Trees had learned to bend their branches, but they were patient, and had all the time in the world. Another body lay near her feet, poked into the bushes. This one was a sleeping bag, its fibrous innards leaking through unhealable scars. You could lose anything here, Meredith thought. You could drop anything—toss it mere yards into this undergrowth—and it would fester and rot and give up its ghosts, which might haunt the broken factory come nightfall, but would never be traced to their source without torches and dogs.

Meredith shuddered. She needed to be clear of this place, this sinkhole of aspiration. And until she was back on the road she didn't feel safe, as if those ghosts she'd summoned—the wraiths of the disregarded—were on her trail, eager to feed on her sorrows, and sense of loss.

■ ■ ■

The hate preacher—sorry: men's rights advocate—had left the park. Meredith was glad. The drip-drip-drip of sour resentment was too much the picture of modern Britain to be laughable long: since Brexit, the nation's self-bestowed reputation for warmth and tolerance had taken a hammering. The British were insular by definition, and if outright hostility to strangers had once been kept in check by a reluctance to appear rude, a narrowly won referendum, fought on a campaign fuelled by lies, made it all right now to tell ethnic minorities to fuck off "home." The inevitable splashback spattered women, gay people, everybody. There'd been a vote, and the nastiness unleashed had not yet gone back in its box. She hoped it would. But from now on, she thought, there would be this unwanted knowledge: that when things got to the wire, the British didn't really have much time for anybody else. By a slim majority, true. But they were the ones in charge.

As she approached the café, she took her cap off and shook her hair free. It would be uncontrollable, staticky, all day now. She would have to wash it to regain any semblance of authority. Her scarf too she removed and stuffed into her bag, and she unbuttoned her raincoat. It was still a damp, unlovely day, but the fetid atmosphere of the canal had made her sticky, and she wanted cold air against her skin. She bought a cup of coffee, and took it outside. Behind steamed-up windows, mothers fussed over infants and brought each other up to speed: how few hours of sleep, how many rows, how much wine. There was love behind much of it, Meredith hoped. Families were a good thing. She only had Maggie, and she didn't even have her any more.

All she had, instead, was a vague cloud of unease, hovering over Dickon Broom. A sense of unease and of something overlooked, as if there had been a word, a look, a gesture which spoke of guilt. Not just the scarf he had worn, which sang to her of Maggie, but something besides. But when she tried to focus on whatever it was, it swam from her grasp. Maybe it was nothing. Maybe she was conjuring all this out of the empty air. Broom was an innocent. Just an average man.

Who prowled around towpaths, examining patches of wasteland.

Who listened to stunted preachers spouting misogynistic crap.

Who threw cigarette ends into duck ponds . . .

It wasn't much, was it?

He had secrets, certainly, but who doesn't? And why, anyway, call them secrets? Why would Broom make an open book of his life to Meredith? He didn't even know her real name: who, really, was keeping secrets here?

On an impulse, she took out her phone and called the officer handling Maggie's case. If it could even be termed that.

"I'm wondering if there's been any . . . progress."

"I see. Ms. Barnes, has your sister been in touch with you at all?"

"I—well, no. No, of course she hasn't. That's the whole *point*—"

"Because I have to tell you, unless and until that happens,

there won't be progress of any sort. Ms. Barnes, your sister is a grown woman, and we have no cause to suspect foul play. You say she's gone missing, but the truth is, you've had no contact with her for years. You have no reason to know what plans she might have. You don't know who she might have met, where she might have decided to live. She might have married, changed her name. We simply don't have the resources to . . . to put families back together. I'm sorry."

"She left her job."

"I have days when I wish I could leave mine."

"The room where she was living, she left her belongings behind."

"But we don't know that, do we? We know she left some things behind, but we don't know what they were. Perhaps she took what she wanted and left the rest. More than she could carry."

"She didn't collect her room deposit."

"Or pay the three months' rent she'd owe on giving notice. That would balance out."

"I just . . ."

She just what? She didn't know any more.

"Ms. Barnes?" The officer's voice grew more gentle, or less strident. "I know this is difficult. But you're worrying about something that in all likelihood never happened. Your sister simply . . . left. That's all."

Behind her there was noise, the usual scrimmage that occurs when a woman with a pram tries to get through a door, and too many people try to help her. She didn't turn to look.

"Ms. Barnes?"

"Thank you," she said. For nothing. She disconnected, then watched while the woman with the pram wheeled it past her and headed towards the park gate. Be careful with your family, she thought. We don't have the resources to put you back together.

At length, she finished her coffee and headed home.

Two years was nothing. This was what she was thinking, pelting through the tunnels beneath London. Two years was nothing. There was a poster for a two-year-old movie on the Jubilee platform at Baker Street: seen daily by thousands, yet somehow unregarded. Two years, you could be there all the time but unnoticed by anyone. You didn't even have to make yourself small. You could just fade into London, pull on its colouring, allow yourself to disappear. Maggie could be right here in this carriage, she could take the seat next to Meredith, and Meredith wouldn't know. London could do that to you: could make you fall from sight, or make you fail to see. All cities, probably. But London, definitely.

She thought about the dead factory too, and its patch of scrubland. More of the capital's invisibles congregated there, to drink, drug, sleep, have sex. What else might it be used for? What had Broom been doing—considering its possibilities? And what good had it done her, ringing his broken doorbells, following his wandering path? He too might just be fading away, slipping into the margin, and all the reasons she had for noticing him were just his hollow attempts to catch hold of something, and keep a grip on the visible world.

The only thing certain to her was that she didn't know what to do now. She couldn't keep on like this—padding around after feeble suspicions. And it was in one of those unsubtle moments that the world sometimes offers, its hamfisted attempts at a joke, that a solution occurred just as the train dashed out of darkness, and into the white-tiled brightness of her station.

If she wanted to know whether Broom had taken her sister, there was an obvious course of action available.

It was simple, really.

She could ask him.

Part five.

1

Maggie wasn't well.

She was almost certain this was true. On a few earlier occasions she had thought she was sick, in need of medical attention, but Harvey had told her all she needed was rest, and maybe paracetamol. Rest? She never did anything but rest. But she was wrong, he explained, she was constantly jagged, her nerves in splinters. This made her feel unwell, when all she was was agitated. If she would learn to take things calmly, and not get into a state, she would feel all right. And he had turned out to be correct, or at any rate, she had not had medical attention, and she had not died.

But this time, she was nearly sure. A hand to her forehead came away damp. Her skin felt clammy. She had lain in bed for hours, but when she rose and looked at the clock, she had only been prone ten minutes. Could that be right? The cut on her finger, which had nearly healed, was throbbing again. She remembered the gruesome fears she'd had, and wondered if they were coming true. Would her finger fester, turn rancid and green? If it had to be removed, would Harvey have the nerve to wield the knife? Or would he prove too weak?

All the men she'd ever been involved with had turned out more interested in their own welfare than hers. Harvey was different, but that didn't make him perfect. She thought she might be able to take her own finger off, but she'd need him there, with towels and ice. Would need him not to faint. Would need him strong.

How would Dickon Broom have coped, she wondered.

She hadn't been going to think about Dickon Broom. Since the trip outside had gone so scarily wrong, she'd determined to banish him from her mind. It would do nobody, neither Harvey nor herself, any good to consider how Dickon Broom would behave, how much better he would deal with all this. And she was glad she hadn't mentioned his name to Harvey. Men didn't enjoy being reminded that there were stronger men around. But now, her temperature on the rise, Broom seemed nearer. If she closed her eyes and reached out her hand, he might take it. He might lead her out of this half-life, and into the daylight.

Perhaps he'd come for her already. Yesterday, there'd been someone looming outside the house. It was hard to be sure, so little light fell through the binbagged windows, but she thought there had been somebody by the front door. Ringing the bell? But there were no bells. Harvey had had them disconnected, the better to make the safe house safe. He had disconnected bells and covered up windows. That was sound and light accounted for. But he had not been able to safeguard against looming.

It couldn't have been Dickon Broom, though, because it was such an ominous thing to do. Nothing good ever loomed. Like no good person lurked.

Maggie lay on her bed again and allowed more hours to pass. Again, they were measured in minutes only. She wished this fever would leave. She wished something would happen. Lately, she'd been dreaming about Meredith. For years they'd been at odds, for reasons that seemed ridiculous now, for reasons that didn't matter. In her dreams, they were friends again. That would be good. She rubbed her eyes and rolled over twice, trying to get comfortable. Her finger pulsed and her eyelid fluttered. She wondered if this was what Harvey meant by *rest*.

Anything could be dealt with, if you broke it into smaller parts.

That was something Broom used to tell his students when he was teaching at MISE. You had a problem, it might be to do with sentence structure or some real-life issue, whatever, the thing to do was break it into smaller parts. Solutions for small things were easier than for big. Everybody knew that. Not everybody put it into practice.

So, Maggie.

He needed her to be somewhere else.

So it was essentially a problem of transport. And while he didn't have a car, he had a licence, and while he didn't have money, he had a credit card. Outlay now, income later. He could hire a car and put her inside it. See? Break the problem down, it's no longer about Maggie. It's simply a matter of looking up local car-hire firms and taking it from there.

He had a vision of driving her, blindfolded, into the depths of the countryside, somewhere miles away, days away, the longest drive the kingdom could offer, and releasing her in a dark wood, and hurrying home alone. She'd be lost, disoriented, sure. It would all be very strange. But she'd be fine, someone would find her, take care of her, and gradually she'd come to realise that the world hadn't Collapsed after all. She'd be so grateful for this, so happy the nightmare was over, that she'd settle down into her new life and forget everything. Face it: she didn't even know his name. Had only the vaguest idea of where this house was. It would be that simple. He would be that safe.

For maybe five minutes Broom sat in an armchair, two floors above Maggie's basement, and allowed this future to take shape.

But it was like the novella he hadn't written. As soon as he tried to give his plan form, its bubble would burst. Hiring a car was all very well, but it would mean there'd be a record. And these days, hire cars, didn't they have GPS? So the firm would always know where you were, where you'd been? Which meant that no matter how far he drove, it would be like painting the road as he went, leaving a trail that could be followed from the moon. It would be worse than having Chinese security forces after him.

And Maggie, anyway. It wasn't like getting rid of a stray dog. Ultimately, he had to be sure that she wasn't going to tell her story. And the only way he could be sure of that would be if she wasn't Maggie any more.

Anything could be dealt with, if you broke it into smaller parts.

Maggie, Maggie.

He thought perhaps he should go down and see how she was today.

"I don't feel well."

"You're fine."

"I've got a temperature. Feel my forehead."

He felt her forehead.

"See?"

"It feels fine," he said. "You're imagining it."

"I should probably see a doctor?"

"Well, how is that going to work? Seriously, Maggie? How are we going to get a doctor here?"

"Don't Five have medical staff?"

"No. I mean yes, of course they do. But I've told you. Five have—"

"Washed their hands."

"Yes."

"So they don't catch germs."

"You're not making any sense."

She looked grim, to tell the truth. Pale and sweaty, and her tracksuit had patches under the arms and under her breasts. It was difficult not to be angry when you saw the state she'd got herself in. Ill, though, he didn't want her to be ill. He only wanted her to be ill if it got very serious, very quickly, very quietly, with him not there.

"Why don't you sit down," he said. "I'll make us a cup of tea."

"Make a cup of tea, make a cup of tea," she parroted. "If I'm not making you a cup of tea you're making me one, but it doesn't make any difference, does it? It's still just a bloody cup of tea."

"Maggie," he said again. "You're not making any sense."

She wilted, and he reached out for her before she hit the floor. All he needed. He steered her to the sofa and let her drop onto it, and then, because he couldn't stand the sight of her, went into the kitchen and did indeed make a bloody cup of tea.

How nice it would be, how calm, how pleasant, to have an ordinary life. To hear Sue say, "It's a lovely morning—shall we go out for breakfast?" and walk arm in arm to a trattoria.

Never going to happen. Could happen. Might.

He took Maggie her tea, and found she was sitting up at least.

"Have you taken any paracetamol?" he asked.

"Couple."

"You'll feel fine again soon."

He handed her the mug, and she took it in both hands, then sat with a glazed expression, as if staring through the walls. "I think my finger might be infected," she said at last.

"Why would you think that?"

"It feels funny."

"Let me look."

She let him look at her finger. It was pink and ordinary, with a healing cut at the tip. Seriously, you'd have to be a woman to make a fuss. It looked like something that had happened weeks ago.

"It's fine," he said. "You're imagining it."

"I'm not."

He suppressed a sigh. He knew from experience this could go on for hours. You're fine. I'm not. You're fine. I'm not. He quite deliberately hadn't made himself a cup of tea. He was leaving in a minute.

She said, "If it needed amputating, would you help me do it?"

"It's not going to need amputating. Don't be ridiculous."

"But if it did."

"It's not."

"You wouldn't, would you?" She turned her head and gazed at him, big-eyed. "It's okay, you know. I don't blame you. It can't be easy for you, either."

He was glad she appreciated that much, anyway. The stuff he had to do for her she didn't even know about. The sacrifices he had made.

"Five let us both down, didn't they?"

And he saw no reason to disagree with this, either.

She sipped her tea, said, "It's very hot"—he had to bite back three responses—and then dipped her finger into it, the one she'd been complaining about, withdrew it, sucked it dry, and blew on it. "Did they do that with Dickon Broom too?"

The world collapsed for real, briefly. Broom felt it whirl and spin.

". . . What did you say?"

"Did they do that with Dickon Broom too? Just leave him to take care of himself? Do they do that with all their agents?"

His heart, his heart. Its pounding must have been visible.

"Where did you get that name?"

"I found it. It doesn't matter. He was here, though, wasn't he? Before me. He was another of Five's agents, and they put him in this safe house, and he's not here any more. Did Five wash their hands of him too? I've been imagining all sorts of things about him, but I don't even know if he's still alive. Maybe they just decided to get rid of him."

"I . . . I . . . What are you even talking about?"

"It doesn't matter. I wasn't going to tell you." She put the cup of tea on the floor. "Thank you for making this. It's horrible, though. You never leave the bag in long enough." She ran a hand through her hair, and then looked at her palm. "I need a bath. I haven't had a bath yet."

"No, sit down." He took hold of her arm, prevented her from getting up. "Tell me about Dickon Broom. Where did you get that name from? It's important."

"Why?"

Jesus!

"Why do you think? You're not supposed to know about him! No one is. It's dangerous information!"

He could hear his own voice rising.

"Harvey! You're hurting me!"

He was gripping her still, gripping tight. He had to force himself to let go.

"I'm sorry."

She rubbed her arm. "I found his name on a library ticket, that's all. In the wardrobe. It must have fallen out of a pocket."

"Oh Christ."

"Did you know him?"

"Oh Christ."

"Did you know him, Harvey?"

He put his head in his hands, closed his eyes, let the world turn. What now?

After a while, she laid a hand on his shoulder. She spoke very softly. "I'm sorry, Harvey. I didn't mean to upset you. I don't know anything about him, really. I just made up stories. Like having an imaginary friend."

". . . That's okay."

"Is he a friend of yours? Is he one of your agents?"

". . . He was."

"But not any more?"

"No. He's dead, Maggie. I'm sorry."

"Oh no."

"I'm sorry. He was a very brave agent, a very brave man. But he's dead."

Maggie sank into him and burst into tears.

For a while, a little while, Dickon Broom cried too.

Later:

"I want to hear about him."

"Are you sure?"

"Yes."

"It's not a happy story."

"None of them are."

So he told her about Dickon Broom.

"He was an agent, yes. One of mine. The best I've ever had. The best anyone ever . . . Anyway. I recruited him, and gave him a job to do. A very important job, Maggie. More important even than yours."

"Was it to do with the Collapse?"

"It had everything to do with it. Everything. Do you remember I told you? That Five had an inkling it was coming, that there was going to be an attack? An economic takeover? And what you did was part of trying to stop that from happening, but the reason I knew about it in the first place, the reason *Five* knew, is because of what Dickon Broom did."

She was nodding sagely, as if this much she already knew. That Dickon Broom had been part of her history all this time.

"What did he do?" she said.

"He infiltrated the Chinese security service."

"But how did he . . . He wasn't Chinese, was he? It's not a Chinese name."

"No. He did it by pretending to be a traitor. By pretending he was spying on us for them, when all the time he was spying on them for us. Like I said, he was a very brave man. It was a very dangerous thing to do."

". . . What happened?"

This is what happened.

"He was discovered," said Broom. "There was a Chinese

agent—a very bad one, an evil, evil woman—she was called Lin Hua. Broom was good at pretending to be someone he wasn't, but she was even better. He thought she believed in freedom and democracy. That her ideals were the same as ours. So he trusted her, and she betrayed him. He was tortured. They tortured him, Maggie. Lin Hua did. Lin Hua tortured him."

She had tears in her eyes again. "She killed him?"

"He managed to escape. Five—we got him out. We broke him out. And he was brought here to recover, but he was too badly hurt, Maggie. He died here. There was nothing anyone could do." His own eyes were wet still too. "He gave his life for his country. He was a very brave man."

"And he told you about—"

"He told us everything he'd learned. Which was a lot. But not enough to prevent the Collapse from happening."

She was all cried out, it seemed. She sat very close to him, and after a while he put his arm around her, and drew her even closer. It was just the two of them in here, and the whole world out there. They were allies. They had to be strong. This couldn't go on much longer.

"So this ticket I found," she said at last. "His library card. How did that even get here? In the wardrobe?"

"I don't know," he said. "It shouldn't have been there. I can't think why it was."

Maggie nodded. "It's the stupid little things you can't find answers for, isn't it?"

He agreed, and said, "Are you feeling better now?"

"I think my fever's gone."

"Good." He kissed her forehead. "Now. This is important. Are you ready?"

". . . Yes."

"We're leaving."

". . . What?"

"We're leaving."

"Leaving here?"

"Yes."

"When? Soon?"

"Soon, yes. Today. Tonight."

"But that's—"

"I need you not to get excited."

"—fantastic! Oh, Harvey, that's the last thing I was expecting you to say!"

"Good. Good. That's good. But you have to not get excited. It's important we both keep calm."

She looked like an infant, sitting up straight, hands clasped in front of her, great big beam on her face. Trying not to be excited.

"Where are we going, though?" she asked. "Not to another place like this?"

"Not like this, no."

"Like what, then?"

"It's another safe house, but not like this. Out in the countryside, like I promised. So we'll be able to get out for walks and fresh air. Nobody will see us. Nobody we need be frightened of, anyway."

"I'm so tired of being frightened!"

"You'll have a new identity. We both will."

"Are you going to be there too? To stay?"

"Yes. We'll be there together."

"Oh, Harvey . . . Will we be pretending to be married?"

"Yes. That'll be our cover story."

"Can we get a dog?"

". . . Maggie, we can work out the details later—"

"It's just that I've always wanted a dog. I've always wanted to live in the country and I've always wanted a dog. I didn't even know I'd always wanted one until just now. It's funny, that, isn't it?"

"I think you're getting excited."

"I know I am. I'm sorry. I'll calm down." She clasped her hands again. "Do I need to pack?"

"You won't need anything, Maggie. We'll have everything we need in the new place. It's all taken care of."

"You've been planning this for ages, haven't you?"

"I'm sorry it's taken so long."

"Don't be silly! I'm just glad it's happening at last. And I know you've had so many things to take care of—"

"I have."

"—but the best thing of all is that you're taking care of me. Thank you, Harvey."

"You don't need to thank me, sweetheart."

"But I do. Thank you thank you thank you. All of this, these last two years, they'll all have been worth it if we can escape now, and lead a happy life."

"Then that's what we'll do," he said. "We'll escape now, and lead a happy life."

He left her then, and went upstairs, and planned the best way to kill her.

The meat mallet would do for the actual deed.

For the rest of it he'd need a saw, a cleaver too.

And plastic sacking. There'd be a mess, he couldn't afford to leave traces.

And bleach, plenty of bleach. To swill everything down with afterwards, and make sure the drains were clean.

And different shops, he thought. I'll have to go to different shops. If you went into one hardware place and filled your basket with cleaver, saw, bleach, plastic sacks, they'd ring the police before you reached the till.

And he would have to go to a money machine first because he needed cash to buy the tools. He didn't want to leave a paper trail.

Cash, then, and different shops. There was no reason, if he was careful, why anyone need raise an eyebrow.

Nobody had missed Maggie Barnes for years. Why would they start now?

The previous day he had walked along the towpath. Sue had stood him up, but that was okay, he thought that was okay—she'd put an *x* on her text—and he had walked along the towpath to the old abandoned factory, like in a folk song. The previous summer there'd been an encampment there, crusties with dogs, smoking dope and drinking cider, but now it was deserted. There was a wilderness behind those broken walls. He wouldn't be surprised if there were already half a dozen missing people in a couple of dozen places back there. That thought squeezed a laugh from him. *Half a dozen missing people in a couple of dozen places.* He'd just be adding to an ongoing jigsaw puzzle. London was full of them, people nobody cared about. The police would never put them back together. Why would they? Nobody cared.

He rubbed at his cheeks. He was very tired. Which wasn't surprising, he had so many things to do. He should make a list, but no. Best not put this on paper.

Another thing he should do was text Sue. Or maybe call her. With all this going on, it was crucial he keep a foot in the real world, that while all these problems were being dealt with, he was still visibly going about his ordinary life. It wasn't as if he needed to establish an alibi, the way criminals do. All the same, it was important to show that everything was normal, to leave no bumps in the day. Nothing anyone could look back on later, and think odd.

He should clean his laptop history too. Not that anyone would ever examine it, but still, he'd searched *Maggie Barnes* once or twice, making sure she hadn't been missed. She hadn't, of course. The Internet didn't care about her any more than anyone else. He sat down to do that now, because that was how he was, methodical, thorough. First, though, he had another look for Sue.

But it was impossible. He had no surname for her, and he had already learned the hard way that there were many people called Sue who worked in advertising in London. Many. The image results alone, you could pore over for hours.

It didn't matter. Sue wasn't going to come wrecking his life the way Maggie had, the way Lin Hua had. He didn't need to research her. He would get to know her slowly, each discovery strengthening the bond they were starting to form. The Internet was destroying traditional relationships, and he wasn't going to get caught in that trap. He scrolled a little way through *Sue, advertising, London*, then prepared to log off, but had another thought. He had her mobile number. Why not search for that?

Wouldn't take a minute.

Late the previous day, a sinkhole had appeared in a suburban street in Newcastle, and already Meredith had seen its photo four times: on her phone and on newspaper front pages. Later she'd see it in the evening press, and the following morning it would doubtless appear in *Metro*—"yesterday's news tomorrow"—so by and by, it would start to seem normal. Sinkholes usually happened elsewhere in the world. But lately, these weirdly circular pits had been appearing all over the country, at the ends of driveways, cars teetering on their brinks. There were scientific reasons: fluctuations in the water table, instability exacerbated by subterranean works. But mostly, Meredith decided, it was because the world had a sense of humour. What better way of pointing out the precarious nature of our lives than by opening up holes where we walked?

She was on her way to see Dickon Broom while having these thoughts. Maybe they would appeal to him, a way into today's topic. *My sister disappeared in the sinkhole of the city.* It was part of the Generation Y trap nobody had been warned about yet: the young were just getting used to life's low ceilings, and now the floors were vanishing beneath their feet. Something philosophical like that, to distract him from the fact that Meredith had lied to him, about her name, about who she was, about why she'd befriended him in the first place. Because she wanted to know what he'd done with her sister. If anything, she reminded herself. You know nothing for a fact.

Her journey had that grindingly inexorable quality that usually signifies trips to the dentist, or to a break-up with a lover. You try to dig your feet into each moment, to prevent it from sliding into the next, but . . . She didn't want to confront Dickon Broom. She suspected that if you scratched his surface hatred would ooze forth, that the things he pretended to—his interests in *animal welfare, human rights, the environment*—would peel away without leaving a mark, and underneath he would be a raw lump of gristle. She didn't know precisely why she felt this, but it had to do with his slow-motion walk, his pedantic drawl, with the way the tips of his incisors appeared when he smiled. Kindness showed in the eyes. It didn't in his.

So no, she didn't want to put herself on the wrong side of Dickon Broom, and explaining to him that their relationship was based on her need to find her sister was unlikely to have a pretty ending. But otherwise, she'd reached a wall. She'd found nowhere to lay a flower for Maggie, nowhere to nail a plaque. Perhaps she never would. But this next step needed to be taken before she accepted that as final.

She reached her stop and left the Tube. On the streets the weather was grizzling once more, its continuing dissatisfaction with the city expressed as damp air, cold pavements, wet windows. At a nearby tricycle, whose bearded owners were brewers of artisanal coffee, unless they were artisanal brewers of coffee—like "organic," the word had become fluid of meaning, and mostly just signified "pricey"—she bought a latte. A delaying tactic, she recognised. But it made little difference. The end was near.

Looking up, she saw Broom heading towards her.

She didn't need to pack, but she packed anyway, if you could call it packing when no case was involved, no bags, no luggage. All Maggie had done, really, was collect her things and lay them on the bed. There wasn't a lot. Her clothes, apart from those she was wearing. Her toiletries. The laptop Harvey had given her, and a small pile of DVDs.

My two years, she thought. These are my last two years.

There were things in the kitchen she supposed were technically hers too, since they hadn't been here when she arrived, and Harvey had provided them specifically for her use. But she didn't think it fair to remove these from the safe house. They included a mug with thick blue stripes, a sieve and a cheese grater. The kettle had been here already, alongside a few pans, and the array of long-handled spoons and stirrers, the wooden rolling pin, had all been lying in drawers for her to find.

She wondered when the next refugee would arrive to take

possession of her little queendom, and hoped, whoever it was, that they'd find safety here. It hadn't all been awful. It had been packed with awful moments, true, but they were mostly to do with discovering things that had happened elsewhere, and would have happened anyway. That Joshua was dead, and that the country had Collapsed. About the discontents rippling outwards, the riots and police strikes, the sinister awareness that a foreign power had quietly taken control. All those poor families thrown onto the streets. She had never asked Harvey what had happened to them. When the Chinese government had stretched out its helping claw, and the banks had struggled off their knees, were those people allowed back into their homes? Or was being a casualty a permanent state?

But she had to make an effort to leave all this behind, alongside the kitchen implements. Joshua apart, none of it had been her fault. In fact—in a small way—she had worked to prevent it from happening, and the fact of her failure was now just dust in history's pan. Nobody could change the past. And it was now up to other people to challenge the future, because for herself and Harvey, the struggle was over. They would make a quiet life in a new place, and hope never to be noticed again. This wasn't cowardice, it was common sense. They had been brave. It was now their turn to be something else.

As for Dickon Broom, she would never forget him. He had given his life for the cause, while she had merely given two years. And while the evil Lin Hua had brought him low, he remained the hero Maggie had imagined, and nothing could take that away. It was to honour that fact that she took the pile of DVDs she'd collected and removed them from the bed. There was little in the safe house to comfort her successor, and she could easily spare them this much. A few old movies and TV sitcoms—they had shaved some hours off her solitude, and could do the same for someone else. She put them in the wardrobe, on its topmost shelf. And then she sat and waited again, because she had nothing else to do.

Broom's mind was busy and that's why he didn't see Sue standing by the barista tricycle. He had places to go, hardware to buy. Back home, the Internet had offered a number of services prepared to identify the owner of the phone number he'd fed it, but the first few demanded payment, and he was hoping to find one which would satisfy him for free. Later, he thought. He'd have time later—afterwards—to scroll through them. He'd need some dull task or other to occupy him then. Dealing with Maggie had increasingly been an unhappy chore, and that wasn't going to change today.

At the cash machine, he found that his debit card wouldn't allow him withdrawals, and he had to use his credit card instead. That would rack up a hefty interest charge, and he cursed under his breath as he counted the notes out—but cash was cash. Now he had it in his hand, it was invisible. He could buy whatever he needed, and leave nobody the wiser.

To keep himself invisible, then, and spread his purchases out, he went down into the underground, and caught a Tube to Oxford Circus. In a crowded department store—where did everyone come from? How come they all had money?—he prowled the kitchenware area, looking at knives, examining blades.

The cleaver he found was heartbreakingly expensive. He was only planning on using it once, for Christ's sake. He wondered what their returns policy was, whether he could bring it back the following day, and for a moment that notion shone with possibility—but he doubted it would fly. Chances were, there'd be markings, discolouring—chances were, Maggie would turn out tougher than she looked. He couldn't return something palpably used, and wouldn't want to explain its usage. He'd need more cash, though, before the day was through. This whole thing was getting ridiculous.

But: outlay now, income later. Get through this, and his house would be his once more. Two flats to let, or one whole property to sell. Either way, quids in, so stop fretting, Broom. Suitably self-chastened, he made his purchase, enduring some flattering banter

("Very serious piece of equipment, sir. A good choice."

"Thank you."

"We get a lot of professionals buying into this range."

"I can imagine.")

in the process, and left the shop via one of its cash machines. There were two of these in the lobby, "for your convenience."

In a hardware shop off the Edgware Road he bought a thick pair of gardening gloves, because he knew from experience how sawing could chafe the hands—he couldn't say how he knew this, couldn't precisely remember wielding a saw, but all the same, he knew that he knew it. Gardening gloves, then—and rolls of thick plastic bags too, and some twine and rolls of duct tape. The parcels he'd be making would need to be tightly bound.

For the saw, he thought he'd return home and use his local shop. The one he'd seen the other day would fit the bill nicely, and would be cheaper than in Central London. And also: support your local tradesmen. That was an environmental issue, one he'd blogged about in the past.

Practising what he preached was a matter of integrity.

After Broom walked straight past her, Meredith experienced one of those odd moments when relief and disappointment merge. She hadn't been ready for an encounter, but at the same time, if he was elsewhere—on a mission—she might be hanging in the wind for hours. And she'd already exhausted the local possibilities: the park, the parakeets. There was only so much coffee she could drink.

So she wandered the strip a few times, drinking the cup she already had. There was a butcher's and a supermarket, Sunrise Stores. A display of garden furniture graced the window display of a hardware shop, and she wondered whether this meant they were trying really hard or had given up altogether. The coffee, she had to admit, was good. Maybe men with beards knew what they were doing after all. And she wondered, too, about gardens, and whether Dickon Broom's house had a garden at the rear, or backed directly onto other housing.

Catching herself thinking this, she started to laugh. Meredith Barnes, she thought. What are you now, a burglar? Was she going to sneak up to Broom's back door, shimmy it open with a handy tool—she could probably pick something up in the hardware shop—and explore the other flats in his house, all the while awaiting his returning tread? It would be the worst kind of suspense show, the kind you've seen a hundred times. The girl pushes open a door and something rushes out—she jumps! Then, hand to heart, relaxes. It's only a cat. Then the villain appears.

She dropped her empty coffee cup in a recycling bin. She needed to talk to Broom, not prowl around his property. She needed to ask what she should have asked a few weeks ago: had he ever seen Maggie while he was lurking round the park café, chatting up lone women? Ever spoken to her? He would be angry, but she was prepared for that. She was angry too: she'd lost her sister. And if he was an innocent, just a lonely man who happened to be in the right place for suspicion to cloud him, well, that was his fault. If not for his creepy manner, which he evidently considered personal charm, she'd have got rid of him during their first minute's conversation and not given him a second thought since.

Thinking all this she felt her heart rate picking up, blood coursing into her cheeks. This was what anger did, it made you feel more alive. Which was not necessarily a comfortable feeling, but surely beat the alternative.

She walked back to Broom's, found herself circling his block once more, almost despite herself—*was* there a way in round the back?—and found there wasn't. There were gardens, or yards, because she could make out the tops of a few small trees and the wigwam tip of a conservatory, but there was no convenient back alley running alongside them. It was just as well. The easiest temptations to resist were those never on offer. The choice now was to head home and come back another day, or just find somewhere to sit and await Broom's return. If she chose the former, she could treat herself to a quiet afternoon: read a book, watch a movie, put life on hold for a bit. What harm would it do? Whatever had happened to Maggie had happened. If Meredith metaphorically—or even literally—pulled a duvet over her head for the rest of the day, no outcomes would be altered. The only difference would be that she'd feel more prepared, and be better able to talk to Broom about who she really was, and what she really wanted.

That was that then. Her circuit had brought her back to Broom's front door, and since she was there anyway, she repeated her actions of the previous day, and walked up his short path, up the steps to his door, and rang his noiseless bell again. There was no response. She glanced down at the blacked-out basement windows, and imagined for a moment she could perceive a shape behind them, a still figure awaiting her departure, but that was more of the tired old suspense show she'd been thinking about earlier. She shook her head. She had made her decision. Nothing could happen today. She would go home.

Ten minutes later, she was on a Tube.

2

Let's have a plan here.

Let's have a plan.

The thing was to get everything over with as swiftly as possible. No getting round it, this would take ages, but do it efficiently and he'd be free and clear by this time tomorrow. The actual deed, the sad bit, would be a matter of a moment. A meat mallet to the temple. She'd never know what hit her, would still be thinking happy thoughts about the life to come when he removed all knowledge from her head forever. It was the best way. The difficult part would be suppressing his own natural instincts, his gentle temperament. That was what he had to overcome. He actually found himself thinking: *Knock that on the head, and you're home and dry.* Funny how the brain made jokes as a coping mechanism. There might be a blog in that. Or maybe not.

So anyway: one swift blow, then get her into the bath. That was where the hard work would happen.

Broom was being realistic here. He could see himself being up all night.

He had travelled back by Tube, the line half-empty this time of day. The cleaver had been carefully packaged in a cardboard box to prevent accidents in transit. This was now in the same carrier bag as his other bits and pieces, the balls of twine and plastic sacks, the gardening gloves, the duct tape. He had bleach too. All he needed was the saw, and he was good to go.

There was so much *detail*, so much *organising*. He had to be methodical. He would leave this shopping in the hallway, so as not to have to keep traipsing up and down the stairs, on top of everything else he had to accomplish.

. . . Clothing. That was another thing. He could have bought overalls but that was just another expense, and another opportunity for someone to remember him. But he had an old tracksuit from when he'd taken up running, something a lot of the students at MISE did. He'd done that two or three times, after which it had found its way to the back of his wardrobe. He could wear that for the hard part. And coming out of the station, he picked up a handful of *Evening Standards*. It would be good reinforcement for the plastic bags, and burn more easily afterwards.

At the hardware shop he bought the saw, paying for it in cash. Had no conversation with the young woman who served him beyond the obvious exchange about Nice Day and what have you. So that was good.

Except, Broom thought, he really had no business being cagey. In a sense he'd got away with this two years ago. Today was just admin. Even Maggie would allow that. What he was going to do next was simply tidying up. It had all gone too far, he'd already admitted as much. He couldn't waste the rest of his life being sorry. It was time to move on.

The saw came in a separate bag so he had two of them as he made his way home, one in each hand. Nicely balanced. The trick was, he decided, to start immediately, not to build up to it, because that way mistakes were made. He'd go into the house, drop the shopping in the hall, then up to his flat—remember to put the tracksuit on—grab the mallet, and back downstairs to get the job done. A blow to the temple. How cattle were dispatched, he'd once read. He took an interest in animal welfare, had signed petitions. After that he'd get her into the bath, collect the tools, and go to work. It wasn't going to be fun, no point kidding himself. He'd need to keep his mind occupied, and not get broody and upset. A radio—he should take a radio downstairs too. There'd be a play or something on, distract him from the task in hand.

And afterwards, once he'd scattered the remains, he'd do something nice for Maggie, because this wasn't all her fault. He'd plant a tree, perhaps, as a memorial, somewhere he could go when he wanted to remember her. He'd have to explain it to Sue, of course, his special place. He'd tell her Maggie had been a friend from university who had died young. Or that she'd been his sister—but no. It was best to keep relationships honest. He would tell her Maggie had been a girlfriend, and leave it at that. Sue would have to learn to respect his privacy.

The plastic handle of the heavier carrier bag was starting to tighten round his hand, interfere with the blood supply, and he had to stop for a moment and lower it to the ground.

And it wasn't like he could just relax after Maggie was taken care of, he reminded himself. He would have to take decisions, whether to sell the house and start afresh, or go about the business of getting tenants in. All sorts of things to consider—landlord regulations to familiarise himself with, and whether or not to go with a letting agency, who would deal with red tape but cream off most of the profit, and how to ensure he got tenants he wanted, who wouldn't be disruptive or turn out criminal. Headache upon headache. Perhaps best to go the former route, and sell up. No income, but more capital. He should read up on the pros and cons, and that's what he was thinking about, getting hold of a book on money management, when he reached his house and looked up and saw Sue at the top of the steps, waiting for him.

She said, "Hi."

". . . Hi."

"You look shocked. Is this a bad time?"

"It's . . . I wasn't expecting to see you, that's all."

"I know. I was just . . . No. I wasn't passing. I needed to talk to you. So here I am."

"Here you are," said Dickon Broom.

He had a shopping bag in each hand, one of which held a tool of some sort, it looked like a saw. She could only see the handle. Funny: she hadn't thought of Broom as a handyman. On the other hand, how well did she know him? They were mutual mysteries. She hadn't even given him her real name yet.

Meredith had travelled two stops on the Tube before getting off and retracing her journey. There was no point prolonging the agony, she decided. With this unfinished business left hanging, she'd get no rest. So back she'd come, and here she was now: waiting on his steps like a faithful dog. And he didn't look pleased to see her, she could tell. He looked—she wasn't sure what. Guilty? No: furtive. He looked like he'd been caught doing something he shouldn't, though that might be nothing more than the reaction of a private man to an unexpected visitor. But he looked unwashed, too, and his fixed grin couldn't have looked faker if it was labelled MADE IN CHINA. She should go, she thought. This was a bad idea: she should go. But how would that help? No: she needed to stay, and draw a line.

We know you like chatting up women in the park.

Did you take my sister? . . .

"Can I give you a hand with that?"

"With . . . ?"

"Your shopping."

"No. No. I can manage. Just a few . . . items."

Broom had to put a bag down to fish his keys from his pocket, and it fell open to reveal two blue bottles of household bleach and what looked like a pair of heavy-duty gloves. He evidently had some major task in hand.

He said, "What was it you wanted to talk about?"

"Can we go inside?"

"I don't mean to be rude, Sue, but I'm really quite busy today."

He glanced down towards the basement windows, then back at her.

"Things to do, you know?"

She said, "And I don't mean to be a nuisance. But I need to speak to you and it really has to be now. Can I come in? It won't take long."

"The place is kind of a mess."

"I'm not carrying out an inspection, Dickon, I just want to have a few words."

He had his keys in his hand now.

"Please?"

"You make it sound very important."

"It is."

He said, "Okay. But you'll have to be quiet coming in."

"Because of the baby in the basement."

He nodded. "Wouldn't want her to start making a fuss."

He left the carrier bags in the hallway, next to the little table. There was no sense altering his plans. Whatever Sue wanted, he'd deal with quickly as possible, and then get rid of her—he could manage that without being rude. She was the one who'd turned up without warning. In any other circumstances, he'd have been delighted: here was cast-iron proof she was interested in him. Romantically, he meant. Sexually. He'd always been good at reading the signs.

"You're going to leave them there?"

He put a finger to his lips.

"Sorry."

But it didn't actually matter. Or wouldn't soon. Next time she came round, he'd tell her the couple had moved out, that there was no longer need to tiptoe. He'd reconnect the doorbells. Join the world again, after having been excluded from it for so long.

Upstairs in the flat, he said, "Sorry about that. I'm so used to being quiet in the hallway, it comes as a bit of a shock when someone speaks out loud."

"I understand."

She was wearing a different coat today. A grey raincoat. He'd seen one like it recently, but couldn't think where. It was funny how, when you first got to know someone, you knew nothing about their wardrobe, about the items of clothing that were their favourites and would soon be as familiar to you as your own. He'd have to raise that topic with her, but not now, because if he allowed the momentum to falter, he'd never get through the day. "What did you want to talk about, Sue?"

She said, "I'm looking for my sister."

It was all in his eyes. Earlier, she'd been thinking about what they didn't hold: kindness. Now, in the empty spaces where that should have been, she read a mixture of things: panic, fear, guilt. Or was it just puzzlement?

He said, "I'm sorry, I don't . . ."

"My sister's missing."

"I didn't even know you had a sister."

"I do. But she's been missing for years."

"For *years*?"

"Two years."

It seemed to Meredith that Broom was organising his responses, deciding on an approach. The one he chose was sympathy.

"Oh my days—you've lost a sister?"

"I'm looking for her."

"Sue, that's awful—that's . . . I'm so sorry. What happened? I mean, did she run away or . . . Did she run away?"

Meredith took a deep breath.

"There's something else I need to tell you. My name's not Sue. I lied to you about that. It's Meredith."

He was silent.

"Dickon?"

"You lied to me."

"Yes," she said.

"About your *name*? Why would you lie to me about your name?"

"I felt I had to. Because I'm trying to find out what's happened to Maggie."

"Your sister's called Maggie."

His voice was flat, deserted, all expression ironed out of it.

"Yes. Maggie Barnes. And she disappeared two years ago."

"You've been looking for her for two years?"

"No. No. It's a long story. I didn't know she was . . . Look. I lied, and I'm sorry about that, but I had my reasons. And there's something I have to know. She lived not far from here. She used to drink coffee in the park café, the one where we met. Did you ever meet her there, ever come across her?"

"You think I had something to do with her going missing."

It wasn't a question but an accusation—she dared think that? He was an innocent man. He had spoken to her in a café, that was all. This didn't make him a monster.

All that in his tone.

She said, "I know it seems ridiculous—"

"You bet it seems ridiculous!"

"—but I didn't know what else to do. I'm trying to pick up her trail, to find out where she went. There are no clues, Dickon. She dropped off the face of the earth and nobody cares."

"She probably just . . ."

"Just what?"

"Well, I don't know! People go off. They do it all the time. What's it got to do with me?"

"I just wondered, that's all. You hang about at that café, the same one she used to go to. I thought you might have seen her there, that's all."

"Seriously, Sue?—Meredith. Meredith? I'm not going to be able to get used to that."

"It doesn't matter."

"Whatever. Whatever. Seriously, is that what this is about? You think that just because I spoke to you in the park, just because we had a conversation there, you think I might have spoken to your sister, what, two years ago? Is that what you think?"

And now she didn't know what she thought. What would someone look like, someone who'd done the things she'd thought he might have done? Would he be this ordinary, this lackluster?

"You were wearing a scarf—you were wearing Maggie's scarf."

"I was . . . I was wearing *what*?"

"That's what I thought. Except I don't know what I think any more. I just thought it was odd, that I was looking for her, and you were in that very place, and, well . . . I wondered. That's all."

"You think I'm some kind of stalker or something?"

"You're getting angry. But try to see it from my point of view. If your sister went missing, you'd do all you could to find her, wouldn't you? You'd follow any trail."

"Well I wouldn't wait *two years*!"

Meredith winced.

"Have you been to the police?"

"Yes. Of course I have."

"And did you mention *me* to them? Did you tell the police you thought I was responsible?"

"Of course not. And I didn't say I think that. All I'm asking is, did you ever see her?"

"Well why didn't you just ask me that when we met? Instead of this . . . *charade*?"

What was she supposed to say? That she'd had a bad feeling? Was that what this was, the famous feminine instinct? What would the man in the park, the preacher on his crate, say about that?

"Dickon—"

"Have you been stalking me?"

"No. It's not like that."

"Well it sounds like that. Have you been *cyber*-stalking me, investigating me? Have you any idea what an invasion of privacy that is?"

"I'm trying to find my sister," she said again. It was all she had to fall back on in the face of his growing anger. But it was starting to feel flimsy, as if this were an elaborate fantasy she had concocted, to provide an excuse for spying on him.

"I don't care," he said. "I don't care why you were doing it. It's no excuse for . . . for *spoiling* things between us."

"We hardly know each other, Dickon. There's nothing to spoil. Look . . ." Look what? She'd read everything wrong. "If you tell me you never saw her, that you don't remember ever talking to her, Maggie Barnes, then I'll believe you. And I'm sorry I've upset you. But I need to hear you say it, okay? I need to hear you tell me you never spoke to her."

"I never spoke to her," he said.

". . . Okay."

"Good enough for you? I never spoke to her, never laid eyes

on her. And I can't believe you think I'd have anything to do with something like that. *Jesus!*"

He'd folded his arms, was trying to hold himself in.

Meredith wondered why she didn't believe him. Wondered why, from the moment she met him, she'd thought him . . . off.

"And all of this just because I bought you a coffee? You know what that is, Sue—or Meredith, or whatever your name is? That's crazy. You're a crazy woman. You're crazy."

". . . Oh my God," said Meredith Barnes.

He saw the shift, he felt it happen.

A moment ago, he'd been starting to skate. It was a shock, it was a betrayal, it was the worst thing he could think of—worse than Lin Hua—but the immediate problem was starting to fade. This woman who wasn't Sue, Maggie Barnes's sister, would leave, and then he could get on with his day. She had robbed him of the future he'd been planning for them, but she couldn't rob him of that part which was his alone: getting his house back. He would focus on that. Everything would be all right once his house was his own. But something had shifted, and he didn't know what she was going to say next.

She said, "My sister had this phrase. 'Crazy coffee.' She'd say that whenever she had a second cup, because too much caffeine made her hyper."

". . . So?"

"You used those words, Dickon. Back in the park, the day we met. We got a refill, and you called it crazy coffee."

"It's a common phrase."

"No it isn't."

"It is."

"It really isn't."

He said, "It's what my mother used to say. That's what she always called the second cup."

"I've never heard anyone say it except my sister. And I'd even forgotten her saying it. But that's why I focused on you. It wasn't just the scarf. That's what caught my attention. And I didn't even realise it until now."

She'd been following a candle she hadn't known was lit. Or a trail of crumbs, like the flakes of pastry left by that enormous man, waddling along on his bike.

This was the reason her first encounter with Broom had left her with needles under the skin.

She said, "That's why I knew you'd met her, spoken to her. It's because you used her words."

"You can't really think . . ."

He trailed off.

She waited.

He said, "It's just a turn of phrase."

"No. It's more than that. What did you do with my sister, Dickon? Where is she?"

". . . Okay," Broom said. "Okay. I'll tell you what happened."

■ ■ ■

He sat on the sofa. She remained on her feet. He stared at his hands, and at the floor, and then, at last, up at her face.

"She was working at this place, Quilp House? Have you heard of it?"

"Yes."

"Okay, yes, of course you have. Only she was having problems. With one of the men who worked there, he was harassing her. Stalking her."

"How do you know?"

"Because she told me, Meredith, okay? She told me all about it. We were friends."

"How? Where did you meet?"

"Where do you think? We met in the park, we were both regulars at the café. We just got talking, nothing strange about it. She shared my table one day when it was crowded, and after that we used to sit together. And I liked her, she was a sweet kid, but there was nothing more to it than that. She was just, you know, a friend. A sister even. I was seeing somebody else back then, I wasn't interested in her in that way."

"And she was being bothered by someone at work?"

"The security guard. Joshua, his name was. He kept hanging round the mail room where she worked, kept making . . . offensive remarks. About how much he'd like to, well. You know. I don't want to repeat what he said. He was disgusting."

"Why didn't she complain? There must have been someone there she could complain to."

"Yes, except Joshua's worked there twenty years or whatever, and Maggie'd only been there a few months. It was his word against hers, and nobody believed her. People always side against the woman. You should know that."

Meredith said, "So what happened?"

"She asked me for help, that's what happened. Because she trusted me, okay? He followed her home one night. She saw him on her street, watching the house where she lived. It's not far from here."

"Why didn't she call the police?"

"You think they were interested? They said sure, make a note of the time, and if it happens again, we'll have a word with him. And that was it. They could not have cared less."

He was growing animated now, moved by Maggie's plight, and angry at the way in which men failed her.

"And so she asked you for help."

"She wanted to leave. Leave her job, leave London. She wanted to move up north, where she'd be safe from him and it would be cheaper to live. But she didn't have any money, and she was too frightened to head off with nothing to fall back on." He looked at her. "She said she was all alone. She never mentioned having a sister."

Meredith said, "What did you do?"

"What do you think I did? I gave her some money. Enough to leave, to get away. She didn't tell me exactly where she was going, because she didn't even know. She just knew she was going to King's Cross, and catching a train up north."

"And she hasn't been in touch since?"

"She sent me a postcard."

"Where from?"

"Scotland, I think."

"You think?"

"I mean yes, Scotland. It was a long time ago."

"How long?"

"Nearly two years."

"How much money did you give her?"

"Six hundred pounds."

"That's a lot," said Meredith. "That's a lot of money to give somebody you met in a park."

"It was a loan. She promised to pay it back."

"And has she?"

"Some of it," Broom said. "Every month, she pays ten pounds into my bank account. Every month. So she's fine, okay? Your sister's fine."

"Not every month," she told him.

". . . What?"

"I went to Quilp House," she said. "I met Joshua."

"Well then, you know I'm telling the truth. He's the security guard, right?"

"Yes. But he didn't strike me as the sort of man you're saying he is."

"But you can never tell, can you? That just proves it. Some men—stalkers. They're never the ones you expect."

"I think sometimes they are," said Meredith. "Do you still have this postcard?"

"No. I don't think so. It was from Edinburgh, I think."

"That's a pity. The police will want to see it. And your bank statements, too, I expect. So they can trace where these payments are being made from."

"Actually—no, you know what? I think I do have that postcard. I think it might be on top of the fridge. Give me a minute."

"No. I'm going now."

"I just need to—"

"No. I'm going."

He strode into his kitchen anyway, but Meredith was already on her way to the door. A postcard? An image of a playing card came into her mind instead. He'd built this tower of lies, each story flimsier than the last, and it had no more substance, no more strength, than a house of cards. She wasn't going to wait around to see what he came up with next. A flutter of panic blew through her, the same gust that had blown his house down. He was mad. Who knew what he was fetching from the kitchen—another lie, another faked history? A weapon? She was scared now. Crazy coffee. Yellow scarf. What had taken her so long?

Maggie, she thought. Oh, Maggie. I hope to God—

She was at the door, and all but gone. But before she turned the handle, Dickon Broom came out of the kitchen and struck her on the head with a wooden hammer.

There.

He knelt beside her. Her eyes were open but there was nothing in them, no life, no noise. He looked at the meat mallet. It seemed clean. The blow hadn't broken skin, though there was blood trickling from her ear. He had used the smooth side of the mallet's head, but this hadn't been a deliberate choice. He had simply swung his arm. There'd been little premeditation.

She was a stupid, stupid woman. If she'd simply had the grace to take his word, she'd have walked out of here twenty minutes ago, and he wouldn't be in this mess.

But there was no reason to think everything couldn't still be contained. There would be more work to do, more effort, but if he kept his head down, sweated through it, it would all be fine.

He wasn't sure, though, that she was dead.

She wasn't moving, true. And didn't seem to be breathing. And when he put a hand to her throat, he couldn't find a pulse. But his own heart was beating so fast, it might be interfering with the signal: there was enough blood pounding his veins to keep two people alive. He'd have to calm down before he could be sure. But how could he do that, halfway through the job? She had doubled his workload at a stroke. Of course his heart was beating. He raised the mallet again. The first time he'd hit her, it had made a hollow *thwock*. If he did it again, and kept doing it until the results were liquid, he'd know for certain she was gone.

Just bring it down, hard on her head, again and again and again.

Don't think about it.

Do it.

■ ■ ■

Although there was no point to it now, although light and noise would make little difference, Broom left the landing dark as he made his way downstairs. The only illumination spilled from his own flat, the door to which he'd left open. The bag of tools was where he'd left it, by the hall table. He'd get to that in good time. Stuff in there he needed, definitely, but right now the mallet was all. There was a woozy quality to his thoughts, but that was the stress of the moment. He was in control. Knew what he was doing. He worked out which key he needed from the familiar ring in his pocket, and let himself into the basement.

"Harvey?"

And there it was, the name she knew him by that wasn't even his, that he'd plucked from two sheets on a notice board, a poet and a ballet. It was true they'd been through a lot together, but really: how could finishing this relationship be wrong, when she didn't even know his name? By any civilised standard, it was the proper thing to do.

"I'm here," he said.

She appeared at the foot of the stairs, coming fully into view as he descended. She'd had a bath and changed her clothes while he'd been gone. The sweatshirt she was wearing was his old one. It had been too big for her when she'd appropriated it, but she filled more of it now than she had then. Another reason.

"What's that in your hand?" she asked.

He was holding the mallet, of course, because that was part

of the plan. From here on in, everything was according to the plan.

"Just something I'll need later. Not important. Are you ready to go?"

"Now?"

"Now this minute, yes."

"Yes, I'm ready."

He reached the bottom step and she flung her arms around him and squeezed him tight.

"I'm so excited, Harvey. I thought today would never come."

"Well, it has."

". . . What's the matter?"

"Nothing. Nothing's the matter."

She released him and took a step back. "You sound different. Has something happened?"

"Nothing's happened."

He realised then that he'd forgotten to change his clothes, that he wasn't wearing the tracksuit.

"Damn!"

"What is it, Harvey? What is it?"

"It's—damn. It's nothing. It's all right. Everything's all right."

Just one more thing to do. He'd have to burn these clothes afterwards, that was all. Or change immediately once this part was done.

Maggie said, "That's a meat tenderiser."

"What?"

"What you're holding. It's for tenderising meat. Why do

you need one of those, Harvey? What are you doing with it later?"

He said—

He said—

He said—

But nothing came. It didn't matter. There was nothing more to say.

He raised the mallet above his head, and swung.

There was something wrong with Harvey.

Earlier he'd been tender and good, and when he'd told her about Dickon Broom he'd done so with such sorrow that Maggie knew Dickon had been not just an agent but close to his heart. And when he had spoken about the new house, the life they were to have, it had been like old times in the park café, when they'd sat at a table together, and there had been sunlight and fresh air and the song of parakeets.

But that had disappeared in the hours he'd been gone. Now his face was a mask she couldn't read, worse even than when he was angry with her, because now he was simply blank and cold, as if somebody else had moved into his head. And she thought—it filled her with terror—she thought that the worst had happened, that he'd been caught by Lin Hua or someone like her, and she'd scrambled his brain, turned his mind inside out, and he was no longer Harvey Wells but an enemy come to destroy her.

Given a minute, she knew, she could bring the old Harvey

back. She would paint him such a true picture of Harvey Wells that all the poison he'd been fed would seep away and he'd be his own self once more. But that minute burst like a bubble. It was already over. She stepped back. Harvey's teeth were showing, the tips of his incisors, the way they did when he smiled, but he wasn't smiling. He changed his grip on the mallet.

When he raised it above his head, she screamed.

When he swung it, it caught the light fitting, and the bulb exploded with a bang and plaster rained down.

All the lights in the basement died at once.

Hot.

Cold.

Floor.

Ceiling.

Fingers.

Head.

Eyes.

Open eyes.

She opened her eyes.

Pain.

Light.

Dark.

Pain.

Blood.

Blood?

Blood.

The blood was on her fingers.

The pain was in her head.

No,

The pain was everywhere.

No,

The pain was in her head.

When she moved her head it went everywhere.

Otherwise, it was just in her head.

Somebody screamed.

Meredith closed her eyes.

When the darkness came he swore loudly and swung the mallet again, but its head thunked into the staircase. A hollow sound echoed through the basement. He could see nothing, but a slithering, beady noise suggested she'd passed through the curtain into the kitchen. That was small and enclosed and the last place she needed to be. Then again, it was the last place she was going to be, so that seemed tidy enough.

"Maggie?" he said.

No reply, but someone was whimpering.

He needed a moment, so his eyes could adjust. Things were not going the way they were supposed to, but that didn't mean they couldn't be reclaimed. All he needed was to keep his nerve. Soon this would be over, and he would tidy up, and all would be well.

"Maggie?" he said. "I'm sorry. But it has to be done. It's the only way out. For both of us."

She didn't reply.

Broom could hear London in the distance. London was always there, always breathing. There was always traffic. There was always something.

He thought that a kind thing to do would be to show her she wasn't alone.

"I'll be coming with you, Maggie. Afterwards," he said. "I have some pills. I'll take them all. I'll follow you."

Still she said nothing.

His scalp felt scratchy, and when he rubbed it with his free hand his fingers flamed with pain, shards of lightbulb glass impaling their tips. He tried to shake them free, then rubbed them against his jeans. It felt like he'd dipped his hand in a bucket of razor blades.

Forgetting to put on the tracksuit was a blip. But the important thing was, he'd avoided the bigger mistakes. He could have crushed Sue's head, but that would have been messy—he needed to collect his shopping first, and spread the bin liners around, to contain the leakage. It was fine: she wasn't going anywhere. Besides, if he'd come downstairs with the meat mallet dripping blood and brain, Maggie would have thought he was a maniac.

Maggie, Maggie.

"Come on out, Maggie," he said.

Was she in the kitchen? Or had she brushed the curtain on her way past?

His dark-vision was adjusting. He knew this basement flat, had lived in it for years. Did she think she could hide from him? He took a step forward and extended an arm, felt with the tip of the mallet the beaded curtain he'd always hated. Like stepping through a dry waterfall.

If she wasn't here, she was nearby.

The single blow to the temple was looking less and less likely, but she had no one to blame but herself.

Maggie, Maggie.

She had scrambled into the tiny kitchen because it was the nearest different space, and her animal instincts had urged her somewhere small and dark. But Harvey was right outside, near enough to touch, and she could hear him muttering and brushing at something, could hear the angry noises he made without moving his lips. Something had possessed him. It had taken no time at all. She imagined him strapped to a chair, head in a clamp, Lin Hua opening him up and tinkering with the connections. If his hammer hadn't caught the light she would be dead now. She would be dead.

He was calling her name.

Maggie was on the floor, clutching her knees. He had left the door unlocked, and if she could get past him and up those stairs—then what? She wouldn't survive in the Collapsed world without him. But he wanted her dead. She had nowhere to be.

"I'll be coming with you, Maggie. Afterwards. I have some pills. I'll take them all. I'll follow you."

His voice was the same as ever—how could Harvey have changed into someone else, and kept the same voice?

"Come on out, Maggie . . ."

Maybe that would be best . . .

The thought winked on then off then on again. They should take the pills together. They should lie on her bed and go the quiet way home, peacefully slide into nowhere, while the safe house cobwebbed round them. Years from now they'd be found hand in hand, shadows of their current selves, surrounded by brambles.

Something made the curtain shiver, and the noise the beads made was like a wave hitting shingle.

"Maggie . . . ?"

An outstretched arm made its way into the darkness.

Somebody screamed.

Meredith opened her eyes.

There was this awful pain, like trying to wheel a heavy suitcase using only her mind.

Dickon Broom had hit her with a hammer.

Really?

Yes,

Dickon Broom had hit her with a hammer.

Her thoughts were clustered on one side of her head, like words hugging a margin.

What had just happened?

Somebody screamed.

Maggie.

Maggie?

Maggie.

She had heard Maggie scream.

There were doors and doors and stairs and doors, but somewhere was Maggie, and she'd just screamed.

Don't let go of your sister's hand.

Meredith closed her eyes.

She opened them again.

It was her own fault, she knew. If she hadn't killed Joshua. If she hadn't been Maggie. If nothing had happened, she wouldn't be here.

And she could leave now. That was what Harvey had promised earlier. And he had come to keep that promise, though not in the way she'd expected.

But really, what difference did it make?

The country had Collapsed. There must still be people—thousands of them—millions—who wanted only quiet lives, the pretence of normal, the ordinary day. To continue as if life remained the same. But she wouldn't be allowed to join them. She would have to answer for the things she'd done, and maybe it was best if it all ended now, just her and Harvey. Here in the safe house, which had become her home.

The curtain rustled, and he was in there with her.

Broom stepped through the curtain. Maggie was a dark shape on the floor, whimpering. He put his free hand on her head and felt her brain pulsing through her scalp. Maggie, Maggie.

It would all be over soon. He didn't wish her any harm, he just wanted her dead. And then he would make Sue—Meredith—dead too, and once the unpleasant business of disposal had been dealt with, his life could start again. It would be lonely, but not for long. He wondered where Lin Hua was now. Perhaps they could start over.

"Maggie, Maggie," he said, and raised the mallet.

Hands and knees.

Crawl not walk

Floor then door.

Door then stairs.

At the top of the stairs Meredith stopped.

It was dark.

There were noises.

She heard:

A crash,

A shriek,

A clatter.

Broom's voice saying:

"Maggie, Maggie."

Meredith's head hurt.

She arched her neck.

Like a wolf.

She screamed:

"Maggie!"

■ ■ ■

Maggie felt Harvey's hand on her head, and waited for the blow.

It wouldn't hurt, she thought. Or if it did hurt, it wouldn't hurt for long.

Or if it did hurt for long, it was going to happen anyway.

She closed her eyes, and for a moment imagined life with a different ending, in a world where the Collapse hadn't happened. There'd be more sunshine, more fresh air. There'd be happier voices. She wouldn't let go of her sister's hand.

"Maggie!"

The scream came from nowhere, as if she'd conjured it out of darkness.

She jerked backwards, and the blow that should have crushed her temple slammed into the cupboard door. On the rebound the mallet slipped from Harvey's hand, and flew into the opposite wall.

Meredith . . .

It didn't sound like Meredith—sounded harsh and animal, as if it were being scraped through a grater—but it was Meredith, she knew it was Meredith, because you always know your sister's voice—you always know your sister.

Harvey swore and threw a punch which hit her shoulder. Without thinking she seized his hand and bit. He cried out and she scrambled past him, through the beaded curtain and into the hallway.

He was after her immediately, shouting again, *Maggie, Maggie*, but still scrabbling—on all fours—she launched herself up the narrow staircase. The door at the top was unlocked, and if she could reach it, if she could open it, perhaps her sister was on the other side . . . Harvey grabbed her sweatshirt, bunching it, pulling her back, but she tugged free as she reached the top. He grunted, lunged forward and took hold of her once more, and there was a sickening crack, something like a chair leg splitting in half, and suddenly his grip came loose and there was a moment during which a heavy object found its balance, wavering upright with no energy keeping it so. The moment passed, and Harvey Wells, whose head had come into contact at speed with the low ceiling by the basement door, tumbled backwards down the staircase and made no further sound.

She looked back, still on her hands and knees, and could see nothing but darkness below.

"Harvey?"

Nothing.

"Harvey . . . ?"

There might have been movement, but she couldn't be sure.

At length Maggie pulled herself up and turned the handle. The door swung open. The hallway was mostly in shadow, but there was light somewhere up above, and this fell down the stairs much like Harvey had, and pooled before the front door. Maggie put a hand to her face. She was crying. She hadn't realised she was crying. There was a noise, and she should have been frightened, but this time she wasn't. You always know your sister.

Three steps took her halfway to the front door. To her left were more stairs. On the landing a woman sprawled, her back against the wall.

"Merrie?"

There was no answer.

Maggie climbed the stairs, one at a time, putting both feet on each step before tackling the next, and the nearer she came to Meredith, the realer her sister became. Blood was smeared across her cheek, but she was awake and breathing and watching as Maggie drew close, and her eyes, like Maggie's own, were wet with tears.

". . . Maggie," she whispered.

"Yes, it's me," Maggie said. She knelt down on the landing. "Are you okay, Merrie?"

"I think so. I might need a doctor. Are you?"

"Yes, I think so. How come you're here?"

"Because you are," Meredith said.

She reached out a hand, and her sister took it.

"Don't let go."

"I won't," said Maggie.

ACKNOWLEDGMENTS

My heartfelt thanks to the real Meredith Barnes, for allowing me to use her name.

And my gratitude, as so many times before, to Juliet Grames, for wise advice.

Continue reading for a preview of Mick Herron's

LONDON RULES

The killers arrived in a sand-coloured jeep, and made short work of the village.

There were five of them and they wore mismatched military gear, two opting for black and the others for piebald variations. Neckerchiefs covered the lower half of their faces, sunglasses the upper, and their feet were encased in heavy boots, as if they'd crossed the surrounding hills the hard way. From their belts hung sundry items of battleground kit. As the first emerged from the vehicle he tossed a water bottle onto the seat behind him, an action replicated in miniature in his aviator lenses.

It was approaching noon, and the sun was as white as the locals had known it. Somewhere nearby, water tumbled over stones. The last time trouble had called here, it had come bearing swords.

Out of the car, by the side of the road, the men stretched and spat. They didn't talk. They seemed in no hurry, but at the same time were focused on what they were doing. This was part of the operation: arrive, limber up, regain flexibility. They had driven a long way in the heat. No sense starting before they were in tune with their limbs and could trust their reflexes. It didn't matter that they were attracting attention, because nobody watching could alter what was to happen. Forewarned would not mean forearmed. All the villagers had were sticks.

One of these—an ancient thing bearing many of the characteristics of its parent tree, being knobbled and imprecise, sturdy and reliable—was leaned on by an elderly man whose weathered looks declared him farming stock. But somewhere in his history, perhaps, lurked a memory of war, for of all those watching the visitors perform their callisthenics he alone seemed to understand their intent, and into his eyes, already a little tearful from the sunshine, came both fear and a kind of resignation, as if he had always known that this, or something like it, would rear up and swallow him. Not far away, two women broke off from conversation. One held a cloth bag. The other's hands moved slowly towards her mouth. A barefoot boy wandered through a doorway into sunlight, his features crumpling in the glare.

In the near distance a chain rattled as a dog tested its limits. Inside a makeshift coop, its mesh and wooden struts a patchwork of recycled materials, a chicken squatted to lay an egg no one would ever collect.

From the back of their jeep the men fetched weapons, sleek and black and awful.

The last ordinary noise was the one the old man made when he dropped his stick. As he did so his lips moved, but no sound emerged.

And then it began.

From afar, it might have been fireworks. In the surrounding hills birds took to the air in a frightened rattle, while in the village itself cats and dogs leaped for cover. Some bullets went wild, sprayed in indiscriminate loops and skirls, as if in imitation of a local dance; the chicken coop was blasted to splinters, and scars were chipped into stones that had stood unblemished for centuries. But others found their mark. The old man followed his stick to the ground, and the two women were hurled in opposite directions, thrown apart by nodules of lead that weighed less than their fingers. The barefoot boy tried to run. In the hillsides were tunnels carved into rock, and given time he might have found his way there, waited in the darkness until the killers had gone, but this possibility was blasted out of existence by a bullet that caught him in the neck, sending him cartwheeling down the short slope to the river, which was little more than a trickle today. The villagers caught in the open were scattering now, running into the fields, seeking shelter behind walls and in ditches; even those who hadn't seen what was happening had caught the fear, for catastrophe is its own herald, trumpeting its arrival to early birds and stragglers alike. It has a certain smell, a certain pitch. It sends mothers shrieking for their young, the old looking for God.

And two minutes later it was over, and the killers left. The jeep, which had idled throughout the brief carnage, spat stones as it accelerated away, and for a short while there was stillness. The sound of the departing engine folded into the landscape and was lost. A buzzard mewed overhead. Closer to home a gurgle sounded in a ruined throat, as someone struggled with a new language, whose first words were their last. And behind that, and then above it, and soon all around it, grew the screams of the survivors, for whom all familiar life was over, just as it was for the dead.

Within hours trucks would come bearing more men with guns, this time trained outwards, on the surrounding hillsides. Helicopters would land, disgorging doctors and military personnel, and others would fly overhead, crisscrossing the sky in orchestrated rage, while TV cameras pointed and blamed. On the streets shrouds would cover the fallen, and newly loosed chickens would wander by the river, pecking in the dirt. A bell would ring, or at least, people would remember it ringing. It might have been in their minds. But what was certain was that there would still be, above the buzzing helicopters, a sky whose blue remained somehow unbroken, and a distant buzzard mewing, and long shadows cast by the stunned Derbyshire hills.

In some parts of the world dawn arrives with rosy fingers, to smoothe away the creases left by night. But on Aldersgate Street, in the London borough of Finsbury, it comes wearing safecracker's gloves, so as not to leave prints on windowsills and doorknobs; it squints through keyholes, sizes up locks and generally cases the joint ahead of approaching day. Dawn specialises in unswept corners and undusted surfaces, in the nooks and chambers day rarely sees, because day is all business appointments and things being in the right place, while its younger sister's role is to creep about in the breaking gloom, never sure of what it might find there. It's one thing casting light on a subject. It's another expecting it to shine.

So when dawn reaches Slough House—a scruffy building whose ground floor is divided between an ailing Chinese restaurant and a desperate newsagent's, and whose front door, made filthy by time and weather, never opens—it enters by the burglar's route, via the rooftops opposite, and its first port of call is Jackson Lamb's office, this being on the uppermost storey. Here it finds its only working rival a standard lamp atop a pile of telephone directories, which have so long served this purpose they have moulded together, their damp covers bonding in involuntary alliance. The room is cramped and furtive, like a kennel, and its overpowering theme is neglect. Psychopaths are said to decorate their walls with crazy writing, the loops and whorls of their infinite equations an attempt at cracking the code their life is hostage to. Lamb prefers his walls to do their own talking, and they have cooperated to the extent that the cracks in their plasterwork, their mildew stains, have here and there conspired to produce something that might amount to an actual script—a scrawled observation, perhaps—but all too quickly any sense these marks contain blurs and fades, as if they were something a moving finger had writ before deciding, contrary to the wisdom of ages, to rub out again.

Lamb's is not a room to linger in, and dawn, anyway, never tarries long. In the office opposite, it finds less to disturb it. Here order has prevailed, and there is a quiet efficiency about the way in which folders have been stacked, their edges squared off in alignment with the desktop, and the ribbons binding them tied in bows of equal length; about the emptiness of the wastepaper basket, and the dust-free surfaces of the well-mannered shelves. There is a stillness here out of keeping with Slough House, and if one were to seesaw between these two rooms, the bossman's lair and Catherine Standish's bolt-hole, a balance might be found that could bring peace to the premises, though one would imagine it would be short-lived.

As is dawn's presence in Catherine's room, for time is hurrying on. On the next level down is a kitchen. Dawn's favourite meal is breakfast, which is sometimes mostly gin, but either way it would find little to sustain it here, the cupboards falling very much on Scrooge's end of the Dickensian curve, far removed from Pickwickian excess. The cupboards contain no tins of biscuits, no jars of preserves, no emergency chocolate and no bowls of fruit or packets of crispbread mar the counter's surface; just odds and ends of plastic cutlery, a few chipped mugs and a surprisingly new-looking kettle. True, there is a fridge, but all it holds are two cans of energy drink, both stickered "Roddy Ho," each of which rubric has had the words "is a twat" added, in different hands, and an uncontested tub of hummus, which is either mint-flavoured or has some other reason for being green. About the appliance hangs an odour best described as delayed decay. Luckily, dawn has no sense of smell.

Having briefly swept through the two offices on this floor—nondescript rooms whose colour schemes can only be found in ancient swatches, their pages so faded, everything has subsided into shades of yellow and grey—and taken care to skirt the dark patch beneath the radiator, where some manner of rusty leakage has occurred, it finds itself back on the staircase, which is old and rackety, dawn the only thing capable of using it without making a sound—apart, that is, from Jackson Lamb, who when he feels like it can wander Slough House as silently as a newly conjured wraith, if rather more corpulent. At other times Lamb prefers the direct approach, and attacks the stairs with the noise that a bear pushing a wheelbarrow might make, if the wheelbarrow was full of tin cans, and the bear drunk.

More watchful ghost than drunken bear, dawn arrives in the final two offices and finds little to distinguish them from those on the floor above, apart, perhaps, from the slightly stuccoed texture of the paintwork behind one desk, as if a fresh coat has been applied before the wall has been properly cleaned, and some lumpy matter has been left clinging to the plasterwork: best not to dwell on what this might be. For the rest, this office has the same air of frustrated ambition as its companions, and to one as sensitive as light-fingered dawn it contains, too, a memory of violence, and perhaps the promise of more to come. But dawn understands that promises are easily broken—dawn knows all about breaking—and the possibility delays it not one jot. On it goes, down the final set of stairs, and somehow passes through the back door without recourse to the shove this usually requires, the door being famously resistant to casual use. In the dank little yard behind Slough House dawn pauses, aware that its time is nearly up, and enjoys these last cool moments. Once upon a time it might have heard a horse making its way up the street; more recently, the happy hum of a milk float would have whiled away its final minute. But today there is only the scream of an ambulance, late for an appointment, and by the time its banshee howl has ceased bouncing off walls and buildings dawn has disappeared, and here in its place is the day itself, which, once within Slough House's grasp, turns out to be far from the embodiment of industry and occupation it threatened to be. Instead—like the day before it, and the one before that—it is just another slothful interlude to be clock watched out of existence, and knowing full well that none of the inhabitants can do anything to hasten its departure, it takes its own sweet time about setting up shop. Casually, smugly, unbothered by doubt or duty, it divides itself between Slough House's offices, and then, like a lazy cat, settles in the warmest corners to doze, while nothing much happens around it.

Roddy Ho, Roddy Ho, riding through the glen.

(Just another earworm.)

Roddy Ho, Roddy Ho, manliest of men.

There are those who regard Roderick Ho as a one-trick wonder; a king of the keyboard jungle, sure, but less adept in other areas of life, such as making friends, being reasonable, and ironing T-shirts. But they haven't seen him in action. They haven't seen him on the prowl.

Lunchtime, just off Aldersgate Street. The ugly concrete towers of the Barbican to the right; a hardly more beautiful housing estate to the left. But it's a killing box, this uncelebrated patch of London; it's a blink-and-you're-eaten battlefield. You get one chance only to claim your scalp, and Roddy Ho's prey could be anywhere.

He knew damn well it was close.

So he moved, pantherlike, between parked cars; he hovered by a placard celebrating some municipal triumph or other. In his ear, driven like a fence post by the pounding of his iPod, an overexcited forty-something screeched tenderly of his plan to kill and eat his girlfriend. On Roddy's chin, the beard he'd grown last winter; rather more expertly sculpted now, because he'd learned the hard way not to use kitchen scissors. On Roddy's head—new development—a baseball cap. Image matters, Roddy knew that. *Brand* matters. You want Joe Public to recognise your avatar, your avatar had to make a statement. In his own personal opinion, he'd nailed that angle. Neat little goatee and a baseball cap: originality plus style. Roderick Ho was the complete package, the way Brad Pitt used to be, before the unpleasantness.

(Gap in the market there, come to think of it. He'd have to have a word with Kim, his girlfriend, about coining a *nom de celeb*.

Koddy.

Rim . . . ?

Nah. Needs work.)

But he'd deal with that later, because right now it was time to activate the lure module; get this creature into the open and bring that sucker *down*. This required force, timing and use of weapons: his core skills in a nutshell . . . Whoever came up with *Pokémon GO* must have had Roderick Ho on their muse's speed dial. The name even rhymed, man—it was like he was born to poke. Gimme that stardust, he thought. Gimme that lovely stardust, and watch the Rodster *shine*.

All reflex, sinew and concentration, Ho shimmered through the lunchtime air like the coolest of cats, the baddest of asses, the daddy of all dudes; hot on the trail of an enemy that didn't exist.

A little way down the road, an enemy that did turned the ignition, and pulled away from the kerb.

That morning, on her way to the Tube, Catherine Standish had dropped in at the newsagent's for a *Guardian*. Behind the counter a steel blind had been drawn to hide the array of cigarette packets, lest a stray glimpse prove a gateway to early death, while to her left, on the topmost row of the rack, the few pornographic magazines to survive into the digital age were sealed inside plastic covers, to nullify their impact on concupiscent minds. All this careful protection, she thought, shielding us from impulses deemed harmful, but right there by the door was a shelf of wine on special offer, any two bottles for £9, and up by the counter was a range of spirits all cheerfully marked two quid down, none of them a brand to delight the palate, but any of them enough to render the most uptight connoisseur pig-drunk and open to offers.

She bought her newspaper, nodded her thanks and returned to the street.

One journey later, she remembered it was her turn to pick up milk for the office—no huge feat of memory; it was always her turn to pick up milk—and dropped into the shop next to Slough House, where the milk was in the fridge alongside cans of beer and lager, and ready-mixed tins of G&T. That's twice without trying, she thought, that she could have bought a ticket to the underworld before her day was off the ground. Most occasions of sin required a little effort. But the recovering alcoholic could coast along in neutral, and the temptations would come to her.

There was nothing unusual about this. It was just the surface tension; the everyday gauntlet the dry drunk runs. Come lunchtime, the lure of the dark side behind her, Catherine was absorbed in the day's work: writing up the department's biannual accounts, which included justification for "irregular expenses." Slough House had had a lot of these this year: broken doors, carpet cleaning; all the making-good an armed incursion demands. Most of the repairs had been sloppily done, which neither surprised nor bothered Catherine much: she had long ago grown used to the second-class status the slow horses enjoyed. What worried her more was the long-term damage to the horses themselves. Shirley Dander was unnervingly calm; the kind of calm Catherine imagined icebergs were, just before they ploughed into ocean liners. River Cartwright was bottling things up too, more than usual. And as for J.K. Coe, Catherine recognised a hand grenade when she saw one. And she didn't think his pin was fitted too tight.

Roddy Ho was the same as ever, of course, but that was more of a burden than a comfort.

It was a good job Louisa Guy was relatively sane.

Stacks of paper in front of her, their edges neatly though not quite neurotically aligned, Catherine waded through the day's work, adjusting figures where Lamb's entries overshot the inaccurate to become manifestly corrupt, and replacing his justifications ("because I fucking say so") with her own more diplomatic phrasing. When the time came to leave for home, all those temptations would parade in front of her again. But if daily exposure to Jackson Lamb had taught her anything, it was not to fret about life's peripheral challenges.

He had a way of providing more than enough to worry about, up front and centre.

■ ■ ■

Shirley Dander had sixty-two days.

Sixty-two drug-free days.

Count 'em . . .

Somebody might: Shirley didn't. Sixty-two was just a number, same as sixty-one had been, and if she happened to be keeping track that was only because the days had all happened in the obvious order, very, very slowly. Mornings she ticked off the minutes, and afternoons counted down seconds, and at least once a day found herself staring at the walls, particularly the one behind what had been Marcus's desk. Last time she'd seen Marcus, he'd been leaning against that wall, his chair tilted at a ridiculous angle. It had been painted over since. A bad job had been made of it.

And here was Shirley's solution to that: think about something else.

It was lunchtime; bright and warm. Shirley was heading back to Slough House for an afternoon of enforced inertia, after which she'd schlep on over to Shoreditch for the last of her AFMs . . . Eight months of anger fucking management sessions, and this evening she'd officially be declared anger free. It had been hinted she might even get a badge. That could be a problem—if anyone stuck a badge on her, they'd be carrying their teeth home in a hankie—but luckily, what she had in her pocket gave her something to focus on; to carry her through any dodgy moments which might result in the court-ordered programme being extended.

A neat little wrap of the best cocaine the postcode had to offer; her treat to herself for finishing the course.

Sixty-two might just be a number, but it was as high as Shirley had any intention of going.

Being straight had had the effect of turning her settings down a notch, and the world had been flatter lately, greyer, easier to get along with. Which helped with the whole AFM thing, but was starting to piss her off. Last week she'd had a cold-caller, some crap about mis-sold insurance, and Shirley hadn't even told him to fuck himself. This didn't feel like attitude adjustment so much as it did surrender. So here was the plan: get through this one last day, suffer being patted on the head by the counsellor—whom Shirley intended to follow home one night and kill—then hit the clubs, get properly wasted and learn to live again. Sixty-two days was long enough, and proved for a fact what she'd always maintained as a theory: that she could give it up any time she wanted.

Besides, Marcus was long gone. It wasn't like he'd be getting in her face about it.

But don't think about Marcus.

So there she was, heading past the estate towards Aldersgate Street, coke in her pocket, mind on the evening to come, when she saw two things five yards in front of her, both behaving strangely.

One was Roderick Ho, who was performing some kind of ballet, with a mobile phone for a partner.

The other was an approaching silver Honda, turning left where there was no left to turn.

Then mounting the pavement and heading straight for Ho.

■ ■ ■

So here's the thing, thought Louisa Guy. If I'd wanted to be a librarian, I'd have been a librarian. I'd have gone to library school, taken library exams and saved up enough library stamps to buy a library uniform. Whatever they do, I'd have done it: by the book. And of all the librarians in the near vicinity, I'd have been far and away the librarianest; the kind of librarian other librarians sing songs about, gathered around their library fires.

But what I wouldn't have done was join the intelligence service. Because that would have been fucking ridiculous.

Yet here I am.

Here she was.

Here being Slough House, where what she was doing was scrolling through library loan statistics, determining who had borrowed certain titles in the course of the last few years. Books like *Islam Expects* and *The Meaning of Jihad*. And if anyone had actually written *How to Wage War on a Civilian Population*, that would have made the list too.

"Is it really likely," she'd said, on being handed the project, "that compiling a list of people who've borrowed particular library books is going to help us find fledgling terrorists?"

"Put like that," Lamb had said, "the odds are probably a million to one." He shook his head. "I'll tell you this for nothing. I'm bloody glad I'm not you."

"Thanks. But why do they even stock these books, if they're so dangerous?"

"It's political correctness gone mad," agreed Lamb sadly.

"I'm rabidly anticensorship, as you know. But some books just need burning."

So did some bosses. She'd been working on this list, which involved cross-checking Public Lending Right statistics against individual county library databases, for three months. It now stretched not quite halfway down a single sheet of A4, and she'd reached Buckinghamshire in her alphabetical list of counties. Thank Christ she didn't have to cover the whole of the UK, because that would have taken even an actual librarian years.

Not the whole of it, no. Just England, Wales and Northern Ireland.

"Fuck Scotland," Lamb had explained. "They want to go it alone, they can go it alone."

Her only ally in her never-ending task was the Government, which was doing its bit by closing down as many libraries as possible.

In the War Against Terror, you take all the help you can get.

Louisa giggled to herself, because sometimes you had to, or else you'd go mad. Unless the giggling was proof you'd already gone mad. J.K. Coe might know, not so much because of his so-called expertise in Psychological Evaluation, but because he was a borderline nutter himself. All fun and games in Slough House.

She pushed away from her desk and stood to stretch. Lately she'd been spending more time at the gym, and the result was increasing restlessness when tethered to her computer. Through the window, Aldersgate Street was its usual unpromising medley of pissed-off traffic and people in a hurry. Nobody ever wandered through this bit of London; it was just a staging post on the way somewhere else. Unless you were a stalled spook, of course, in which case it was journey's end.

God, she was bored.

And then, as if to console her, the world threw a minor distraction her way: from not far off came a screech and a bump; the sound of a car making contact.

She wondered what that was about.

Hi Tina

Just a quick note to let you know how things are going here in Devon—not great, to be honest. I've been told I'm being laid off at the end of the month because the boss's sister's son needs a job, so someone has to make way for the little bastard. Thanks a bunch, right?

But it's not all bad because the gaffer knows he owes me one, and has set me up with one of his contacts for a six-month gig in—get this—Albania! But it's a cushy number, doing the wiring on three new hotel builds, and it'll be cheap living so I'll

Coe stopped midsentence and stared through the window at the Barbican opposite. It was an Orwellian nightmare of a complex, a concrete monstrosity, but credit where it was due: like Ronnie and Reggie Kray before it, the Barbican had overcome the drawback of being a brutal piece of shit to achieve iconic status. But that was London Rules for you: force others to take you on your own terms. And if they didn't like it, stay in their face until they did.

Jackson Lamb, for instance. Except, on second thoughts, no: Lamb didn't give a toss whose terms you took him on. He carried on regardless. He just *was*.

Tina, though, wasn't, or wouldn't be much longer. Tina wasn't her real name anyway. J.K. Coe just found it easier to compose these letters if they had an actual name attached; for the same reason, he always signed them Dan. Dan—whoever he was—was a deep cover spook, who'd moled into whichever group of activists was currently deemed too extreme for comfort (animal rights, eco-troublemakers, *The Archers*' fanbase); while Tina—whoever *she* was—was someone he'd befriended in the course of doing so. There was always a Tina. Back when Coe had been in Psych Eval, he'd made a study of Tinas of both genders; joes in the field were warned not to develop emotional attachments in the group under investigation, but they always did. You couldn't betray someone efficiently if you didn't love them first. So when the op was over, and Dan was coming back to the surface, there had to be letters; a long goodbye played out over months. First Dan moved out of the area, a fair distance off but not unvisitable. He'd keep in touch sporadically, then get a better offer and move abroad. The letters or emails would falter, then stop. And soon Dan would be forgotten, by everyone but Tina, who'd keep his letters in a shoebox under her bed, and Google-Earth Albania after her third glass of Chardonnay. Rather than, for example, dragging him into court for screwing her under false pretences. Nobody wanted to go through that again.

But of course, joes don't write the letters themselves. That was a job for spooks like J.K. Coe, whiling away the days in Slough House. And lucky to be doing so, to be honest. Most people who'd shot to death a handcuffed man might have expected retribution. Luckily, Coe had done so at the fag-end of a series of events so painfully compromising to the intelligence services as a whole that—as Lamb had observed—it had put the "us" in "clusterfuck," leaving Regent's Park with little choice but to lay a huge carpet over everything and sweep Slough House under it. The slow horses were used to that, of course. In fact, if they weren't already slow horses, they'd be dust bunnies instead.

Coe cracked his knuckles, and added the words *be able to save a bit* to his letter. Yeah, right; Dan would save a bit, then meet an Albanian girl, and—long story short—never come home. Meanwhile, the actual Dan would be undercover again, on a different op, and the ball would be rolling in a new direction. On Spook Street, things never stayed still. Unless you were in Slough House, that is. But there was a major difference between J.K. Coe and the other slow horses, and it was this: he had no desire to be where the action was. If he could sit here typing all day and never have to say a word to anyone, that would suit him fine. Because his life was approaching an even keel. The dreams were ebbing away at last, and the panic attacks had tapered off. He no longer found himself obsessively fingering an imaginary keyboard, echoing Keith Jarrett's improvised piano solos. Things were bearable, and might just stay that way provided nothing happened.

He hoped like hell nothing would happen.

The car smeared Roderick Ho like ketchup across the concrete apron; broke him like a plastic doll across its bonnet, so all that was holding him together was his clothes. This happened so fast Shirley saw it before it took place. Which was as well for Ho, because she had time to prevent it.

She covered five yards with the speed of a greased pig, yelling Ho's name, though he didn't turn round—he had his back to the car and his iPod jammed into his ears; was squinting through his smartphone, and looked, basically, like a dumb tourist who'd been ripped off twice already: once by someone selling hats, and a second time by someone giving away beards. When Shirley hit him waist-high, he was apparently taking a photo of bugger-all. But he never got the chance. Shirley's weight sent him crashing to the ground half a moment before the car ploughed past: went careering across the pedestrianised area, bounced off a low brick wall bordering a garden display then screeched to a halt. Burnt rubber reached Shirley's nose. Ho was squawking; his phone was in pieces. The car moved again, but instead of heading back for them it circled the brick enclosure, turned left onto the road, swerved round the barrier and went east.

Shirley watched it disappear, too late to catch its plate, or even clock the number of occupants. Soon she'd feel the impact of her leap in most of her bones, but for the moment she just replayed it in her head from a third-party viewpoint: a graceful, gazelle-like swoop; lifesaving moment and poetry in motion at once. Marcus would have been proud, she thought.

Dead proud.

Beneath her, Roddy yelled, "You stupid cow!"

The internet was full of whispers.

No, River Cartwright thought. Scratch that.

The internet was screaming its head off, as usual.

He was on a Marylebone-bound train, returning to London after having taken the morning off: care leave, he'd claimed it, though Lamb preferred "bloody liberty."

"We're not the social services."

"We're not Sports Direct either," Catherine Standish had pointed out. "If River needs the morning off, he needs it."

"And who's gunna pick up his workload in the meantime?"

River hadn't done a stroke of work in three weeks, but didn't think this a viable line of defence. "It'll get done," he promised.

And Lamb had grunted, and that was that.

So he'd taken off in the pre-breakfast rush, battling against the commuter tide; heading for Skylarks, the care home where the O.B. now resided; not precisely a Service-run facility—the Service had long since outsourced any such frivolities—but one which placed a higher priority on security than most places of its type.

The Old Bastard, River's grandfather, had wandered off down the twilit corridors of his own mind, only occasionally emerging into the here and now, whereupon he'd sniff the air like an elderly badger and look pained, though whether this was due to a brief awareness that his grasp on reality had crumbled, or to that grasp's momentary return, River couldn't guess. After a lifetime hoarding secrets the old spook had lost himself among them, and no longer knew which truths he was concealing, which lies he was casting abroad. He and his late wife, Rose, had raised River, their only grandchild. Sitting with him in Skylarks' garden, a blanket covering the old man's knees, an iron curtain shrouding half his history, River felt adrift. He had followed the O.B.'s footsteps into the Secret Service, and if his own path had been forcibly rerouted, there'd been comfort in the knowledge that the old man had at least mapped the same territory. But now he was orphaned. The footsteps he'd followed were wandering in circles, and when they faltered at last, they'd be nowhere specific. Every spook's dream was to throw off all pursuers, and know himself unwatched. The O.B. was fast approaching that space: somewhere unknowable, unvisited, untagged by hostile eyes.

It had been a warm morning, bright sunshine casting shadows on the lawn. The house was at the end of a valley, and River could see hills rising in the distance, and tame clouds puffing across a paint box sky. A train was briefly visible between two stretches of woodland, but its engines were no more than a polite murmur, barely bothering the air. River could smell mown grass, and something else he couldn't put a name to. If forced to guess, he'd say it was the absence of traffic.

He sat on one of three white plastic chairs arranged around a white plastic table, from the centre of which a parasol jutted upwards. The third chair was vacant. There were two other similar sets of furniture, one unused, and the other occupied by an elderly couple. A younger woman was there, addressing them in what River imagined was an efficient tone. He couldn't actually hear her. His grandfather was talking loudly, blocking out all other conversation.

"That would have been August '52," he was saying. "The fifteenth, if I'm not mistaken. A Tuesday. Round about four o'clock in the afternoon."

The O.B.'s memory was self-sharpening these days. It prided itself on providing minute detail, even if that detail bore only coincidental resemblance to reality.

"And when the call came in, it was Joe himself on the line."

". . . Joe?"

"Stalin, my boy. You're not dropping off on me, are you?"

River wasn't dropping off on him.

He thought: this is where life on Spook Street leads. Not long ago the old man's past had come barking from the shadows and taken large bites out of the present. If this were common knowledge, there would be many howling for retribution. River should be among them, really. But if his own murky beginnings had turned out to be the result of the O.B.'s tampering with the lives of others, they remained his own beginnings. You couldn't argue yourself out of existence.

Besides, there was no way of taking his grandfather to task for past sins now those sins had melted into fictions. The previous week, River had heard a story the old man had never told before, involving more gunfire than usual, and an elaborate series of code names in notebooks. Ten minutes on Google later revealed that the O.B. had been relaying the plot of *Where Eagles Dare*.

When the old man's tale wound itself into silence, River said, "Do you have everything you need, grandad?"

"Why should I need anything? Eh?"

"No reason. I just thought you might like something from . . ."

He tailed off. Something from home. But home was dangerous territory, a subject best avoided. The old man had never been a joe; always a desk man. It had been his job to send agents into the unknown, and run them from what others might think a safe distance. But here he was now, alone in joe country, his cover blown, his home untenable. There was no safe ground. Only this mansion house in a quiet landscape, where the nurses had enough discretion to know that some tales were best ignored.

On the train heading back into London, River shifted in his seat and scrolled down the page of search results. Nice to know that a spook career granted him this privilege: if he wanted to know what was going on, he could surf the web, like any other bastard. And the internet was screaming. The hunt for the Abbotsfield killers continued with no concrete results, though the attack had been claimed by so-called Islamic State. At a late-night session in Parliament the previous evening,

Dennis Gimball had lambasted the Security Services, proclaiming Claude Whelan, Regent's Park's First Desk, unfit for purpose; had sailed this close to suggesting that he was, in fact, an IS sympathiser. That this was barking mad was a side issue: recent years had seen a recalibration of political lunacy, and even the mainstream media had to pretend to take Gimball seriously, just in case. Meanwhile, there were twelve dead in Abbotsfield, and a tiny village had become a geopolitical byword. There'd be a lot more debate, a lot more hand-wringing, before this slipped away from the front pages. Unless something else happened soon, of course.

Nearly there. River closed his laptop. The O.B. would be dozing again by now; enjoying a cat's afternoon in the sun. Time had rolled round on him, that was all. River was his grandfather's handler now.

Sooner or later, all the sins of the past fell into the keeping of the present.

"You stupid cow!"

He'd been thrown sideways and the noise in his head had exploded: manic guitars cut off midwail; locomotive drums killed midbeat. The sudden silence was deafening. It was like he'd been unplugged.

And his prey was nowhere to be seen, obviously. His smartphone was in pieces, its casing a hop-skip-jump away.

It was Shirley Dander who'd leaped on him, evidently unable to control her passion.

She crawled off and pretended to be watching a car disappear along the road. Roddy sat up and brushed at the sleeves of his still-new leather jacket. He'd had to deal with workplace harassment before: first Louisa Guy, now this. But at least Louisa remained the right side of her last shaggable day, while Shirley Dander, far as the Rodster was concerned, hadn't seen her first yet.

"What the hell was that for?"

"That was me saving your arse," she said, without looking round.

His arse. One-track mind.

"I nearly had it, you know!" Pointless explaining the intricacies of a quest to her: the nearest she'd come to appreciating the complexities of gaming was being mistaken for a troll. Still, though, she ought to be made to realise just what a prize she'd cost him, all for the sake of a quick grope. "A bulbasaur! You know how rare that is?"

It was plain she didn't.

"The fuck," she asked, "are you talking about?"

He scrambled to his feet.

"Okay," he said. "Let's pretend you just wanted to sabotage my hunt. That's all Kim needs to know, anyway."

". . . Huh?"

"My girlfriend," he explained, so she'd know where she stood.

"Did you get a plate for that car?"

"What car?"

"The one that just tried to run you over."

"That's a good story too," Roddy said. "But let's stick with mine. It's less complicated. Fewer follow-up questions."

And having delivered this lesson in tradecraft, he collected the pieces of his phone and headed back to Slough House.

Where the day is well established now, and dawn a forgotten intruder. When River returns to take up post at his desk—his current task being so mind-crushingly dull, so balls-achingly unlikely to result in useful data, that he can barely remember what it is even while doing it—all the slow horses are back in the stable, and the hum of collective ennui is almost audible. Up in his attic room, Jackson Lamb scrapes the last sporkful of chicken fried rice from a foil dish, then tosses the container into a corner dark enough that it need never trouble his conscience again, should such a creature come calling, while two floors below Shirley Dander's face is scrunched into a thoughtful scowl as she replays in her mind the sequence of events that led to her flattening Roderick Ho: always a happy outcome, of course, but had she really prevented a car doing the same? Or had it just been another of London's penis-propelled drivers, whose every excursion onto the capital's roads morphs into a demolition derby? Maybe she should share the question with someone. Catherine Standish, she decides. Louisa Guy too, perhaps. Louisa might be an iron-clad bitch at times, but at least she doesn't think with a dick. Some days, you take what you can.

Later, Lamb will host one of his occasional departmental

meetings, its main purpose to ensure the ongoing discontent of all involved, but for now Slough House is what passes for peaceful, the grousing and grumbling of its denizens remaining mainly internal. The clocks that each of the crew separately watches dawdle through their paces on Slough House time, this being slower by some fifty percent than in most other places, while, like the O.B. in distant Berkshire, the day catnaps the afternoon away.

Elsewhere, mind, it's scurrying around like a demented gremlin.

Other Titles in the Soho Crime Series

Stephanie Barron
(Jane Austen's England)
Jane and the Twelve Days of Christmas
Jane and the Waterloo Map

F.H. Batacan
(Philippines)
Smaller and Smaller Circles

James R. Benn
(World War II Europe)
Billy Boyle
The First Wave
Blood Alone
Evil for Evil
Rag & Bone
A Mortal Terror
Death's Door
A Blind Goddess
The Rest Is Silence
The White Ghost
Blue Madonna
The Devouring
Solemn Graves

Cara Black
(Paris, France)
Murder in the Marais
Murder in Belleville
Murder in the Sentier
Murder in the Bastille
Murder in Clichy
Murder in Montmartre
Murder on the Ile Saint-Louis
Murder in the Rue de Paradis
Murder in the Latin Quarter
Murder in the Palais Royal
Murder in Passy
Murder at the Lanterne Rouge
Murder Below Montparnasse
Murder in Pigalle
Murder on the Champ de Mars

Cara Black cont.
Murder on the Quai
Murder in Saint-Germain
Murder on the Left Bank

Lisa Brackmann
(China)
Rock Paper Tiger
Hour of the Rat
Dragon Day

Getaway
Go-Between

Henry Chang
(Chinatown)
Chinatown Beat
Year of the Dog
Red Jade
Death Money
Lucky

Barbara Cleverly
(England)
The Last Kashmiri Rose
Strange Images of Death
The Blood Royal
Not My Blood
A Spider in the Cup
Enter Pale Death
Diana's Altar

Fall of Angels

Gary Corby
(Ancient Greece)
The Pericles Commission
The Ionia Sanction
Sacred Games
The Marathon Conspiracy
Death Ex Machina
The Singer from Memphis
Death on Delos

Colin Cotterill
(Laos)
The Coroner's Lunch
Thirty-Three Teeth
Disco for the Departed
Anarchy and Old Dogs

Colin Cotterill cont.
Curse of the Pogo Stick
The Merry Misogynist
Love Songs from a Shallow Grave
Slash and Burn
The Woman Who Wouldn't Die
Six and a Half Deadly Sins
I Shot the Buddha
The Rat Catchers' Olympics
Don't Eat Me

Garry Disher
(Australia)
The Dragon Man
Kittyhawk Down
Snapshot
Chain of Evidence
Blood Moon
Whispering Death
Signal Loss

Wyatt
Port Vila Blues
Fallout

Bitter Wash Road

David Downing
(World War II Germany)
Zoo Station
Silesian Station
Stettin Station
Potsdam Station
Lehrter Station
Masaryk Station

(World War I)
Jack of Spies
One Man's Flag
Lenin's Roller Coaster
The Dark Clouds Shining

Agnete Friis
(Denmark)
What My Body Remembers
The Summer of Ellen

Michael Genelin
(Slovakia)
Siren of the Waters
Dark Dreams
The Magician's Accomplice
Requiem for a Gypsy

Timothy Hallinan
(Thailand)
The Fear Artist
For the Dead
The Hot Countries
Fools' River

(Los Angeles)
Crashed
Little Elvises
The Fame Thief
Herbie's Game
King Maybe
Fields Where They Lay
Nighttown

Mette Ivie Harrison
(Mormon Utah)
The Bishop's Wife
His Right Hand
For Time and All Eternities
Not of This Fold

Mick Herron
(England)
Slow Horses
Dead Lions
Real Tigers
Spook Street
London Rules

Down Cemetery Road
The Last Voice You Hear
Why We Die
Smoke and Whispers

Reconstruction
Nobody Walks
This Is What Happened

Stan Jones
(Alaska)
White Sky, Black Ice
Shaman Pass
Frozen Sun

Stan Jones cont.
Village of the Ghost Bears
Tundra Kill
The Big Empty

Lene Kaaberbøl & Agnete Friis
(Denmark)
The Boy in the Suitcase
Invisible Murder
Death of a Nightingale
The Considerate Killer

Martin Limón
(South Korea)
Jade Lady Burning
Slicky Boys
Buddha's Money
The Door to Bitterness
The Wandering Ghost
G.I. Bones
Mr. Kill
The Joy Brigade
Nightmare Range
The Iron Sickle
The Ville Rat
Ping-Pong Heart
The Nine-Tailed Fox
The Line

Ed Lin
(Taiwan)
Ghost Month
Incensed
99 Ways to Die

Peter Lovesey
(England)
The Circle
The Headhunters
False Inspector Dew
Rough Cider
On the Edge
The Reaper

(Bath, England)
The Last Detective
Diamond Solitaire
The Summons
Bloodhounds
Upon a Dark Night

Peter Lovesey cont.
The Vault
Diamond Dust
The House Sitter
The Secret Hangman
Skeleton Hill
Stagestruck
Cop to Corpse
The Tooth Tattoo
The Stone Wife
Down Among the Dead Men
Another One Goes Tonight
Beau Death

(London, England)
Wobble to Death
The Detective Wore Silk Drawers
Abracadaver
Mad Hatter's Holiday
The Tick of Death
A Case of Spirits
Swing, Swing Together
Waxwork

Jassy Mackenzie
(South Africa)
Random Violence
Stolen Lives
The Fallen
Pale Horses
Bad Seeds

Sujata Massey
(1920s Bombay)
The Widows of Malabar Hill

Francine Mathews
(Nantucket)
Death in the Off-Season
Death in Rough Water
Death in a Mood Indigo
Death in a Cold Hard Light
Death on Nantucket

Seichō Matsumoto
(Japan)
Inspector Imanishi Investigates

Magdalen Nabb
(Italy)
Death of an Englishman
Death of a Dutchman
Death in Springtime
Death in Autumn
The Marshal and the Murderer
The Marshal and the Madwoman
The Marshal's Own Case
The Marshal Makes His Report
The Marshal at the Villa Torrini
Property of Blood
Some Bitter Taste
The Innocent
Vita Nuova
The Monster of Florence

Fuminori Nakamura
(Japan)
The Thief
Evil and the Mask
Last Winter, We Parted
The Kingdom
The Boy in the Earth
Cult X

Stuart Neville
(Northern Ireland)
The Ghosts of Belfast
Collusion
Stolen Souls
The Final Silence
Those We Left Behind
So Say the Fallen

(Dublin)
Ratlines

Rebecca Pawel
(1930s Spain)
Death of a Nationalist
Law of Return
The Watcher in the Pine
The Summer Snow

Kwei Quartey
(Ghana)
Murder at Cape Three Points
Gold of Our Fathers
Death by His Grace

Qiu Xiaolong
(China)
Death of a Red Heroine
A Loyal Character Dancer
When Red Is Black

John Straley
(Sitka, Alaska)
The Woman Who Married a Bear
The Curious Eat Themselves
The Music of What Happens
Death and the Language of Happiness
The Angels Will Not Care
Cold Water Burning
Baby's First Felony

(Cold Storage, Alaska)
The Big Both Ways
Cold Storage, Alaska

Akimitsu Takagi
(Japan)
The Tattoo Murder Case
Honeymoon to Nowhere
The Informer

Helene Tursten
(Sweden)
Detective Inspector Huss
The Torso
The Glass Devil
Night Rounds
The Golden Calf
The Fire Dance
The Beige Man
The Treacherous Net
Who Watcheth
Protected by the Shadows

Hunting Game

Helene Tursten cont.
An Elderly Lady Is Up to No Good

Janwillem van de Wetering
(Holland)
Outsider in Amsterdam
Tumbleweed
The Corpse on the Dike
Death of a Hawker
The Japanese Corpse
The Blond Baboon
The Maine Massacre
The Mind-Murders
The Streetbird
The Rattle-Rat
Hard Rain
Just a Corpse at Twilight
Hollow-Eyed Angel
The Perfidious Parrot
The Sergeant's Cat: Collected Stories

Timothy Williams
(Guadeloupe)
Another Sun
The Honest Folk of Guadeloupe

(Italy)
Converging Parallels
The Puppeteer
Persona Non Grata
Black August
Big Italy
The Second Day of the Renaissance

Jacqueline Winspear
(1920s England)
Maisie Dobbs
Birds of a Feather